D0629927

By Hans Hellmut Kirst

Revolt of Gunner Asch
Gunner Asch Goes to War
Return of Gunner Asch
The Officer Factory
The Night of the Generals
What Became of Gunner Asch?
Soldier's Revolt
The Last Card
Brothers in Arms
The Wolves
Last Stop Camp 7
No Fatherland
The Adventures of Private Faust
Hero in the Tower
Damned to Success
Everything Has Its Price
The Night of the Long Knives
The Affairs of the Generals
Party Games

PARTY GAMES

Hans Hellmut Kirst

TRANSLATED BY J. MAXWELL BROWNJOHN

Simon and Schuster   New York

Copyright © 1978 by C. Bertelsmann Verlag GmbH
translation © 1979 by William Collins & Sons, Ltd.
Published by Simon and Schuster
A Division of Gulf & Western Corporation
Simon & Schuster Building
Rockefeller Center
1230 Avenue of the Americas
New York, New York 10020

SIMON AND SCHUSTER and colophon are
trademarks of Simon & Schuster
Designed by Irving Perkins
Manufactured in the United States of America
1 2 3 4 5 6 7 8 9 10

Library of Congress Cataloging in Publication Data

Kirst, Hans Hellmut, date.
Party games.

Translation of *08/15 in der Partei.*
I. Title.
PT2621.I76N8313   1980   833′.914   79–28231

ISBN 0–671–25267–4

Foreword

THIS IS the story of a few weeks in the life of Konrad Breitbach, who had realized that words can destroy as well as delude. To resist this process by borrowing his enemies' methods struck him as a legitimate and essential form of self-defense.

The immediate effect of Konrad's maneuvers was an alternation of farce and tragedy, and death itself joined in the laughter that greeted them.

The alarums and excursions described here can be accurately dated. They took place during the late spring and early summer of that memorable year 1933.

The scene is a small town in the backwoods of East Prussia—now Polish, but then part of Germany. Its name, Gilgenrode, will not be found on any surviving maps of that vanished world. It is a composite of two East Prussian towns, Gilgenburg and Osterode, where the author spent his boyhood and adolescence.

This novel has a collaborator of sorts—by name, Adolf

Hitler. All excerpts from his celebrated work, *Mein Kampf,* are reproduced verbatim from the standard edition, complete with chapter and verse. If there is any satire in the story that follows, much of it stems from the lamentable fact that too few people read the book until too late.

PARTY GAMES

1

"Look, you two, I'm not ramming my advice down your throat. Just asking you to try and see my point of view. After all, I am your father."

Richard Breitbach gave his sons an encouraging smile. Master saddler, taxpayer, churchgoer and patriot, Breitbach was one of Gilgenrode's most respected citizens. The days when people had called him a ball of fire were long gone. The flames had dwindled to an occasional flicker, but there were still some who suspected this stocky, pleasant-faced man of stirring up trouble as an antidote to boredom.

"Don't get me wrong," he went on. "It's just that everything connected with these loudmouthed saviors of the nation strikes me as childish and idiotic." He gazed at his sons like a preacher adjuring his flock to put their faith in the

11

wisdom of God. "Sometimes I feel we're living in a madhouse. A lot of what our brown-shirted brethren say sounds plausible, I know, but they aren't to be trusted."

Konrad, his younger son, cocked an eyebrow. "You mean we shouldn't believe a word of their propaganda, however convincing we find it?"

Breitbach's paternal self-assurance remained temporarily intact. "Our fellow citizens are as unpredictable as a bunch of school children. I find it hard to sort them into sheep and goats myself, boys, but even you should be able to spot the difference between an idealist and a crook."

"Really?" Konrad's friendly persistence was beginning to make his father fidget. "You really think you can draw the line as neatly as that—here in Gilgenrode? Personally, I find it just as easy to imagine a crooked idealist as an idealistic crook."

Breitbach seemed to be having trouble with his breathing. He loosened his tie, a patriotic confection of red, white and black stripes. Spring was yearning to become summer, and sunlight streamed into the normally somber confines of his living room, whose plain interior was dominated by leather upholstery and polished oak.

His "boys" were grown men. The elder, Johannes, was tall, broad-shouldered and strikingly handsome, with dreamy eyes and a face that might have been carved in wood by some medieval craftsman. Johannes was nearly thirty years old and artistically inclined.

Young Konrad came from a different mold. He not only looked small but was so. Barely five-foot-four in his socks, he made a fragile but agile impression, like a skillfully animated puppet. Not that Konrad seemed to mind; few of the town's inhabitants had so far taken much notice of him. "Konrad's a nice young pup," his father used to say.

12

"Thoroughly housebroken, but still a bit wet behind the ears."

Breitbach senior had a soft spot for dogs. Now, though, as he sat ensconced in his big leather armchair, his attention was firmly centered on Johannes. His elder son's future was in question, quite apart from loyalty, integrity and any other article of faith handed down by successive generations of Breitbachs. He looked Johannes straight in the eye.

"Speaking as one member of the family to another," he said, "a shit's a shit in any language—and that goes for Heinrich Sonnenblum."

Johannes drew himself up, radiating courage and determination. "Look, Father, let's put the record straight. You used to be friends before you declared war on each other. The reasons are immaterial. Don't force me to elaborate—I'd find it extremely embarrassing, and so, I suspect, would you. All I'm asking is, why should children be dragged into their parents' vendettas?"

"No reason, on the face of it," Breitbach conceded. "None at all, under normal circumstances, except that this isn't just a squabble over some woman. You can forget *that* red herring, Johannes. Sonnenblum and I are diametrically and irreconcilably opposed. He's a rabid Nazi and I'm a staunch German Nationalist. They say he's sworn to wipe out me and my family, you included."

"Who's 'they'?" Johannes demanded. "People have been saying a lot of things lately, but it doesn't alter the fact that I love Erika Sonnenblum and she loves me."

His father glowered. "You mean she's actually told you so?"

"We both know the truth, so why should we discuss it?"

Konrad cleared his throat. "The simplest solution would

be to produce a *fait accompli*. Why don't you clinch matters by getting her good and pregnant?"

Johannes rounded on him. "Keep your dirty-minded suggestions to yourself!"

"Don't be so naïve," Konrad retorted calmly. "If you're really in love and you want to get hitched, why not steal a march on the preacher? It's the local custom."

Breitbach stared at his sons in surprise. Although he had reckoned with some stiff resistance from Johannes, if not quite on this scale, Konrad's contribution was totally unexpected. He found it strange and somehow ominous.

But Johannes had to be taken far more seriously. He was a sensitive soul and highly susceptible to fits of emotion. This had its dangers, especially in a place like Gilgenrode, which had lately become a happy hunting ground for those whom Breitbach regarded as ideological con men in brown uniforms.

"Look," he said, "Sonnenblum has been blind or perverse enough to bet his shirt on the Nazis. He's a pretty good dentist—I'll grant him that, being a fair-minded man —but his political opinions are a downright disaster, and Erika's his own flesh and blood."

"And I'm yours." Johannes looked indignant. "Does that mean I have to think the way you do? Why should our views be identical?"

A chasm opened in front of Breitbach's worried eyes. "My dear boy, don't tell me *you've* been bitten by the Nazi bug?"

"No," Johannes said firmly. Even as a child he had shuddered at the feel of a moist frog on his palm, and he had much the same sensation now. "I've always tried to act like a civilized human being. The Nazis are cultural outsiders—of course I'm against them."

"Good." Breitbach breathed a sigh of relief. "Then I

14

suppose you had better hear the worst. Last night, just as I was coming out of the Fatherland Café, that bastard Sonnenblum buttonholed me in the middle of the square. Would I kindly note the following, he said: he had now been appointed District Director of the National Socialist German Labor Party, so Erika was going to marry someone worthy of the daughter of a senior Party official. In other words, a Nazi!"

"But that's monstrous!" Johannes sounded half horrified, half belligerent.

"What are you going to do about it?" asked Konrad. No lamb could have looked more innocent. His limpid blue eyes seemed to mirror the depths of a serene Mediterranean sky. "Any ideas?"

Breitbach grunted impatiently. "Give the girl her marching orders. That would save us all a lot of unpleasantness."

Johannes flushed. "Certainly not, Father, I wouldn't dream of it. Besides, the present situation may only be temporary."

"Let's hope to God you're right," boomed Breitbach. "Those jumped-up Brownshirts won't last more than a few months—a couple of years at most."

The old warhorse and his elder son exchanged a searching stare. They almost jumped when the third member of the party, that diminutive and underrated chip off the Breitbach block, ventured another interruption.

"So Sonnenblum fancies himself as his beloved Führer's local representative and insists on consigning his equally beloved daughter to someone who's alight with the spirit of National Socialism. You aren't that someone, Johannes, and you never will be. Father's relieved and I accept the fact, so where does that leave us?"

Johannes frowned. "What are you driving at?"

"Look at it this way. A sheep—meaning Sonnenblum—

15

has strayed into a pigsty and seems to like it there so much he plans to stay. Putting it baldly, there are two alternatives: we extricate the sheep or clean out the pigsty. Either way, somebody has to get his feet dirty."

"You're being oversubtle," snapped Breitbach, instinctively sensing a dangerous development. "Forget Sonnenblum. Let him wallow in filth if he wants to."

"But not Erika," Johannes said gravely. "We belong to each other."

Konrad grinned. "Which is why I aim to amuse myself and salvage my brother's love life at the same time." He said it as though reciting his multiplication tables. "I'm going to join Herr Sonnenblum's party."

"The hell you are!" roared Breitbach, every inch the outraged patriarch. "I forbid it!"

"Objection overruled, Father. I'm old enough to be a free agent. Quite apart from that, it's time I had a little fun."

"Everything's going fine," announced Heinrich Sonnenblum, dentist and District Director of the Gilgenrode Nazi Party. "People are beginning to see the light, Mother. Know who raised his hat to me just now—very respectfully, I might add?"

"No idea, Heinrich, but I'm sure you'll tell me. Not now, though, you're getting under my feet."

Gertrude Sonnenblum, his widowed mother, was busy cooking lunch in the kitchen. She was a squat, pear-shaped little woman with a wrinkled face, a pair of beady eyes and a mouth like a surgical incision.

"You have no business in my kitchen," she went on. "How many more times do I have to tell you? Better stick to tinkering with other people's teeth—or that receptionist of yours, if you can get within arm's reach of her."

Heinrich Sonnenblum chuckled complacently. He

16

thought he knew his mother pretty well. She might have hair on her teeth, as the local saying went, but she also had the proverbial heart of gold. Her barbed remarks were generally reserved for their family sparring matches.

"All right, Mother, just to satisfy your burning curiosity: the man who tipped his hat to me was your friend Parson Bachus!"

"I can well believe it," she said tartly. "Maybe he wants to head your propaganda department—anything's possible these days."

Heinrich was a tall man, but as pear-shaped as his mother. He had narrow shoulders, broad hips and the face of an honest, earnest civil servant. Gertrude eyed her only child with a trace of kindly forbearance. She loved him dearly but was far too concerned for his welfare to show it.

Poor boy, she thought. He had always been his own worst enemy—always combined a lack of sophistication with a desire for social recognition. It now seemed that his urge to rid the world of rotten teeth had taken a political turn. Gertrude sometimes fretted at Heinrich's absolute conviction that right was on his side. For all that, he was her son. It was her duty to see that he didn't make a fool of himself, especially now that he was a widower.

"It worries me when you smirk like that," she said. "What makes you think you're entitled to look so smug?"

But nothing could quench her son's high spirits. "How about opening a bottle in honor of the occasion?" he suggested, knowing that Gertrude was never averse to a decent drop of Rhine wine.

"Now I've heard everything," she retorted. "Wine in the middle of the day? Most men drink to celebrate something or forget it. Which is it this time?"

Heinrich did his best to explain over lunch, which began with a concentrated, cream-thickened vegetable soup. Then

17

came braised beef smothered in mushroom sauce, followed by Heinrich's favorite sweet, a freshly baked apple flan topped with whipped cream. He prepared to chomp his way blissfully through the entire menu. As far as his digestion was concerned, all was right with the world.

Gertrude Sonnenblum, be it noted, was a cook renowned for her ability to produce hearty meals that stuck to the ribs. Superbly tasty but never overladen with condiments that would have destroyed their basic flavor, they were served in the most tempting way possible. Heinrich regarded it as an absolute imperative to love and revere his mother, if only for her culinary skill. He raised the glass she had allowed him and cried, "To our great German future!"

"Nonsense, boy!" she growled. "No need for that. We're all on our own here. I've always thought you had a future—as a dentist—but now you spring this on me."

He hastily changed the subject. "Mother, your cooking's a dream, quite irresistible, but it can't banish all my worries. Take Erika, for a start."

His daughter Erika had just turned twenty. Heinrich considered her beautiful, though not—to his regret—in a conspicuously Germanic way. She was dark-eyed and fine-boned, and her voice lacked firmness and resonance. She taught the kindergarten class at the local primary school.

"I've got great plans for her," Heinrich confided. "Erika's future must be worthy of my own. I owe it to my official position."

Gertrude glared at him. "One politician's more than enough for any family. If you're fond of the girl you'll keep her out of this. Her future's all mapped out; she's going to marry a decent young man—and I know who. Then she'll set up house and raise a family. That's what she was born and bred for."

18

"Was I born to be a dentist?" he retorted—sharply through a mouthful of beef. "Mother, there's a new wind blowing in this beloved land of ours. Thank God I spotted it in time!"

"You're drunk," said Gertrude, taking possession of the wine bottle, "drunk on distilled Hitler. All right, out with it. What do you have in mind for the girl?"

"I want her to be a credit to me, that's all—take over the local branch of the German Girls' League, say, or play an active part in our Women's Association."

"But you know who she's in love with?"

"I do, more's the pity." Heinrich's eyes darted in search of some more beef. "She's involved with that deadbeat Johannes Breitbach, a notorious idler with cultural pretensions. He writes sloppy, sentimental articles for the local press. He also plays the organ—in church, if you please!"

"It's the only one in town."

"Granted, but why does he have to play it at all? To crown everything, I hear he writes poetry. Not very manly, would you say? What do you expect me to do, thrust my darling daughter into the arms of *that* flabby aesthete? He'd have to turn over a new leaf, I can tell you—him and his whole rotten family."

Gertrude emitted a mirthless bark of laughter. "I see it all now. You've been waging a private war with Richard Breitbach for years, and now you're trying to win it by exploiting your new position."

He dismissed the imputation with a sweeping gesture. "You misjudge me, Mother. You always do."

"Oh no, my boy, I don't misjudge either of you. You and Richard are like dogs in a manger, especially when it comes to women. You married each other's girlfriends out of spite. Whatever one of you wanted, the other wanted too,

19

and your unfortunate wives had to pay the price. No wonder they both died young."

"That's an old story."

"Yes, but it never stops. Look at you now—both pushing fifty and still chasing the same bit of skirt."

"Fräulein Fischer means more to me than a receptionist," Heinrich declared in a tone of gentlemanly reproof. "I also admire her personal qualities."

"Oh sure, you want to go to bed with her. But so does Richard Breitbach, and that's the only reason for this embarrassing performance. Aren't you carrying things too far?"

"With all due respect, Mother, I reject your insinuations. I've always aimed high—always been a perfectionist. It's the way I'm made."

"This perfectionism of yours—does it apply to Erika?"

"Of course. Only the best is good enough for my daughter, which rules out Breitbach's artsy-craftsy son."

"Anyone else in mind?"

"Well, yes—Hermann Keller, for instance. Our new Stormtroop Commander, appointed with my blessing. He's definitely the coming man here—after me."

"That's quite enough!" Gertrude's eyes flashed fire. "You must be crazy. How can you even dream of letting that tomcat loose on my granddaughter?"

"Please don't get so worked up, Mother," Heinrich said hurriedly. He stared into space with an almost visionary expression, grimly determined to make National Socialist history. "You mustn't underestimate me. I may be your son, but I'm not a child any more. I have to plan ahead—far ahead. May I have another glass of wine?"

"This diner's closed," snapped Gertrude. "Not just for today, either. You're banned till further notice—till you come to your senses. I never want to hear Keller's name mentioned again, certainly not in connection with Erika. I mean that, Heinrich, so be warned!"

The Breitbach saddlery near the Protestant church north of Market Square consisted of an office, two adjoining workshops, and the so-called studio. The firm employed a score of first-rate craftsmen, whose output sold worldwide at de luxe prices.

Breitbach senior spent most of his time in the office, whereas Konrad could generally be found in the studio. Here he put the finishing touches to the saddlery's finest products, investing them with considerable artistic polish. He was currently working on a large and ornate saddle.

It did not distract him in the least when his elder brother appeared. Johannes stood over him, gazed at him intently and proclaimed, "I'm worried, Konrad. So is Father."

"Quite right too." Konrad kept his eyes on his work. "I wonder if you really know why."

"It's you. You must have been joking when you announced your intention of joining the Party. It wasn't very funny, if you ask me."

"But I didn't ask you, Johannes. Nor did I ask what *you* hope to achieve by your poetic effusions, your stirrings of conscience, your spiritual torments and temptations. You're welcome to the lot, because you are what you are. I hope you manage to remain yourself for as long as possible."

Konrad's deft fingers continued to embellish the saddle in front of him with designs woven in silver wire. Commissioned by a Texas rancher, it was to be adorned with bulls: lying, grazing, rolling, trotting, charging.

"Strange creatures, bulls. They have an instinctive aversion to the color red. With me, it's brown."

Johannes looked really alarmed. "Listen, Konrad, you're an artist in your own field. As for me, I hope to be a writer

21

some day—a writer with something worthwhile to say. Just because a political sewer's burst, why should we soil our hands?"

"Megalomaniacs should never be ignored or underestimated, Johannes. Believe me, they won't ignore you or anyone else who strikes them as different—or *degenerate*, to use their favorite term. That's what you've got to bear in mind. You have to run with the pack—you even have to take the lead if necessary."

"I find that a totally alien idea."

"You're an aesthete, that's why. Cultivate your cosmic conscience. Concentrate on your poetry and Erika, and leave the dirty work to me. I'm planning to beat these sewer rats at their own game."

"The only battle I could wage would be a spiritual one."

Konrad grinned. "Curiously enough, it's always the most gutless people who issue gutsy calls to arms."

"That's nonsense," Johannes protested indignantly. "Don't be so damned impertinent. You ought to know me better."

"I was only paraphrasing a book you may have heard of: Hitler's *Mein Kampf,* otherwise known as the new German Bible. Some people not only believe in its contents but act on them."

"They can't be such fools."

"They are. Words have the same effect on them as hard liquor. There's brain fever around, Johannes, and it's spreading fast. I happened to be present when Father had his shouting match with Sonnenblum in the square."

"You never said."

"I was ashamed to. They looked like a pair of aging stags in the rutting season. I ask you—those two! School friends who lived next door and served together in the trenches, and both of them itching to lock horns, gore each other—even kill each other."

"How awful," said Johannes, wrinkling his nose. "You mean there were other people standing around watching, and nobody tried to step in?"

"Oh yes, one of our workers *tried*, but he's in the hospital—not too badly hurt, I'm glad to say. Keller broke his arm. In self-defense, of course. Keller's boss of the local stormtroopers now, had you heard? He's right at the top of my black list."

"How about you? What did you do?"

"Not a thing. I hadn't the slightest desire to get beaten up too. However, I was forcibly reminded of a key sentence in Hitler's *Mein Kampf*, page two-two-five: 'For my part, I decided to enter politics.' "

Hermann Keller, commander of the Gilgenrode SA detachment, or Brownshirts, was seething with rage—a frequent emotion and one for which he had lately developed quite a taste. This time he was bent on a showdown with the president of the local sports club. A contingent of Stormtroopers forged along behind him, eyes shining with missionary zeal and biceps bulging, ever prepared to guard their German homeland, perfect their skill at arms and spring to the defense of sound political dogma.

"Some patriot you are!" Keller snarled at the sports club president. "Did I say patriot? Don't make me laugh! You're a public enemy, a subversive. What made you think you could hoodwink us, the Führer's authorized representatives?"

The sports club president, who was pale with apprehension, took care to look servile. "Can't you be a bit more specific?" he begged. "Please, Hermann!"

Keller's voice became even sharper and more caustic but no louder; he was already in full cry. Being an ex-sergeant of infantry and a renowned drill instructor, he was widely experienced in bullying subordinates of every kind. That experience was now paying off.

"Number one, I object to being addressed as Hermann while acting in an official capacity: I'm Stormtroop Commander Keller to you. Number two, I'm hopping mad. My men and I have been using this sports ground twice a week for military training purposes. Now I'm informed it belongs to a Jew named Sass. True or false?"

"Well—er, yes, Stormtroop Commander, you're right." The sports club president looked suitably contrite. "But I didn't think it mattered. Herr Sass—"

"What was that? Did I hear you say *Herr* Sass?"

Keller's victim swiftly corrected himself. "Sass, I mean. He leased the land to us years ago at a nominal rent, without any strings. We lent it to your outfit free of charge, if you don't mind me mentioning it."

"Shame on you!" roared Keller, with an elaborate show of disgust. "And you call yourself a German? Get out of my sight, you filthy Jew-lover!"

The latter was a venomous, even dangerous epithet—the sports club president knew that full well. He scampered off as though a dozen Dobermans were baying at his heels.

Keller pursued his retreating figure with the sort of virile laughter he normally reserved for boozy evenings in the canteen, then turned to his Stormtroopers. Gilgenrode already boasted some sixty of the breed, which was distinguished by firm jaws, tight lips and a trusting expression.

"Close on me!" he commanded.

They promptly formed an earnest, bovine semicircle round the leader of the herd.

"Men," proclaimed Keller, "this lousy Jewish field isn't

worthy of a unit that has sworn an oath of allegiance to the Führer. What we need is a decent SA clubhouse, a proper roof over our heads—an all-weather, all-year-round training center. I'm going to see we get one."

He dismissed his comrades with the following injunction: "And now, have yourselves a good time. The first three beers and schnapps are on the Party. Present your chits at headquarters tomorrow morning and you'll get a refund. I like to do things through the proper channels."

They all trooped happily off.

For his own part, Hermann Keller had decided to set the town an example. He duly changed into civilian clothes and repaired to the Fatherland Café in Market Square, where he sat down at one of the few unoccupied tables and ordered a beer in characteristically stentorian tones.

"And get me the owner of this dump!"

The proprietor was Felix Kimminger, a young man whose inherited wealth and financial acumen had made him one of Gilgenrode's three or four most successful businessmen. The café was not his only capital asset. He also owned the German Eagle Hotel and its three-star restaurant, a brace of groceries, a footwear and clothing store, and several bars. There was nothing particularly impressive about his pasty face and flabby physique, but his eyes had a foxy glint.

"Good evening, sir," he said suavely. "Anything I can do for you?"

"Maybe. Do you know who I am? No? Then it's time you did." Keller launched into a semiformal introduction. He gave his name and, with unmistakable relish, disclosed his official status.

Kimminger was deference in person. "Delighted to make your acquaintance, Herr Keller. I've heard a lot about you. May I invite you to be my guest for the evening?

Nothing's too good for a man like you and a town like ours."

Gilgenrode, situated in the southern reaches of East Prussia, was surrounded by dense but undepressing forests through which the sunlight filtered as through radiant stained-glass windows. The little town was mirrored and its image multiplied by the shimmering waters of a sizable lake. Two smaller and more modest lakes lay placidly in the background, marking a transition to lush pastures and well-tended fields that seemed to exhale peace and tranquillity.

Commonly regarded as an earthly paradise, this region was inhabited by countless creatures: the timid deer, the nimble hare, the artful fox. In and around its lakes, ducks dabbled busily, herons strutted proudly and cranes rose trumpeting to greet the sun. Knee-deep in meadow grass, speckled black-and-white cows looked on without alarm as horses cantered past. Even the local cats and dogs lived at peace, having been reared together from birth, and could often be seen sprawled in quiet communion outside cottage doors.

Gilgenrode itself, though some way off the main road to Königsberg, the East Prussian capital, numbered nearly seven thousand inhabitants. Parson Bachus was not alone in referring to them as "souls." They all prayed to the Almighty, mostly in the Protestant manner, and continued to do so undisturbed until the advent of these newfangled "Nazis," who wanted to be everything at once: national, socialist, and German. A few citizens were heartily amused by the antics of dentist Sonnenblum and his so-called National Socialist German Labor Party, but their smiles soon faded.

This they did as soon as the local Storm Detachment, or SA, acquired a worthy commander in Hermann Keller, the former drill sergeant who now worked for the municipal water and electricity board. Word soon spread that he was not a man to be trifled with.

Kimminger was all the more eager to ingratiate himself with the Nazi chieftain, who now sat facing him in an unmistakably imperious pose.

"Anything you want, Stormtroop Commander. You only have to say the word. An SA dinner dance at cost price? Leave it to me. A really generous donation to your worthy cause? By all means—why not?"

"You misunderstand me, Herr Kimminger." Keller's manner had become ominously brusque. This fat slob was reacting as expected—sweating hard and talking money. He assumed an official tone. "Would you by any chance be trying to bribe the Movement?"

"Nothing could be further from my thoughts!"

A broad grin appeared on Keller's billy-goat face, which sat squarely on his shoulders. His hands were powerful and prehensile, his jaw and neck muscles strongly developed. He made a frightening impression when he drew himself up to his full height, especially in the presence of those without Party affiliations. At such times, his every word became a command.

"It's like this. You're president of the Germania Rowing Club, which is anything but a haunt of the toiling masses. I'm giving you a chance to show you're on the right side. Ours, I mean."

Keller went on to explain that he had conducted a thorough survey. The rowing club's lakeside site was the finest piece of real estate for miles around, and the clubhouse itself was a gem. Also forming part of the complex was a barnlike building sometimes used for storing boats, but usually empty.

"And that's what I'm after, Kimminger—that shed of yours."

27

"An admirable suggestion, Stormtroop Commander." The hotelier's tone was unctuous in the extreme. "I'll certainly recommend that the committee give you and your men the run of the place—without any financial liability on your part, naturally. However, should the committee raise objections—"

"They won't, not unless you all want to risk being branded public enemies. I'm sure I don't have to tell you what that would mean."

Kimminger's fertile imagination could readily picture the probable consequences. Even in the new Germany, however, certain areas were off limits. Knowing this, he decided to trade on it.

"Unfortunately," he purred, "there's a small fly in the ointment. Our club site, including the premises you're after, doesn't belong to us. It's only on loan from someone whose motives may be utterly disinterested or thoroughly selfish—who can say? I refer to Herr Sass."

"That Yid?" Keller bellowed the words like a wild beast, reducing everyone within earshot to stunned silence. "Not him again!"

Kimminger thought it wise to add a soothing rider. "Never mind, Stormtroop Commander, I'm sure the matter can still be arranged."

"It better be," said Keller, red with fury. "You think I'm going to crawl to some swine of a Jewish plutocrat when the welfare and efficiency of my men are at stake? We'll give that bloodsucker a chance to atone for some of his crimes against our race. I want that shed, Kimminger, and you're going to get it for me!"

Heinrich Sonnenblum had recently enlarged his office-cum-apartment, No. 7 Market Square, by the addition of several rooms. Their previous occupant, a headmaster who prided himself on his political neutrality, had been induced to vacate them without too much trouble. A few veiled threats had sufficed.

"NSDAP District Headquarters, Gilgenrode" had been promptly installed in the three vacant rooms at Party expense. Headquarters comprised a waiting room, an outer office complete with a not unattractive secretary chosen for her Nordic appearance, and the inner sanctum of the District Director, to wit Heinrich Sonnenblum, whose dental office could be reached via a communicating door.

Little activity reigned on either side of this door. Few Gilgenroders elected to have their teeth pulled by Sonnenblum the dentist; just as few consulted Sonnenblum the Party boss. Telling himself that all was still in its infancy, Sonnenblum patiently waited for developments.

He continued to do so even when informed, in his District Director's capacity, that a visitor named Breitbach had called to see him. He stared incredulously at his blond and braided secretary.

"If the person concerned is Richard Breitbach the saddler, I don't see public enemies—not unless they're ready to toe the line." He meant, of course, the Party line.

"No, sir, it's the youngest member of the family. He'd like a word with you."

Sonnenblum admitted him without delay. Konrad was his mother's godson, which placed him under something of an obligation. Besides, he was a nice little fellow. The dentist's mood quite mellowed at the sight of him standing there with such a docile, submissive look on his face.

"Konrad, dear boy!" Sonnenblum's voice was as dulcet as the dawn breeze soughing in the reeds around Lake Gilgenrode. "You know I've always had a soft spot for you, but if it's about your father, save it. He and I are past talking. We're worlds apart."

29

"I'm here on my own account, not his. He didn't want me to come."

"He didn't?" The dentist-turned-politico beamed with delight. "You came in spite of him? May I ask why?"

"Out of conviction, you might say."

To Sonnenblum, "conviction" was a verbal beacon, a key word of signal importance. It simply wasn't true, as some of his more malicious neighbors alleged, that he had become a Nazi merely because he had always been compelled to play second fiddle to Richard Breitbach! Breitbach had even eclipsed him in the Veterans Association, purely because he, Sonnenblum, had emerged from the last war—already referred to by forward-looking people as the *First* World War—with the rank of second lieutenant, whereas Breitbach, by some stupid quirk of fate, had made lieutenant.

Anyway, thought Sonnenblum, at least he had been quick to identify the most effective champion of all the German soldier stood for. Hitler alone would ensure that no one had fought or sacrificed his life for the Fatherland in vain —Hitler alone, locally represented by Sonnenblum himself, not by weak-kneed joiners and committeemen like Breitbach, who did nothing at their meetings save get drunk and bawl patriotic songs.

"Conviction, that's the ticket!" The District Director contemplated his visitor with a mild and meditative eye. "Sooner or later, every worthwhile person encounters his moment of truth, and you, my boy, are a worthwhile person —my dear old mother always says so. Am I to take it that we share the same ideas?"

"I suppose we do, District Director."

Sonnenblum flushed with pleasure at the use of his title. "So may I, in spite of your father, welcome you as a faithful devotee of the Führer?"

"If you like to put it that way," Konrad replied blandly. Heinrich Sonnenblum drew a deep breath, profoundly moved. As a man who preened himself on his political perspicacity, he grasped the significance of what had happened. It meant nothing less than a rift in the Breitbach ranks. Now that one of his sons could be played off against him, his lifelong rival and sometime friend would be bound to lose ground. The logic of power politics required that this latest development be exploited to the full.

"Unless I've misunderstood you, my dear boy, you want to join us, even though your father will be far from pleased."

Konrad nodded. "I'm old enough to suit myself, but that's not the only reason."

"How gratifying! What an auspicious sign!" A radiant vision of the future loomed up before the dentist's eyes. "You've obviously grasped the shape of things to come. What prompted this decision?"

"I realize we've reached a crucial stage in our history—one that presents us all with a choice. 'Whatever man wants, he hopes for and believes in!' I quote from page one-seven-seven of what is probably the most influential book of this or any other century, Adolf Hitler's *Mein Kampf*."

The District Director looked thunderstruck. "You mean you've actually read it?"

"Several times."

Sonnenblum's office contained many copies of Hitler's book. Piles of them littered his desk, readily available as gifts on ceremonial occasions. They were all in mint condition except the one he had sometimes opened at random.

"So you know the Führer's work. Breathtaking, isn't it?"

"You can say that again!" Almost reverently, Konrad fitted his fingertips together and stared into space. "It

31

kept me on the edge of my chair. Take page thirty-five, for instance: 'I can fight only for what I love, love only what I respect, and respect only what I know.' There you have it, I told myself."

"Yes indeed!" Sonnenblum chimed in happily. The confident gleam in his eye was more than a measure of his delight at the prospect of taking Breitbach down a peg. Over and above that, he was dominated by the desire to find a political associate and comrade in arms who was worthy of himself. "My dear Konrad, you're positively steeped in the true National Socialist spirit."

"I'm only a novice," Konrad said modestly. "However, I am a regular subscriber to the *Völkischer Beobachter,* the Movement's most influential paper, and *Angriff,* Dr. Goebbels's Berlin daily. I even take Julius Streicher's *Stürmer.* Mines of information, all of them."

"Splendid, absolutely splendid!" Sonnenblum shuffled around in his directorial chair, overcome with joyful agitation. "You're a born Party member. I welcome you to our ranks with open arms."

"Thank you, District Director." Konrad sounded infinitely grateful. He too had realized that the die was cast and his Rubicon already behind him. Involuntarily, his thoughts turned to page 117 of Hitler's gospel: "In this world, a reluctance to tread thorny paths too often implies the abandonment of one's goal."

Sonnenblum made a benedictory gesture that seemed to come straight from the heart. "If you like, I could take you on to my personal staff. How about the public enlightenment and propaganda section? Someone called Patzer has carved out a niche there, but I don't trust him. He's a windbag with suspiciously intellectual leanings. He even tries to lecture *me!* Patzer needs understudying with a view to replacement. How would that suit you?"

"Later, perhaps." Konrad's air of gratitude deepened. "I'd rather start at the bottom if I may. Let me serve my apprenticeship as an ordinary Party member. I'd also like to join the SA, but only as a trooper to begin with. We'll see how things turn out."

"Bravo!" cried Sonnenblum. "You're absolutely right. In welcoming you to our ranks, my dear Konrad, I'm taking certain problems into account. Your father's bound to make trouble, but even that can be handled as long as we stand shoulder to shoulder."

This concluded a pact which was soon to have bizarre results. It was sealed with the vigorous handshake customary among all self-respecting German males.

RICHARD BREITBACH, master saddler, was sitting with Fräulein Beate Fischer, dental receptionist, at a secluded table in the restaurant of the German Eagle Hotel. They were dipping into a choice East Prussian dinner: cream of chicken soup followed by wild duck with prunes, then almond pastries fresh from the oven.

Breitbach, who was in a mood to enjoy himself, could afford such fare. He was probably the wealthiest man in town apart from Sass, the Jew. Besides, he enjoyed spending money on Beate. She was likable, presentable, and extremely attractive to the opposite sex. Most people put her in her middle twenties, though she was well over thirty. Her physical charms had a timeless quality.

Beate had now been Sonnenblum's dental receptionist for several years. Sonnenblum, too, was courting her hard in private, much to Breitbach's satisfaction. This was one victory over his erstwhile friend and long-time enemy of which he felt reasonably assured. Breitbach set great store by his financial resources and masculine powers of persuasion. He leaned toward Beate with tender solicitude.

"Did you enjoy it, my dear?" he inquired, registering deep concern for her welfare. Beate liked gentlemanly manners, and Breitbach could produce them to order—far better, he felt, than that man Sonnenblum. "Was everything the way you like it?"

"Very much so," she said graciously, but she coupled this verdict with a hint that her palate was as refined as her appearance. "Except that the soup could have been better seasoned and the duck spent five minutes too long in the oven."

Breitbach wondered at her unerringly good taste—and at his own in choosing her. Everything about Beate invited admiration. Her oval face with its seductively full lips, the sensual flair of her nostrils, her big doelike eyes—all gave promise of sweet surrender.

However understandable, this was a misleading impression. Beate was far from soft and yielding at heart. Her outward appearance was a carefully cultivated disguise, a purveyor of almost unlimited promise that kindled the wildest hopes but fulfilled very few of them. Beate demanded a heavy investment in perseverance as well as cash.

"I adore being with you, Richard dear, but you know how much I dislike being treated like an article of merchandise. Please remember where we are!"

Breitbach gave a start and hastily removed his hand from her thigh. He tended to forget that, however broadminded she might be in private, she was a stickler for propriety in public. This meant hands off. Beate wanted love

36

and devotion, but she also wanted the unqualified respect of the world at large.

"Forgive me, sweetheart. You're such a gorgeous creature. I find you quite irresistible."

"That's nice to know, but we aren't man and wife."

Which was the salient point. Beate wanted to get married, but not at any price. She had a precise idea of her value and intended to extract it in full. Although Richard Breitbach was a good catch and far from averse to marriage, he wasn't the only fish in the local pond. There was Sonnenblum too. That meant she had to choose between one of Gilgenrode's wealthiest citizens and someone who might soon, if he seized his golden opportunity, become the most influential man in town.

Just as she was turning this over in her mind, Sonnenblum telephoned the German Eagle and asked to speak to her.

"Impudent lout!" Breitbach greeted the news with a leonine growl of resentment. Then, catching an admonitory glance from Beate, he quickly tried to laugh it off. "I mean, it's ridiculous. What makes him think he can butt in at this hour? Let me take the call for you, sweetheart."

"No," she said, sweet as an angel. "Not unless you *insist*. If so, I won't stop you."

"Leave him to me. I'll show him what I think of him pestering us at dinner."

The conversation went as follows:

Breitbach: "Sonnenblum? You've got a nerve, poking your nose into Fräulein Fischer's private life. She's not your personal property."

Sonnenblum: "No, but she works for me. I need her urgently."

Breitbach: "What, in the middle of the night? Is this

37

part of your new political philosophy? I thought you people claimed to have a social conscience. Beate's a lady and you use her like a slave. Watch out, my friend, she doesn't take kindly to this sort of treatment. You really want me to pass on your latest piece of effrontery?"

Sonnenblum didn't reply for several seconds. It sounded as if he had hung up. Finally, aware that Breitbach must be reveling in his silence, he broke into a spate of words.

"What gives you the right to speak for her? Who the hell do you think you are? As far as she's concerned, just another contender, and certainly not the odds-on favorite!"

Breitbach: "You've no sense of decency! What do you mean, just another contender? Who's in the running apart from us?"

Sonnenblum: "That shook you, didn't it! And don't think I'm putting you on—they're like flies around a jam pot, even if she does seem to be giving us priority."

Breitbach: "Not us, man—*me!*"

Sonnenblum: "I can only tell you this much: if *I* don't get her, *you* sure as hell won't either. I'll see to that."

Breitbach's parting shot was charged with menace. "Know what you can do, District Director? Go screw yourself!"

Gertrude, Sonnenblum's mother, was working on her granddaughter at the breakfast table. Her son was still sleeping it off. He had made a number of lengthy phone calls the previous night. After that, sustained by a crate of beer and two bottles of schnapps, he had held a protracted conference with propaganda chief Patzer and Stormtroop Commander Keller.

He could hardly be expected to join his womenfolk for breakfast, which in Gertrude's view was the grossest folly. As mistress of the house, she subscribed to the age-old dietary precept: *Eat like a king in the morning, a nobleman at noon and a beggar at night—that way, you'll stay healthy.*

Heinrich's absence did have one advantage, though, because it left her alone with Erika. Gertrude made the most of their tête-à-tête, fussing over the girl like a mother hen.

"All right, out with it. How do you see your future—I mean, in the light of your father's latest antics?"

"I really don't know, Gran. He expects so much of me these days. It preys on my mind, to be frank."

"You can always be frank with me."

Erika, at twenty, was still, in all probability, a virgin. Outwardly gentle as a lamb and dainty as a poodle, she conveyed an impression of total innocence. She was an admirable primary-school teacher, but her experience of life was minimal. Gertrude prompted her with a nod.

"Well?"

"Well," said Erika, "there's always Johannes."

"The elder Breitbach boy? A thoroughly nice type. You find him attractive?"

"Yes." Erika's cheeks turned dawn pink. "At least, I think so."

The old woman cocked her head. "What on earth do you mean, you think so? Don't you know for sure? Haven't you been to bed with him yet?"

"Really, Gran!" Erika sounded horrified.

"So Johannes is as much of a fool as ever." Gertrude slowly wagged her head. "What does he do when you're alone together—read you poetry? My God, he must be even sillier than I thought."

"He—he says he doesn't want to force my hand."

"A gentleman to the marrow, eh?" Gertrude gave a derisive snort. "Your grandfather moved heaven and earth when he got the itch to marry me. He dogged my footsteps,

39

prowled around the house, badgered my father—even threatened to punch his teeth in—and all because of me! What do you two do, aside from holding hands?"

"Never mind that, Gran. Father says I've got to marry someone worthy of his new position."

"You don't mean he's brought up the subject of Hermann Keller?"

"How did you know?"

"He dared to hint as much to me. I thought it was a joke in poor taste, but it seems he really meant it. Well, what do you think? How does the idea appeal? Do you find it worth considering, even?"

"No, Gran. If the choice was mine, I'd take Johannes."

"And I'm going to see you get him." The old woman was trembling with rage. "So our Party boss thinks he can regulate your private life, does he? Don't worry, I'll scotch his little game."

Erika gave her a look of gentle entreaty. "Please do, before it's too late."

"Mind you," said Gertrude, stroking her chin, "there is the other Breitbach boy. Do you see anything of him?"

"Konrad?" Erika nodded. "We bump into each other from time to time. He reminds me of a frisky little squirrel—friendly and playful. Funny about him, isn't it? Who'd have thought he'd end up on Father's team!"

Gertrude's jaw dropped. "You mean he's joined the Party? Are you sure?"

"Oh yes, he's even volunteered for the Brownshirts. Father's thrilled. He calls him a man after his own heart."

"Good heavens, girl, you obviously don't have a clue what this means—but then, I don't suppose anyone round here would, with the exception of me. Konrad's more than my godson, he's a kindred spirit. Why don't you settle for him instead of Johannes? That would solve everything."

"Me marry Konrad? He looks like an overgrown school-boy."

"That's just what makes him such a menace. He's a strange youngster—full of guts, and cunning as the devil. Take a closer look at him and you'll see what I mean."

"On the seventh day," croaked Emil Spahn, striving to hit a note of ritual solemnity, "Almighty God, the creator of heaven and earth, paused for a look at his handiwork, and what did he see? Paradise invaded by sin! Lecherous wearers of fig leaves, defilers of their own daughters, murderers of their own kin! Yea, verily, the world is a nest of vipers!"

The scene was an inn called the Last Resort, which stood immediately opposite the magistrate's court and was one of at least three dozen similar taverns in Gilgenrode. Emil Spahn was the town drunk. He could produce his jeremiads at the drop of a hat and was often rewarded with a schnapps by those who found them entertaining. With his furrowed dachshund face and bleary mastiff eyes, he was a professional malcontent who had earned his jester's license by dint of dogged perseverance.

"The Lord our God is truly great!" he proclaimed to all who were willing to be amused. He usually had an audience of three or four. Schnapps cost only ten pfennigs a shot, and Emil's barroom performances were worth at least that much.

"But the self-styled sons of God," he pursued, "are a mean, miserable bunch of creeps. You don't need a mirror to convince yourself of that. Just take a look at me!"

So saying, Emil retired to the far corner of the taproom with the five schnapps he had earned, there to commune with himself in brooding silence. To his surprise, he was joined by Konrad Breitbach, who gave him a friendly nod.

"You're really hitting the bottle these days, Emil. I don't blame you, the way things are, but why drink that awful potato brandy? You deserve a lot better than rotgut."

Although Emil did not emerge instantly or completely from his alcoholic daydreams, he seemed cheered, if not amused, by the sight of the youngster beside him.

"Wha—what would you be wanting with me, you miniature mind reader? I saw through you long ago. You didn't miss much, even as a toddler."

"And you, Emil, can read our fellow citizens like a book but you're scared to tell them the truth. Why?"

Emil reached hurriedly for his next glass of schnapps. "I'm a pathetic specimen, Konrad. I expect you've noticed. I may live in squalor, but I'm not tired of living—in fact I'm not even miserable. I've got a cat, you see, a lovely little creature. She doesn't look like much, but she makes me happy—gloriously happy. Are you asking me to risk all that?"

"No, but you might be able to inject a little meaning into your life. I'm sure I don't have to tell you what a noble age we're living in."

"Shit on it," said Emil, tersely and with utter conviction. "It's bad enough trading on God the way I do. I don't propose to get mixed up with the devil as well—he's poison. What am I, anyway? A worthless, drink-sodden halfwit."

Konrad registered friendly concern. "I wouldn't ever repeat that aloud if I were you. You're branding yourself an inferior specimen, and that can be dangerous nowadays. To quote from page two-eighty of a book by a gentleman named Adolf Hitler, 'The ruthless segregation of incurable invalids would be a boon to posterity.' You want to be included?"

42

"Not me!" Even another potato brandy failed to dispel Emil's sudden alarm. Tremulously, he asked, "What can I do about it, Konrad?"

"I'll tell you. Instead of taking the Lord's name in vain, you can apply your still considerable intellect to the task of embarrassing some of our home-grown political bigwigs."

Emil threw up his trembling hands. "I may be a confirmed idiot, but I'm not dumb enough to tangle with that bunch of thugs. One word out of place and they'd put me in the hospital. I can't afford to risk it, if only for Susie's sake."

"Susie?"

"My cat."

"You don't have to, Emil. Do just the opposite: bang their drum, boost their egos, praise them to the skies! They won't be able to touch you."

The more Emil drank, the clearer-headed he seemed to become. A distant look came into his drooping eyes. "You want me to lick their boots, is that it?"

"More or less. You shouldn't find it hard, especially if I supply you with the right ammunition—slogans, quotations and so on. You'll still be the voice of the people, but with a difference. It'll be Emil the progressive, Emil the mouthpiece of the new Germany. Are you on?"

"I certainly am, as long as you keep me primed with the right kind of liquor. Who do I start on?"

"How about Keller?"

"Keller?" Emil repeated, staring at Konrad in high delight. He even forgot to reach for another glass. "You couldn't have picked a better target. I'll praise him till he curls up and dies, the bastard. I live right on top of him. He's the bane of my life. He hates Susie. That settles it!"

Stormtroop Commander Keller felt exhilarated. The members of the Gilgenrode SA section were going through their paces like a circus act.

This morning he had been summoned to another conference with his District Director. Sonnenblum valued him highly—of that he felt sure. He was not kept waiting long in the outer office. Sonnenblum soon appeared in a dentist's white coat, which he quickly doffed to reveal his brown Party uniform.

"Just now," he announced, still speaking as a dentist, "I had to treat Sass, the Jew. I extracted one of his teeth." In his District Director's voice, he added, "It went against the grain, of course, but he claimed to be in agony. I could hardly deny him my professional services, but I did refuse him any form of anaesthetic. There's a certain logic there, wouldn't you say?"

"Congratulations," barked Keller. "I've always admired your qualities of leadership, but you're obviously a born diplomat as well."

This was no flattery—at least, Sonnenblum did not take it as such. It was all part of the master-race vernacular. Each of the Führer's "sworn henchmen" was at pains to buttress the other's self-esteem.

"Comrade Keller," Sonnenblum said in stirring tones, "I know I can depend on you, come what may."

"What is it this time?" Keller retorted jocularly, man to man. "Does the parson want to join the Party and am I meant to stop him, or do I have to lean on him because he still refuses to apply for membership? You only have to say which."

"Appropriate action, Hermann, that's what's needed. You've hit the nail on the head." These touches of familiarity did not betoken personal liking so much as the sort of veterans' camaraderie the Führer himself liked to demon-

44

strate when it promised to pay off. "It's one of the Breitbachs this time—Konrad, to be precise."

"That little jerk?" Keller thought it legitimate to look faintly amused. "What do you want done with him? Like me to work him over?"

"On the contrary, I propose to sponsor his application for Party membership. Not only that, but I'm assigning him to your SA unit. Well, what do you say?"

"Does he have to join, or does he actually want to?" Keller eyed his boss curiously. "I can't picture that undersized runt in an SA uniform, but you must have your reasons."

"I do indeed. Konrad's the son of Richard Breitbach, a sworn opponent of the Party. We'd be crazy to turn him down, considering he's approached us of his own free will. This way we undermine the enemy camp. Now do you see?"

"Brilliant!" cried Keller, moved by this stroke of genius. "Just you send him to me. I'll show him what it means to be a fine, upstanding representative of the German race."

"That's the spirit," said Sonnenblum, but he added a word of warning. "Don't scare him off, though. Handle the boy with kid gloves, even if he turns out to be a dead loss. He may come in useful as bait."

"I quite understand, District Director." Keller succeeded in conveying how privileged he felt to operate under such resolute and perceptive leadership. "It's just another sign of the progress we're making. Onward and upward, eh? Very gratifying, I'm sure. People are coming to respect us— I might almost say, love us."

"Love us?" Sonnenblum knit his brow. "In what way?"

The Stormtroop Commander was clearly intoxicated by this theme. "Well, whenever we march through town with me up front, the women go goggle-eyed. They drool over us, I tell you! It's the uniform that does it—in my case, of course, uniform plus personality. A lot of them find it irresistible."

"Who, for instance? I'd be interested to know."

"Well, take Frau Abromeit, the baker's wife—a fluffy little blonde on the outside and a raging volcano underneath. She flings herself at me every time she gets a chance. Then there's Frau Buchner, the headmaster's wife, who looks hoity-toity and plays the piano—Mozart and so on. She's hotter than a dozen unspayed cats. So are the mayor's sister-in-law and the parson's wife and daughter, not to mention the receptionist at Kimminger's hotel—some 'receptionist,' believe me! They all open their legs when I give the word. Tell me one that won't!"

"What about Fräulein Fischer?" Sonnenblum asked tensely, bristling like a tomcat.

"Not her, of course." Keller's answer came back pat. He was well aware of his boss's infatuation, as were many of the town's inhabitants. In this respect, Gilgenrode held few secrets. "She's different; you wouldn't get anywhere with *her* in two minutes flat. A true representative of German womanhood, Fräulein Fischer, even if she doesn't look the part. She's got class—but I don't have to tell you that."

"All the same," Sonnenblum persisted, "wouldn't you like to . . . if you could, I mean?"

"Of course, District Director. No use pretending, not with you. A lovely piece like her? I wouldn't be human if she left me cold, but there's such a thing as loyalty. As a loyal subordinate, I naturally keep off the grass. Where she's concerned, you've got right of way."

"It hasn't stopped you taking her out to dinner, so I'm told. I also hear you sent her flowers—and candies."

"Yes, and a bottle of *crème de menthe*." Keller made this admission point blank. "But I only did it out of respect and

46

admiration for you. You think a lot of the lady. I'd say it was only natural for me to treat her properly."

"Well I don't like it!" Sonnenblum announced, speaking with a touch of asperity now. "I'm not so much thinking of your attentions to Fräulein Fischer, who certainly deserves every possible courtesy and consideration. What really worries me, Keller, is your promiscuous way of life—all these indiscriminate escapades with the opposite sex."

"I'm a man," Keller replied simply. Never one to sell himself short, he added, "And what a man!"

But Sonnenblum was unappeased. He raised his voice as though administering the Party oath. "You command our stormtroopers. As their senior officer, you have a duty to set an example. Are you, or are you not, prepared to do so?"

Keller, who had been lolling in a chair with his legs at full stretch, hurriedly assumed a more decorous pose.

"I've always done my best to—"

He broke off. It dawned on him that Sonnenblum was leading up to a proposition of some kind. He didn't know its value, but it had to be pretty substantial.

"So how should I behave—in your opinion?"

"In keeping with your unique and responsible status in this town," Sonnenblum replied gravely. "You must confine your attention to women of obvious social and racial merit. You owe it to the Movement."

"Your wish is my command, District Director. Can you point me in the right direction?"

"I could give you the names of several admirable and desirable women, my dear Keller—three of them at least. In the first place, there's the young widow who heads our National Socialist Women's Association . . ."

"Ilse Peller? A splendid creature, absolutely splendid, but a shade too old—for my taste, that is."

"Then how about Eva Schwarz of the German Girls'

League? Well brought up, easy on the eye, chock-full of the right spirit—"

"Yes, but a bit too young for me. Besides, she's not my type—always spouting slogans. Who wants to lay a Party handbook, let alone marry one! Eva's out, so who does that leave?"

"I mention the third person for form's sake only." Sonnenblum looked stern, as if daring Keller to misunderstand him. "It's Erika, my daughter."

Keller's face took on an air of heroic determination. "Of *course*, your daughter! A lovely-looking girl, one in a million, I'm sure. You mean you think we might—"

"I never even hinted at such a possibility, my dear Keller. However, Erika means a lot to me. I'd naturally welcome it if her choice fell on someone who was worthy of her in my eyes as well as hers."

"In that case," Keller declared, with the rash exuberance of one who glimpses a rosy future, "I'll try and work my way up to her level. There's nothing a man can't do if he sets his mind to it. The Führer says so, and the Führer's always right."

Richard Breitbach had enjoyed a substantial lunch of crisp roast pork and potato dumplings—the latter home-made, of course—at the invitation of Parson Bachus. Heavily fortified with bodily sustenance and spiritual guidance, he returned to his saddlery and headed for the studio.

Here, as expected, he found Konrad, who was busy adorning a saddle with fleurs-de-lis. This one had been commissioned by a Provençal count and would fetch at least twelve thousand francs.

"You're a damned fine craftsman," Breitbach said admiringly.

"Thanks to you, Father."

"Craftsmanship's worth plenty, but shouldn't I have taught you something more? What about politics and human nature?"

"You've taught me a lot, Father—far more than you suspect."

"Then I don't understand why you've teamed up with Sonnenblum. Have you really joined the Party?"

"I have."

"So you've made up your mind. We're on opposite sides of the fence."

Konrad looked up from his saddle, with its nut-brown leather and fine tracery of plaited silver wire, and gave his father an almost pitying smile. Breitbach, who wasn't used to condescension from his younger son, found it quite exasperating.

"Why should I be against you?" Konrad demanded. "What makes you think I'm on Sonnenblum's side? I'm Johannes's brother, that's all, and I want to see him happy."

Breitbach, as head of the family, felt obliged to launch a massive counterattack. "Any alliance with that damned man must be ultimately directed against me. I flatly forbid you to join forces with him."

"In the first place, Father, I'm not joining forces with him." Konrad might have been patiently coaching an apprentice. "Secondly, I'm twenty-five; you can't forbid me to do anything. Last but not least, I'm very much your son, but in my own way."

"So? What if I present you with a straightforward choice? I could turn my back on you, slam the door on you—cut you out of my will."

"But you won't. I'm not just your own flesh and blood, I'm the best man you've got. Who's going to run this place when you retire—Johannes? You couldn't afford to kick me out."

Breitbach swiped irritably at a fly that was buzzing around his head. "My God, boy, what's eating you?"

"I'm simply making allowances for our family position, which couldn't be more promising. You're a rabid anti-Nazi, Johannes does his best to sit on the fence, and I march beneath the crooked cross."

"You call that promising!"

"Try to see it in the right light, Father." Konrad grinned cheerfully. "Whichever way things work out—and I won't be surprised if the worst happens—one of us is bound to come out on the winning side. It'll then be up to him to dig the other two out, even if they're in it up to their necks."

Breitbach looked impressed despite himself. "Fancy dreaming up an idea like that. You must be insane!"

"No, Father, just moving with the times. What's sane about an age in which a man like Hitler can command universal respect and admiration? 'If we perish, the beauty of this world will subside with us into the grave.' You can read that on page three-sixteen of his literary masterpiece. If people can swallow that sort of trash without a murmur, it's well to be prepared for a few surprises. I wasn't a Boy Scout for nothing."

Emil Spahn gave a preliminary demonstration of his new-found spirit of patriotism, but not before fueling himself with a pint of brandy. With that inside him he felt equal to any game of chance, even dicing with the devil.

His performance took place at the Wheatsheaf, a tavern near the ruined castle of a knightly order on the western outskirts of town. It was much frequented by local farmers, who would round off a profitable day at the cattle market by going there in quest of diversion and entertainment. Emil gladly provided them with both.

This time, however, his act made them vaguely uneasy. Instead of babbling about heaven and hell, the Creation and its disastrous consequences, he gave vent to some rather more risky but equally diverting remarks.

"What a glorious, God-given land we live in! Everything here grows and thrives and blooms. We boast the sturdiest peasants, the biggest potatoes and the fattest livestock: cows with udders like Zeppelins, joyfully guzzling pigs, innocently grazing lambs. Our cup runneth over, my friends. We could rest content with our lot. But, as if that were not enough, stalwart German patriots have arisen in our midst!

"Let us sing their praises, my fellow citizens—or Compatriots, to use the Party-approved term. I congratulate you all, and myself. At long last, every man among us can feel like a genuine German male, every woman can take pride in her Teutonic femininity, and all our beloved children can rest assured of their status as pledges of our national future. That future may be rosy. It may also be as red as the blood that pulses in our German hearts. And whom do they beat for?

"For our Führer, of course, or for those who represent him and act in his name. We must put our trust in them. What matters is spiritual harmony and a shared sense of higher values; what counts is the call of the blood. The men I refer to, first and foremost, are our peerless District Director and his no less incomparable Stormtroop Commander. Both of them are perfect embodiments of the spirit that now presides over our national destiny!"

There was absolute silence in the taproom. Even the landlord was staring open-mouthed at his equally disconcerted customers, whose empty glasses threatened to remain unfilled. Then Emil broke the spell.

"We must drink to the health of our glorious home-grown Hitler and his worthy lieutenant. I'm sure we'll owe them an even greater debt of gratitude before they're through, so who'll do the honors?"

"Drinks all round!" called a cheerfully uninhibited voice. It belonged to Werner Rogalski, a noted breeder of pedigree cattle. "A large schnapps for everyone and a treble for our Emil!"

Rogalski turned to Emil and raised his glass. "You really poured it on, didn't you? All that stuff about Sonnenblum and Keller. Take care somebody doesn't turn off your tap for good one day."

Erika Sonnenblum and Johannes Breitbach had met in the municipal gardens. This public park, which overlooked Lake Gilgenrode, comprised several acres of crunchy gravel paths, lush grass, leafy lime trees and luxuriant flowerbeds. Its most important amenity was a row of park benches, important because rumor had it that a substantial proportion of Gilgenrode's population had been sired on, beside, beneath or behind them.

Nocturnal gloom enveloped the young couple as though tactfully shielding them from prying eyes. The sky was a dark but luminous blue that bathed their faces in magical radiance. The leaden waters of the lake gleamed softly and sensually in the faint moonlight. Erika and Johannes were breathing rather fast.

"Well, here I am." Erika's tone was demure but full of hidden promise. "You asked me to come, so I did."

"Thank you," said Johannes. "Thank you more than I can say." He groped for her hand, which she surrendered with alacrity. "I hope you won't get into trouble with your father. He doesn't approve of me."

"Forget about Father," said Erika, boldly seizing the initiative. "Can you hear my heart beating? It's beating because of you. Would you like to feel?"

Before he could reply she took his hand and guided it to her left breast. Erika's bosom proved to be rather on the small side and, thus, not fully consonant with state-approved standards of beauty, but that meant nothing to Johannes. A delicious thrill ran down his spine.

"You're wonderful!" he whispered. He yearned to fling himself on top of her, tear open her blouse and cup both hands around her breasts, which to him seemed the height of perfection. Instead, panting hard, he hurriedly disengaged himself.

"Dearest Erika, I respect you far too much to compromise you by irresponsibly yielding to my baser instincts."

"Oh God," sighed Erika, "I don't understand you. You can't have my father's blessing whatever you do, but you can have my love. Which matters more to you?"

District Director Sonnenblum had gone to Party headquarters in Allenstein. As soon as he was safely out of the way, Keller boarded the official car that had recently been put at his disposal. It was a four-door, six-passenger Mercedes sedan, and fully appropriate to a man in his exalted position. Color: funereal black.

Piloted by Keller himself, the imposing vehicle pulled up outside 9 Market Square, where Beate Fischer occupied two rooms plus kitchen and bathroom. Keller pressed the horn.

Beate took her time before finally emerging in a jaunty pearl-gray two-piece suit with a matching blouse beneath —an easily unbuttonable one, Keller was pleased to note. Nonchalantly, she climbed in beside him.

"Well," she said, expertly batting her eyelashes, "what's on the menu today?"

"Why not wait and see?"

"All right." Beate sank back against the upholstery but kept her knees firmly clamped together. "Go on, then, surprise me."

Keller did his best. He roared off, chuckling in a hearty, masculine way as he flung the car around. Gripped by a racing driver's exhilaration, he boldly cut corners and weaved in and out with a total disregard for other traffic.

A mere five miles out of town they came to one of the Gilgenroders' favorite haunts. Nestling beside a small expanse of water known as Lovers' Lake, the Brown Jug was an idyllic country inn much patronized by the townsfolk on high days and holidays. The pellucid waters of the Brotherhood Canal made it easily accessible from Lake Gilgenrode by skiff or steamer.

Once Kimminger had added this inn to his empire, its kitchen acquired a reputation for all-round excellence and its cellar for the variety and profusion of its stock, notably a beer named Fountain of England, brewed at Elbing, and several pure and potent spirits distilled in accordance with rustic formulas. Those whose tastes lay farther afield could order wines, both still and sparkling, from the German Rhine.

On the first floor of the Brown Jug, Kimminger had been shrewd enough to install three luxuriously appointed bedrooms. These he let without difficulty, either to honeymoon couples or to local bigwigs and businessmen accompanied by their girlfriends of the moment. Beate, who had never been in one of them, conveyed as much to Keller.

"I hope you don't expect *me* to end up in bed with you," she said with smiling candor. "Or do you really think I'm that sort?"

"Of course not," he assured her, secretly undeterred despite the ringing conviction in his voice. Beate's tight little buttocks bobbed ahead of him as he conducted her to the inn. He couldn't resist giving them a quick squeeze. Beate promptly came to a halt and stared at him wide-eyed.

"I *beg* your pardon! We haven't reached that stage yet, my friend, not by a long shot. If you're looking for a cheap thrill, count me out."

"I wouldn't dream of it," Keller said gravely. "I admire you too much."

Her smile carried a hint of warning. "Good, I'm relying on you to keep my reputation intact."

Keller called loudly for a bottle of German champagne, which came at once. He clinked glasses, drank, and choked. She patted him on the back—only lightly, but his hopes revived.

"I always believe in putting my cards on the table," she said. "It can't have escaped you that two other gentlemen have been taking a serious interest in me."

"Who cares!" Keller cried boldly, determined to impress her. He tipped the contents of his champagne glass down his throat and called for the menu. "Breitbach's a definite has-been; our new Germany doesn't hold any future for him. As for the other one,"—he meant Sonnenblum, but refrained from uttering the name—"he's trying to adapt himself to the needs of the time but he doesn't have the strength or stamina. He'll be trodden into the carpet, you mark my words."

"Who by—you? Aren't you afraid you're biting off more than you can chew?"

"No need to worry about that, not now. I feel you're interested, or at least sympathetic. That's an incentive in itself, but if you were prepared to help my efforts along— well, I could move mountains!"

"What sort of help do you mean?"

"It's entirely up to you." Keller put his arm around her, and this time she didn't recoil. "For instance, you could become the wife of a stormtroop commander who'll soon be a district director, if not a regional director. The sky's the limit with me. How about it?"

Beate leaned against him in an exploratory fashion. "All right, first convince me you're really the biggest man around. Then we'll see."

"Great!" exclaimed Keller. "Absolutely terrific!" He jerked his thumb heavenward. "How about sealing our little pact upstairs, just for a couple of hours?"

"Get away with you!" Beate gave him an arch smile. "As the potential wife of a potential district director, I can't afford any premarital hanky-panky."

"Beate, you're wonderful!" He gave an ultravirile guffaw. "Just my type, that's what you are. Saving it up for me, eh? What a splendid couple we'll make!"

For once, Beate decided to overlook his uninvited use of her Christian name. The evening had put her in a magnanimous frame of mind, which was why she wanted to cut it short. "Would you mind driving me home now?"

The outing had been a success, Keller decided. He summoned the waiter and pushed ten marks across the table, saying casually, "Keep it. The rest put down to Kimminger." Back came a deferential "Yessir!" He escorted Beate outside and, after a vain attempt to embrace her, said, "See? They all toe the line if you know how to treat 'em. This is only the start, though."

He climbed drunkenly into his official Mercedes and settled himself behind the wheel. "Okay, hop in."

Beate, who was still standing in the road, shook her head. "That's not very refined of you, I must say!"

"How do you mean?"

"Anyone with ambitions to be a gentleman," she said,

in restrained reproof, "makes a point of opening the car door for his lady friend and closing it behind her before he gets in himself."

The effect was magical. Keller obediently scuttled around the car and held the door for her. "Sweetheart, you've got real old-fashioned German class! There isn't a woman who'd suit me better."

"Render unto Caesar the things that are Caesar's, and to God the things that are God's. . . ." Still savoring the aftertaste of his latest sermon, which had, he felt convinced, struck a perfect balance between the temporal and the spiritual, Parson Bachus strolled across Market Square after morning service.

Bachus walked with a slight stoop suggestive of permanent humility, but his long legs soon carried him to the south side of the square. Here he paused outside the house occupied by Siegfried Sass, the businessman and philanthropist. It was typical of the civic architecture to be found in the center of Gilgenrode, with two stories, small windows and a fairly narrow front. The heavy door bore a carving of the sun and moon, either rising or setting; it was hard to tell which.

The façade of Sass's respectable-looking house was whitewashed as though to exemplify the resplendent cleanliness of the region. In East Prussia, so the saying went, you could dine in the gutter without a tablecloth.

But the very respectability of this far from flashy home made a lot of people suspicious. The Jew owned half of Gilgenrode, they told themselves. With his kind of money he could have bought himself a lakeside mansion, a pleasure palace in the surrounding forests—even a villa on the Côte d'Azur.

As it was, he stayed put in Gilgenrode, living in some

seclusion. He had no family, no children, no identifiable heirs. His only companions were a grizzled manservant and an equally ancient woman who was reputed to be the best cook in East Prussia—not that Sass, imprisoned in his snug but stuffy hermitage of velvet, leather and French polish, gave any evidence of gluttony.

It had probably escaped everyone in town except Konrad and Johannes Breitbach that Sass's walls were adorned with some truly remarkable paintings, among them a Goya, a Turner, a van Gogh, and two Renoirs. It was even less probable that anyone knew of the portrait hanging in his bedroom, on which his eye often lingered. Though painted in the previous century, it bore a strong resemblance to Beate Fischer.

Sass spent most days admiring his pictures or walking for hours on end—bareheaded usually, as if that were the only proper way to salute a landscape of such tranquil beauty. He also read a great deal. All in all, his finances seemed to claim little of his time.

On this particular Sunday morning, Sass went to answer the bell himself, a slightly round-shouldered figure with snow-white hair and eyes as clear as spring water. He opened the door and found himself face to face with Alois Bachus.

"Surprised, eh?" The parson's tone was as bright as his ingratiating expression. "I'm sure I'm the last person you expected to see. Still, you know the kind of man I am."

"No," said Sass, but not unkindly, "I can't say I do. Who knows anyone else, if the truth be told?"

Bachus looked rather taken aback. Unnerved by his own audacity in seeking this interview, he sank into the nearest armchair, while Sass, who had shown him into the drawing room, remained standing.

"You really must wake up to what's going on, Herr

Sass," the parson said imploringly. "It won't be long before this country is completely dominated by a gang of ruthless, self-seeking individuals who'll pocket anything and destroy anyone in their path. That includes you and those like you. You're in the gravest danger."

"What about you, Herr Bachus? Doesn't a Christian have any cause for concern?"

Bachus looked grim. "At the present time," he said, "our Christian community seems split between those who profess their faith in God and those who espouse the nationalist ideal. My own allegiance is to God alone."

"I see. And what bearing does that have on my own position?"

"You must put yourself in my hands, Herr Sass. I'm the only person here you can trust implicitly."

"How do you mean, put myself in your hands?"

"The Protestant Church has remained inviolate in this country for centuries. It's an institution commanding the deepest respect, a source of continuing influence, a place of sanctuary. We merit and enjoy the fullest possible confidence."

"Come, come," said Sass, only half in jest, "surely you're not trying to recruit me into your flock?"

Whether or not the fine spring weather was to blame, Bachus mopped his brow. His face shone like a well-greased pan. "I would only say this, Herr Sass. Our Church is secure. Not even a man of Hitler's caliber would dare lay hands on it. We shall survive him just as we have survived previous threats to our existence. In the meantime, we must take precautions, and so must you. That's why I'm here."

Although it gave him no great pleasure to see Bachus squirm, Sass had no intention of meeting him halfway. "What exactly was the point you wished to make?"

Bachus mopped his brow again. "I'm offering you a form

59

of insurance, financial as well as personal. In practical terms, I'm ready to help you save your assets from the Nazis before they can seize them—which they will before long."

"Are you suggesting that I sign over all my worldly goods to you—I mean, your church?"

"Yes, but only as a means of preserving them intact. You'd be leaving them in safe hands—until the dust clears, of course. I don't mean to be importunate, my dear sir. It's just a suggestion, but I urge you to consider it—quickly, before it's too late."

"I'll certainly give it careful thought," Sass replied with a rather mournful smile. "Please do the same."

KONRAD BREITBACH's induction into the Brownshirts took place one evening in May. In this, Hitler's first year at the helm of the new Germany, May was everything the ancient Germans had been wont to call the "Month of Joy." Nature threatened to erupt like a verdant volcano, fraught with sensual delights, and the Brownshirts' thirst for action—or that of their commanding officer—was no less unconfined.

Stormtroop Commander Keller, surrounded by his men, was waiting for Konrad at the new SA headquarters. He had swiftly and permanently converted the boathouse to his own use by clearing and renovating it from top to bottom. In accordance with a maxim that was currently acquiring the force of law—"Only the best will do for the best"—it had been transformed into a first-rate drill hall and training center.

"There you are, Comrade Breitbach!" called Keller. Although his greeting was as cordial as the District Director had prescribed, he couldn't repress a faint look of surprise and resentment at his latest recruit's appearance. "All right, lad, let's give you the once-over."

Konrad was dressed in a brand-new SA uniform, clearly of the finest quality: calfskin boots, riding breeches, tailored shirt, gleaming belt and shoulder-straps, peaked cap. The whole of this glamorous brown ensemble had been supplied by the State Ordnance Department in Munich but modified to produce a perfect fit by Werner Simoneit, the best tailor in town. As if to underline the difference between himself and the average stormtrooper, Konrad was carrying a book under his arm.

To this extent he cut an impressive figure, even by the lights of an eagle-eyed stormtroop commander. The only incongruous feature was that all this sartorial splendor encased a pocket-sized figure whose military bearing left much to be desired. Keller saw at once that he would have to make a man of Konrad. That, after all, was one of his specialities. With a face unclouded by any presentiment of the havoc his latest acquisition would cause, he turned to address the rest of the contingent.

"Men," he said, "this is our new recruit. His name and family background don't matter. The main thing is, he's a volunteer. That makes him one of us, so welcome, Comrade Breitbach! You'll get a chance to stand us all a drink after parade, but first things first." Keller smiled grimly. "Duty calls!"

In this case, "duty" began with some drill movements more appropriate to a unit undergoing basic infantry training. "Fall . . . in! Right . . . dress! Count . . . off! At . . . ease! Atten . . . shun! Eyes . . . right! Eyes . . . front!" The men were then reported present and correct by the senior platoon commander, whose salute Keller acknowledged with Napoleonic aplomb.

Then: "Fifteen minutes' foot-drill by platoons. Polish up those turns on the march. Move!"

The platoon commanders took individual command of their men, haranguing them in a barrack-square baritone modeled on Keller's, "Stomachs in, chests out, thumbs on your trouser seams, heads up, eyes front, keep a tight asshole!"—and similar verbal gems.

Keller's platoon commanders were three in number. "Mule" Müller, a bank clerk by day, owed his nickname to the frequency and force with which he used the toe of his boot. "Softy" Schulze, a provision merchant, mistook his overweening personal ambition for simon-pure idealism. Finally, there was "Muscles" Feinemann, a journeyman butcher of cheerful disposition. As one for whom the slaughtering of dumb animals was a legally controlled procedure, he was soon to feel that his license extended to inferior members of the human race.

All three men were dominated by Keller, and they obeyed him to the letter—as now, when he decreed further drill movements designed to turn milksops into men. They were next enjoined to practice the "German" or Hitler salute. This entailed standing at attention, keeping your eyes glued to your superior officer or the flag, and shooting out your right arm, fingers together and stiffly extended. Height of fingertips: level with the right eyebrow—not a millimeter above or below. "And keep those paws still. If anyone moves, I'll kick his ass into a swastika! Right! Get cracking!"

The stormtroopers did so, spurred on by the raucous cries of their platoon commanders. Keller himself stood watching with his thumbs hooked into his belt and his legs planted firmly apart. The new recruit claimed his special attention. Konrad had discarded his book and was joining in with a will. He even showed a certain aptitude, Keller couldn't deny it. The boy might make a useful addition to the ranks. At least he was a trier.

"Dis . . . missed!" Keller commanded, after working his men into a lather for a solid hour. "Let's tank up."

The necessary arrangements had been made. Thanks to generous donations from the majority of Gilgenrode's inhabitants, the Brownshirts could afford to do themselves proud off duty. This time there was a steaming cauldron full of sausages—at least two per head—and some crusty farmhouse loaves still warm from the oven. Keller personally broke the bread into large chunks and tossed them to his men.

They munched away in a companionable group, clustered round their commanding officer, who had additionally decreed a bottle of beer all round. "Just to keep your strength up," he explained. "The hard stuff comes later."

Like all the Führer's henchmen, Brownshirts were encouraged to use the familiar mode of address among themselves, regardless of rank. This simplified matters for everyone including Konrad. He turned to Keller with a look of artless inquiry.

"Excuse me, Stormtroop Commander, but I'm a bit puzzled by your training program. Are you sure you aren't barking up the wrong tree?"

Keller paused in his labors—he was carving a sausage into thick slices—and swung around incredulously. "*Me,* barking up the wrong tree? What the hell gives you that idea, you little jerk—I mean, Comrade Breitbach?"

Surveying the faces around him, Konrad failed to detect a spark of good will, least of all among the platoon commanders. "Softy" Schulze, whose nickname was an ironical allusion to his hard-nosed attitude, gave a menacing laugh.

"Thinks he knows better than the old ones, eh?"

"I realize I'm only a beginner," Konrad said quickly, "but we all have to start sometime. I could be wrong, of course. I simply took the liberty of asking a question—a fair one, as I see it."

Keller's appetite seemed suddenly to have deserted him. He pushed his plateful of dissected sausage aside but left it within reach. "What *is* all this crap, Comrade?"

"I'm only pointing out, Stormtroop Commander, that some of the things we're doing here may be off target."

"Off target?" rumbled "Mule" Müller. "The SA have a job to do, youngster. Question that, and I'll scramble your balls with my boot. You wouldn't be the first."

"Steady, Comrades!" Keller said loftily. "Let Konrad have his say; the District Director believes in free speech. Well, go on."

Konrad responded with a smile of almost moronic innocence. "I'd never be presumptuous enough to question the spirit or objectives of the SA—far from it! I'm only trying to be constructive. It's just that the methods you use strike me as—well—to put it mildly, not well-directed enough."

"Softy" Schulze's face darkened. "Jesus, he's got the verbal trots!" The other stormtroopers gazed at their commander, ready to do his bidding.

"Don't make me laugh, Breitbach," said Keller, looking thoroughly unamused. "What the devil are you driving at?"

"I'm merely raising the following point for discussion. The SA can't, by its very nature, be a military organization. It isn't meant to be a substitute army. All military functions must be left to the armed forces proper. The SA is the spearhead of the Party. As such, it must undergo physical training and be employed in a suitable manner."

Keller drew himself up, bristling. He could feel his men's eyes upon him, and he responded accordingly. "What are you trying to say, man? Who put that bullshit into your head?"

"I wouldn't call it bullshit myself, Stormtroop Commander."

"But *I* would, and what I say goes. Come on, who put this Jewish hogwash into your head?"

Konrad gave another boyish smile. "I read it in a book."

"He read it! Did you hear that? He *read* it!" Keller prompted his audience with a glance and was rewarded with gales of scornful laughter. "My God, that beats everything! The boy actually reads—books, what's more! Well, who wrote that crap?"

"Our Führer," Konrad replied, simply and to devastating effect. The platoon commanders looked thunderstruck, and their juniors flinched as though cowering away from a shellburst. The joke had turned sour, they all realized that. One mention of the Führer's hallowed name was enough to put them in deadly earnest.

Keller, who also looked chastened, strove to salvage the situation with a clumsy attempt at camaraderie. "Isn't it possible you've misunderstood our Führer in some way? These things happen, Comrade—I wouldn't hold it against you."

"My source is Adolf Hitler's *Mein Kampf*." Konrad picked up his discarded book and brandished it like a blunt instrument. He opened it with a deftness that spoke of long practice, reveling in the silence and consternation around him.

"Here it is in black and white, Comrades, on page six-eleven of our new German Bible. The words are italicized, which denotes their special importance. Permit me to quote verbatim: 'Its training'—meaning ours—'must be based, not only on military considerations, but on those expedient to the Party.'

"So much for my first quotation, Comrades. Our beloved Führer follows it up with some detailed remarks which corroborate everything I've taken the liberty of pointing out so far. Would you like me to go on?"

"That's enough," thundered Keller, "Quite enough." He knew there was no arguing with Hitler's *Mein Kampf*. Although he was as ignorant of the book as most Christians are of the Bible, anything it contained in the way of orders and instructions merited unquestioning obedience. "We must think this over, Comrades. Thoroughly!"

Sixty foreheads creased with mental effort, only to relax at Keller's next words.

"That'll do for today. Of course I know the Führer's splendid book—every last word of it—but it's part of my job to read between the lines. We'll discuss it again next time."

He nodded encouragingly at all his men save one. Konrad he studiously ignored. Then he stalked, with an air of grim resolve, to his Mercedes.

"What brings you here?" Siegfried Sass's tone was mildly ironical. "Did you expect to see me quaking with terror, or are you hoping to enlist me in the resistance? I'm too old for either, I'm afraid."

Richard Breitbach shook his head. "Wrong both times, Herr Sass. This is purely a business matter."

Sass eyed his visitor, whom he could remember as a child nearly fifty years ago. He regarded Breitbach as an excellent craftsman and a good businessman, but also as an incorrigible scrapper whose pugnacity tended to cloud his otherwise keen intelligence.

"You tickle my curiosity, dear boy. Several people have made me propositions lately. What's yours?"

Breitbach helped himself to a glass of port and a Dutch

cigar, both of outstanding quality. Then he came straight
to the point.

"It's about Number 7 Market Square. You own the
freehold, I believe."

"What makes you think so?"

"The land register lists it as the property of a real-estate
company run by Dr. Breile, and Dr. Breile has acted as
your legal adviser for years; his father used to be your
father's attorney. That makes it fair to assume you own the
building which houses Sonnenblum's dental practice, also
the district headquarters of the Nazi Party."

"I'm beginning to understand," Sass said slowly. "I mar-
vel at your effrontery, dear boy. I'd never have believed it,
even of you; you plan to kick the man out!"

"I'm thinking of trying. A Jew couldn't afford to do so
without getting his fingers burnt—or worse—whereas I
can make so much trouble for our so-called District Director he'll wish he had never been born."

Sass poured himself a glass of port, but only sniffed it
appreciatively. "It pains me to admit it, but I'm tempted.
Very well, I could do you the favor you ask—in fact I might
even be willing to take a small loss on the transaction."

"There's no question of that," Breitbach said firmly. "I
wouldn't dream of it. We'll have the property valued by a
third party of your choosing and I'll pay the market price.
I refuse to do it any other way."

The elderly Jew was looking even older than his years.
He heaved a sigh. "My dear young friend, you're ven-
turing into the lions' den. Lions do more than savage
people, they eat them alive."

Beate Fischer was sterilizing and rearranging Sonnenblum's instruments, which had scarcely been used during
his latest ill-attended office hours. She was still at it when

Gertrude Sonnenblum padded in and installed herself behind the desk of her absent son, who was once more playing the Party potentate.

The old woman subjected "that girl," as she called Beate, to a protracted stare. Her beady eyes narrowed.

"Looking at you from here, girl, I can understand a lot of things. Your breasts are on the small side, but they look nice and firm. Your backside's the same—not much meat but a decent shape. But your real assets are those great big goo-goo eyes and that dainty little nose with its sexy-looking nostrils. You're like a bird of paradise in a henhouse. No wonder you drive men crazy."

Beate was quite unabashed. After three years as Sonnenblum's receptionist she had given up trying to divine what went on in his mother's head. However crudely expressed, Gertrude's mental processes were bewilderingly complex.

"Frau Sonnenblum," said Beate, as she swabbed some congealed blood and saliva from a pair of dental forceps, "I sometimes wonder why you don't take a stronger line with your son. Tell him to kick me out of his surgery—and his private life. I think he'd do it if you really put your foot down."

"Why should I? I'm not a selfish old fool. I love my son, and I'd like to see him happy—even with you, if that's possible. I doubt that it is, though."

"What makes you so sure?"

"That's easy. You're much the same as I was at your age, even in looks—I'll show you some photos sometime. I was just as much of a man-eater as you. Things were different then, that's all."

"What do you expect me to do? Your son has hinted at marriage. Quite frankly, I can't make up my mind. Does that reassure you?"

"I'm not worried, my dear, but Heinrich should be. He is,

too, thanks to you. He's jumpy, indecisive, unsure of himself. I find that a welcome sign. It suits my book perfectly."

"You mean it doesn't matter how I treat him—it's all right with you?"

"More or less." An almost maternal note crept into Gertrude's gruff but amiable voice. "I probably know more about you than you do yourself. Your mother and I were friends before you were born. She was working as housekeeper to another friend of mine—Herr Sass. That's partly why I've always had a soft spot for you."

"I didn't know," said Beate, frowning. "What are you getting at?"

"Don't waste time wondering, girl. Stay the way you are and turn my son into a mental wreck. With luck, he'll pick up the pieces and come to his senses again. If anyone can ruin his Party prospects, it's you. I'm banking on it."

Stormtroop Commander Keller had been summoned, not invited, to present himself at Sonnenblum's office. The usual sequence was an exchange of salutes and handshakes followed by a cordial, confidential, comradely exchange of ideas. But not this time.

Sonnenblum sat hunched behind his desk like a broody hen. He curtly acknowledged his SA chief's snappy salute with a casual wave of the hand, as though wielding a fly swatter. Then he glanced at his wrist watch and the desk clock in front of him. "Nine minutes late, Keller. I don't like unpunctuality."

The Stormtroop Commander grinned broadly. "I was held up—woman trouble—had to pry her loose. . . ."

"I repeat, nine minutes late." Still unmollified, Sonnenblum left Keller standing where he was. "I summoned you here for a discussion of official business. Uniform is the

regulation attire on such occasions. I'm properly dressed, you aren't. I don't like that either."

Keller couldn't believe his ears, but he was almost certain he knew the real reason for Sonnenblum's ire. The District Director had presumably got wind of his excursion to the Brown Jug with Beate Fischer. Somebody must have blabbed, and God help the bastard when Keller discovered his identity! Hurriedly, he went into his old pal's routine.

"You must have got out of bed the wrong side, District Director. You know you can trust me all the way. I'm right behind you."

"Yes, so you can stab me in the back at the first opportunity." Sonnenblum seemed anxious to develop into a leader figure modeled on the Führer himself. This entailed a recognition that power breeds envy and powerful men have enemies; that everyone in authority has at least one would-be successor breathing down his neck. The dentist's face hardened. "Well, nobody's going to catch me napping, so get that straight."

"You're too suspicious," said Keller, who had paled a little. "Even with someone like me, who couldn't be more loyal. Is that why you saddled me with Konrad Breitbach?"

"Konrad?" Sonnenblum brightened. "What about him? Is he giving you a hard time?"

"That's a mild description of the little swine's behavior —at his very first parade, what's more. I'm pretty sure he's a deliberate troublemaker. Were you trying to test me, or something? He actually had the nerve to—"

"I know, I heard all about it. He submitted a report on his first parade with your unit at my request, and I don't see what you're beefing about. Why should it be deliberately provocative to quote from our Führer's masterpiece—

71

a book I revere and am constantly re-reading? Do you have any criticisms to offer?"

"Of course not!" Keller said quickly. "But the way he tried to make us look like a bunch of ideological idiots, me included—well, it was too much!"

"Did you *feel* idiotic, Keller?"

"Naturally not, or I'd have buttoned his lip for him. I'm very sensitive when it comes to things like that. Besides, I definitely get the impression he respects my rank."

"There you are, then." Sonnenblum was glorying in his sense of superiority. "We've finally acquired a Party member and stormtrooper who devotes some thought to the ideals of our Movement, and we should welcome the fact."

Young Breitbach was going to prove useful, he reflected. He badly needed someone capable of easing his burdens and shielding him from the rivals who were jostling for his directorial position.

Two of these he considered particularly dangerous. One was Peter Patzer, who headed the propaganda section but was merely a schoolmaster with delusions of political grandeur. The other was this gorilla in front of his desk. Keller had no scruples about trespassing on his, Sonnenblum's, private life—that much was abundantly clear. He decided to read the riot act.

"Our Führer's *Mein Kampf* demands universal respect. The truths it proclaims must be accepted without question. I insist on that."

Keller was quick to agree. "If any misunderstandings have arisen, District Director, I sincerely regret them. I beg you never to doubt my loyalty or devotion."

The District Director emitted a harsh, scornful laugh. "My sole concern is the Party's reputation, Keller, and that's where you fail to measure up. I don't mean your outing to the Brown Jug with Fräulein Fischer. What I find so reprehensible is your attempt to extort a free meal from the proprietor. That could furnish the enemies of our Movement with plenty of live ammunition."

"That fat slob Kimminger! If he's had the gall to spread lies about me, I'll break every bone in his body. You see, District Director, we're always being shat on!"

"Not *we*, Keller—*you*. And not without reason, I'm afraid. You're a pretty good stormtroop commander. I'd be sorry to lose you."

The shaft went home. Keller turned brick-red. "I don't deserve this, District Director—Comrade."

"You're a grown man, Keller. Far be it from me to meddle in your private life, but I'd welcome it if you finally settled down. You need a stable relationship—one that befits your official position."

"I know!" Keller cried fervently. Sonnenblum was making yet another allusion to his daughter, he grasped that at once. "To be honest with you, I feel a bit chary of courting such a refined, respectable young lady. Still, if you really think I ought to try my luck—"

"Try anything you like, Keller, as long as it doesn't rebound on me. Think it over carefully."

Mentally armed as well as alcoholically primed by Konrad, Emil Spahn went into action once more. His chosen venue, a hostelry near the old municipal gardens, was patriotically entitled the Prussian Grenadier.

The Prussian Grenadier was patronized by middle-class citizens who enjoyed a certain local repute, among them Oskar Matzke, butcher and veteran of the trenches; Hellmut Kunigkeit, locksmith and weekend angler; and Horst Krüger, distiller and connoisseur of his own liquid produce.

Another regular was Erwin Schulze, provision merchant. He and his wife ran a smallish grocery store not far

73

from Market Square. It was a hard life, but things had been looking up since "Softy" Schulze became a platoon commander in the SA.

Into the tavern—heavy benches, thick tabletops, rough plank floor, smoke-blackened curtains, scrubbed wooden bar—sidled Emil Spahn, but not before making a precautionary announcement:

"I can pay. I've got more than enough for a skinful."

"Who's dead?" quipped one of the regulars. "You must have come into a fortune."

Emil surveyed the room with the solemnity of a preacher in his pulpit. "We're all of us heirs, Compatriots—heirs to a new golden age! How glorious it is to be alive in such times! The trees have more leaves than usual, the cattle look friendlier by far, the flowers bloom more brightly, the hearts of men beat higher. What more could we ask?"

He proceeded to order a large schnapps and pay for it in advance—he even left a tip. Then he poured it down his gullet and blearily scanned the bar. He seemed gratified when he caught sight of Platoon Commander Schulze.

"Permit me," he said loudly, "to salute one of our Storm Detachment's foremost representatives, a man deserving of the highest admiration and deepest respect. Where, I ask myself, should we be without him and his like? It doesn't bear thinking of!"

"All right, man, all right." Schulze spoke with a mixture of complacency and irritation. "You can cut the rest of the crap, I'll stand you a double."

Emil raised both hands in benediction, then picked up his brimming glass and toasted the Platoon Commander.

"You hear that, Compatriots? It only goes to show what noble souls are gathered here—loyal henchmen of the greatest of them all. I refer, of course, to our paragon of a storm-

74

troop commander, Hermann Keller, a shining example to his men and an inspiration to every German female worthy of the name. Even children look up to him in awe!"

"And so they should," Schulze said stoutly, but he expelled the words with an angry hiss. "All right, Emil, no need to go on driveling, you've made your point. Get one thing straight, though: the SA isn't Keller on his own—it's all of us. Now drink up and shut up."

This drew protests and encouragement from the other patrons of the Prussian Grenadier. "Encore! Encore! It may be drivel but it passes the time. Go on, Emil, get it off your chest!"

Emil complied with alacrity. "The Stormtroop Commander is a living symbol of our new and blessed era. Many German women—here in Gilgenrode, at any rate—regard this fine, upstanding man as the light of their lives. Our revered Platoon Commander Schulze's wife is not, of course, among them."

Schulze glared at Emil over a forest of beer and schnapps glasses. His face turned as pale as the faded sandstone of the Baltic coast, then pink as a crag illumined by the setting sun. *"What* did you say?" he yelled, flexing his powerful hands. "What are you insinuating, you drunken sod?"

Emil looked shocked. "Nothing," he protested. "I'd never dare. I was merely paying tribute to the exceptional qualities of your wife, Herr Schulze, coupled with those of your matchless commanding officer. Please don't misunderstand me."

"Carry on!" the barflies chorused eagerly. "We'll keep your glass filled up."

But Schulze, very much the contrary of his nickname now, had had enough. He scowled menacingly. "If that cretin opens his filthy mouth once more, I'll beat him into a pulp—and the same goes for anyone who encourages him, understand?"

The same evening, Stormtroop Commander Keller strode into the Fatherland Café near the town hall, where his open-necked shirt and casual attire created a deliberately challenging impression. He sat down at a table in the center of the café, hands on thighs, bulging chest flung out, keen eyes scanning the clientele.

"Get Kimminger," he commanded the headwaiter.

"As far as I know, sir," the headwaiter cautiously replied, "Herr Kimminger's over at the Eagle—his hotel."

Keller brushed this obstacle aside like a tank. "I'm waiting. I'm a patient man, but don't push your luck."

The headwaiter withdrew at top speed, noting as he did so that another three undesirables had forged their way into the café, all of them clearly Keller's men. They made themselves nonchalantly at home and took possession of a table with the *élan* of assault troops seizing enemy territory.

Although the headwaiter did not know exactly who they were, he very soon found out. They were "Mule" Müller, "Softy" Schulze and "Muscles" Feinemann, the SA platoon commanders.

A wave of disquiet engulfed the solid citizens present, among them a doctor with his wife and daughter, a bank manager and his assistant, a timber merchant and two customers, the owner of the Lakeland Steamship Company, and a town councilor dating the mayor's secretary. All of them sensed that even here, in this haven of respectability, many things were not as they had been.

General uneasiness deepened when the café was overrun by another nine invaders—reliable toughs selected by

Keller's three senior subordinates. They looked around, grinning fiercely, and sat down wherever there happened to be a vacant chair. Once seated, they spread themselves, elbowing the men aside and staring pointedly down the cleavages of their worthy womenfolk. Within a few minutes, at least a dozen customers had hurriedly paid and left.

At this stage, Kimminger bustled in. The headwaiter's alarm call had forced him to cut short a promising tête-à-tête at the German Eagle Hotel. He had just been showing a certain Frau Schulze his stamp collection. The forthcoming interview promised to be less enjoyable—he could tell that at a glance.

He hurried over to Keller and bowed obsequiously. "It's always a pleasure to welcome you to my humble establishment," he assured him in a sibilant, confidential undertone. "The place is entirely at your disposal."

Keller's response was unmistakably hostile. "Kimminger," he snapped, "did you have the gall to report me to the District Director for accepting a dinner at the Brown Jug? If so, you're a mean, dirty, double-dealing bastard. Unless, of course, you can produce a convincing explanation."

"I can indeed!" The hotelier unburdened himself like a limpid stream threading its untroubled way through jagged rocks. "The other day, while I was chatting to Herr Sonnenblum about this and that, I took the liberty of mentioning how delighted I was that he wasn't the only one to avail himself of my services—that they had recently been enlisted by no less a person than his Stormtroop Commander."

Keller stiffened. "How does Sonnenblum come into this?"

"Well, Herr Keller, I always do my best to oblige. I've

been giving the District Director a ten percent discount on his entertainment expenses for quite some time. The same concession will apply to you, of course."

This disclosure filled Keller with deep satisfaction. It was just as he had expected. "I see. So you don't want us to smash up your cozy little joint after all—which we could if we wanted, if you left us no choice."

"For God's sake, Herr Keller, anything but that!" Kimminger looked agonized. "Your good will means a lot to me."

"How much is a lot? Could you put a figure on it?"

"I was thinking of a twenty-five percent discount for you personally and ten percent for your men. Would that do?"

"It might," Keller said grudgingly. "Except that my men wouldn't feel at home in this dump—it's too stuffy, too genteel. They need a recreation center where they can really let their hair down."

"Leave it to me, Stormtroop Commander." Gilgenrode's leading restaurateur gave this assurance with relief. His unerring nose for a good thing told him that a deal was imminent—not an especially profitable one, but worth it in the long run. If Hitler were as firmly in the saddle as he seemed, it would pay to do his comrades in arms a favor.

The stormtroopers' private canteen—destined to be christened the Strong Man's Arms—was as good as open. The inaugural festivities would take place in a few days' time.

There were still moments when Heinrich Sonnenblum, dentist and District Director, was assailed by a fleeting urge to reveal himself a mere mortal like any other. He felt this with Beate Fischer, of course, but his prospects had lately grown dim.

The most favorable time for the intimacies he craved

had proved to be the period following afternoon office hours, which he extended by skimping his patients' treatment and pestering them out of the chair.

At such auspicious moments he would dart toward Beate in hot-breathed anticipation, put his arms around her, clasp her to him and seek her lips with his. She suffered his kisses but watched him intently meanwhile. Sonnenblum did not at first notice this. He was far too busy proving that he, and he alone, could unlock the gates to heaven on earth.

"You . . ." he would moan, trying to ignite her with his own passion as he strove—always unsuccessfully—to accelerate the process of seduction. "I'm burning up inside for you!"

It had been like this for a year now, ever since Beate's last substantial raise. The identical *modus operandi* was invariably accompanied by almost identical phrases. In love as in other fields, Sonnenblum was no great wordsmith; he fancied himself as more a man of action. Having prudently cleared his desk in advance, he would nudge Beate toward it with the obvious intention of bedding her down on its spacious top.

Their arrival at the desk was the signal for him to unbutton her blouse. Beate wore silky, flimsy, clinging blouses all year round, just as she never wore a slip or a misleadingly upholstered bra. With her firm but slender figure, she had no need.

This time, however, as her breasts seemed to bob out at him and he bent to brush them with his lips, she evaded him with a sudden violent twist of the body. Sonnenblum glissaded off her, tripped, and landed on the linoleum.

"Sweetheart," he protested, staring up at her in amazement, "what's the matter with you?"

"The door isn't locked."

He continued to gaze at her like a worried ox denied its due bale of hay. "The whole town's at liberty to know what we're up to in here, as far as I'm concerned. I make no secret of my love. Doesn't that count for anything with you?"

"You're just like all the rest," she retorted sharply, buttoning her blouse. "A sex object, that's all I mean to you, and it sickens me. I won't be treated like a public convenience. I've got too much self-respect!"

Sonnenblum tottered to the chair behind his desk and slumped into it, choked by the sensation that he had been grossly misjudged. What else was he but a loving, generous man in search of tenderness and affection? What did she take him for, a lecherous brute, a womanizer, a sexual scalp-hunter?

"What are you doing to me?" he groaned.

Beate retreated still farther. "Can't you see what *you're* doing to *me?*" she said fiercely. "You treat me like a handle you can grab whenever the mood takes you—*me*, whom you claim to respect! Never try to force your attentions on me again, Heinrich."

Sonnenblum felt like a deep-sea diver being hauled to the surface with fatal rapidity. His lungs ached and his blood-vessels seemed to be bursting inside his skull like ripe tomatoes.

"You can't mean it."

"I most certainly do." She finished buttoning her blouse with the air of one who had shut up shop—God alone knew for how long! "This had to happen sometime, Heinrich, for your sake as much as mine. It's the only way to rebuild our relationship, believe me."

"But I don't understand." Sonnenblum had been smitten with some nameless fever. His hands fluttered like leaves in a gale.

"You must just be patient, my dear. There's nothing a man can't do if he's genuinely in love, and that's the only kind of man I want."

And that, Sonnenblum reflected, breathing heavily, could mean no one but himself.

ERIKA HAD conveyed to Johannes Breitbach, local poet and intellectual, that her grandmother was expecting him for coffee—just him, nobody else. He duly presented himself at 7 Market Square with a bunch of lilies the color of egg yolk.

"My compliments, fair lady."

Gertrude Sonnenblum's response was characteristic. "Don't you fair lady me! I'm an old crone, but all the smarter for that. Nobody gets around me with pretty speeches and flowers that smell like a funeral parlor. You could have saved yourself the trouble and expense, Johannes."

Her use of his Christian name was altogether natural, not just a product of the age gap. In the old days, when the Breitbachs and the Sonnenblums were still on friendly terms, they had spent most Sundays together. Gertrude had looked on Konrad as a late-born son, always with interest and recently with admiration. Although she took care not to show it, she was intensely proud of her godson. Her affection for Johannes, on the other hand, had a tender quality. He had been a strange, dreamy boy with velvet skin, timid, graceful movements, and a pair of melting eyes that seemed to yearn for understanding.

Gertrude poured a cup of coffee and pushed it toward him. "You haven't changed much since you were a youngster. That can be an asset, but it can also work the other way."

"I'm nearly thirty, Aunt Gertrude. That makes me old enough to found a family of my own. To do that I need a wife—you know who I mean. May I count on your support?"

"Johannes, my dear boy!" Gertrude wavered between amusement and impatience. "You're far more naïve than I feared. If what I think matters to you—yes, you have my blessing."

Their discussion was interrupted by the arrival of Parson Bachus, who breezed in and uttered some euphonious words of apology. He didn't mean to intrude, of course; he'd gladly return another time. Gertrude beckoned him in.

"You aren't intruding, certainly not on me."

Bachus disliked Johannes, and the sentiment was mutual. Each regarded the other as a moral coward, whether in the pulpit or in print. Johannes rose and asked to be excused, but Gertrude put him firmly in his place.

"You're staying. I haven't done with you yet."

Now it was the parson's turn to receive a cup of her splendidly strong coffee, accompanied—not that Gertrude bothered to consult him first—by a large glass of corn liquor as clear as ice water. This was his usual ration per visit.

Sipping pleasurably, Bachus started to expatiate in unctuous tones on God and Gilgenrode.

He emphasized, at first without interruption, what a pleasure and privilege it was to call so regularly on the lady of the house. On this occasion, his pleasure had been enhanced by the presence of young Herr Breitbach. It only went to show how little credence should be attached to the ugly rumors of a feud between two families which had been united in harmony and friendship for so many years. "And that is an extremely hopeful sign, particularly today, when misunderstandings tend to spring up like mushrooms—or should I say toadstools?—after a downpour."

Gertrude looked intrigued. "What else would you include under the heading of toadstools, Herr Bachus? The Nazis, perhaps?"

"Come, come, my dear Frau Sonnenblum!" Bachus flung up his arms as though putting Beelzebub to flight. "How could I possibly bring myself, in this house and in your hearing, to insult your worthy son by describing him as a poisonous natural phenomenon? I said nothing of the kind, as our young friend here will bear witness."

"You don't have to butter me up," said Gertrude. "There's no need to spare my feelings, let alone pay lip service to my son's present status. After all, he wasn't a district director when I brought him into the world. If you really want to call the Nazis toadstools, good for you! We think alike."

Parson Bachus ached to steady his nerves with another schnapps, but he was refused the consolation he longed for. Teetering a little like a traveler lost in the desert and close to collapse, he took his leave.

"You see, Johannes?" said Gertrude, with the grim satisfaction of a lone wolf. "There's another one who's trying to

85

curry favor with the powers that be—in other words, my son—and hoping to do it through me. *Me!* Well, there's nothing doing in that direction. Have I made myself clear?"

Next day, the conspicuously unobtrusive figure of Hermann Keller could be seen lurking near the school gates. He was lying in wait for Erika Sonnenblum, who was, he had discovered, supervising a physical-education class in the gymnasium—or, to use official jargon, toughening the youthful bodies of Hitler's youthful devotees.

The SA chief loitered in the lee of a wall, crouching slightly like a long-distance runner on the starting line. The sight of Erika, when she finally appeared, seemed to galvanize him. He reached her in seconds, barred her path, grinned at her invitingly, and raised his arm in a regulation salute.

"Heil Hitler, Party Member Sonnenblum!" he cried, miming joyful surprise. "What luck! I happened to be in the neighborhood on official business, and who should I bump into but you! Mind if I walk you home?"

Erika retreated a step, but only—he felt sure—for a better look. She inspected him with a schoolmarm's practiced eye.

"I think you should know, Herr Keller, that I'm not a member of your party."

Keller was undeterred. "Still," he boomed, "you are the daughter of our ranking Party official, whose closest associate I have the honor to be. As such, I hope you'll let me see you home."

"In a little town like ours?" Erika had taken refuge behind an invisible schoolroom desk. "People might get the wrong idea. I'm virtually engaged, as you've probably heard."

"I realize that, of course." Keller gave a skull-like grin.

Her telltale "virtually" had not escaped his keen ear, so he felt he could afford a blunt threat. "But I'm sure you won't turn me down. Your father wouldn't be at all pleased if he heard—not that *I'd* tell him, naturally."

They left the school behind and headed for Market Square past the moldering ruins of an ancient castle and the neatly kept middle-class homes bordering the playing fields. Erika was very silent—she could hardly be otherwise, because Keller subjected her to a verbal bombardment. They were living in a new, turbulent, tempestuous era, one that called for the total dedication of heart and mind, body and soul. Its overriding commandment was that persons of superior national stock should unite. She, Erika, was undoubtedly one such. He, Keller, was another. Ergo, they were two of a kind!

"I'm sure you know what I'm getting at."

But Erika feigned total incomprehension. She found this all the easier because they had now reached 7 Market Square, which housed her father's surgery, his District Director's office, and her family home.

"I found it all very interesting, Herr Keller," she replied curtly.

"Just a modest start, Fräulein," he assured her, eager for final victory, "but a promising one. I hope you agree."

Richard Breitbach had fixed an appointment with Dr. Breile, Sass's lawyer. Their meeting took place outside normal office hours, because they were anxious to avoid being seen or interrupted by a third party. After a conspiratorial handshake, they got down to business.

"All your requirements have been met," the lawyer told Breitbach. His thick-lensed glasses and apologetic voice made a rather helpless and confiding impression, but that was probably deceptive. "To be specific, you may purchase the property known as Number 7 Market Square if you so desire."

"I do indeed."

"The present owner of the property advises against such a step. So do I, for your sake."

Breitbach doggedly shook his head. "I'll buy at any price."

"At the proper price, Herr Breitbach. This has been fixed by a qualified valuer, as you suggested, and authenticated by a notary public. Nobody will ever be able to accuse you of trading on the plight of a Jewish fellow citizen."

"Good, then let's complete the deal."

"Very well, the deed of sale is ready for signature." The lawyer squeezed a reluctant smile. In a predatory age like the present, transactions of this kind were fraught with danger. "Is there anything more I can do for you, Herr Breitbach?"

"Yes, you can give me some information." Breitbach's eyes twinkled enigmatically. "What really interests me is this: did Sonnenblum know his landlord was a Jew?"

"He may have." Breile spread his hands in an ambiguous gesture. "Let's put it this way: he probably knew the truth but conveniently dismissed it from his mind."

"Could that be proved?"

"I wouldn't exclude the possibility. Supporting evidence may exist somewhere—perhaps in my files."

"Can you find it for me?"

"I'm only a lawyer," Breile said cautiously, "not a supplier of ammunition for personal vendettas, however locally important. Still, why not? If the documents you require *should* come to light, they may well find their way into your hands. But don't expect me to admit having turned them over to you. If anyone asks I shall flatly deny it."

"And I," Breitbach said quickly, "shall never claim otherwise, I assure you. All you need do is deliver."

The full-dress Party conference—subject for confidential discussion: "How to Permeate the Public with National Socialist Sentiments"—opened early in the evening and did not break up until long past midnight. It could fairly be described as momentous.

Venue: the district director's office, imposingly bedecked with a photo portrait of Adolf Hitler and a swastika flag. Attendance list: Keller, Hermann, Stormtroop Commander; Stenz, Ludwig, Treasurer; Patzer, Peter, Propaganda; Peller, Ilse, Women's Association; Schwarz, Eva, German Girls' League. Also present in a supernumerary role: Breitbach, Konrad, Party Member and Stormtrooper.

Sonnenblum had represented Konrad to his associates as someone more than usually permeated with National Socialist sentiments. Quite what he had done by including him, neither he nor anyone else was yet aware. Only Peter Patzer, Director of Public Enlightenment and Propaganda, had an uneasy presentiment of trouble in store.

Till now, the dissemination of National Socialist ideals in Gilgenrode had been Patzer's exclusive domain; it was a labor of love. He was a tireless public speaker, and he spewed forth arguments in a continuous stream, though many people secretly dismissed him as a mere poseur whose appearance of having digested the world's accumulated store of wisdom was a gargantuan confidence trick.

Patzer's misgivings were not lost on Sonnenblum, who rejoiced in them. He often found Patzer overbearing and pushy. There had even been occasions when he dared to interrupt his chief, ostensibly carried away by crusading zeal, and that the District Director found hard to endure.

Resolutely, Sonnenblum steered for his objective. He began by passing some brief but favorable remarks. They were making definite strides, welcome and undeniable progress, but their achievements still fell short of perfection. They already enjoyed public recognition—nay, esteem —but there was plenty of room for improvement.

"Can anyone suggest a way of speeding things up?"

Konrad donned an air of puppylike docility and said nothing. Ludwig Stenz, the Movement's stalwart treasurer, confined himself to a staccato "Shit! More loot!"—meaning that the Party's coffers needed replenishment.

Sonnenblum never took exception to such crudities. He was just as unmoved by the complaints of Women's Association chief Peller ("German womanhood has still to receive its due recognition!") and the sacred avowals of Girls' Leaguer Schwarz ("Our young people expect great things, really great things, of the new era!")

"Quite so," he said unblushingly, and turned to Keller. The Stormtroop Commander declined to commit himself right away.

"I reserve judgment. I always prefer to be guided by you, District Director."

Sonnenblum screwed up his eyes as though scanning some distant horizon, then glanced inquiringly at the propaganda chief he had appointed in a weak moment. "Well, Comrade, do *you* have any ideas?"

Forever burning with initiative, Peter Patzer felt that his hour had struck. "The Goebbels of Gilgenrode," as he liked to style himself, unleashed a torrent of words. Conscious that his job was at stake, he harangued his audience as though addressing a Nuremberg rally.

"We must steadfastly strengthen and reinforce our beloved Party at district level. We must boost its influence and efficiency. We must turn the people of Gilgenrode into a race of National Socialists!"

Treasurer Stenz grunted like a cabhorse nuzzling its nosebag. "Like I always say, more loot!"

Patzer beamed at this confirmation of his remarks. "Our most urgent need is for new members, comrades who will actively assist us and lend us financial support. What I propose, therefore, is an aggressive and intensified recruitment and fund-raising drive."

The treasurer gave vent to an even more audible grunt —any talk of "loot" was music in his ears—but the head of the Women's Association sniffed resentfully.

"Speaking for myself," said Ilse Peller, "I've already managed to more than double our membership in the last three months."

Girls' Leaguer Schwarz was looking faintly pensive, not to say concerned. "I'm rather worried by all this emphasis on the material side of things. Our campaign must be primarily idealistic, surely!"

"Shit," muttered Stenz, rolling his eyes in disgust.

"All the same," said Keller, "we do have to fight for some kind of definite objective."

The Stormtroop Commander shrewdly left it at that. He had been watching Sonnenblum closely and could sense the District Director's growing animosity toward his airy-fairy, self-assertive propaganda chief. Patzer's lofty and expansive manner conveyed that the Party was his personal fief— that he, not Sonnenblum, was its real top dog, which he wasn't. Neither one nor the other, thought Keller.

Sonnenblum seemed animated by similar ideas but did not feel called on to voice them; the true leader knew how to delegate. He comfortably folded his arms on his chest and glanced at Konrad.

"Any comments on the points raised by Party Member Patzer?"

Konrad looked around with an air of boyish apology, then opened his briefcase and produced various papers—a sheaf of press clippings, several Party circulars, three political-indoctrination manuals—and a book. His voice was as melodious as a harp in the wind.

"I do have one small criticism—that is, if I haven't misunderstood our honored Director of Propaganda."

Patzer felt affronted and provoked. "Criticism?" he demanded in a querulous tremolo. "Criticism of my carefully considered remarks—after all my years of experience in this field; after all my successful and well-attended public meetings in Gilgenrode and its environs? Very well, let's hear the nature of your criticism."

"With all due deference to your fine past record," said Konrad, "anyone can make a mistake."

"Anyone but me!" cried Patzer, heatedly dismissing such a possibility. "Not as regards the true national spirit and its permeation of our local community. Where that's concerned, no one here can touch me!"

Konrad modestly bowed his head. "You seem to be confusing two different categories. Party supporters and Party members, I mean."

"What's the difference?" Patzer prepared to fight tooth and nail, spurred on by the others' challenging stares. "It's six of one and half a dozen of the other. They all subscribe to the same beliefs; they all rally round and contribute to our funds. That's as clear as daylight!"

The District Director was feeling more than a little piqued by Patzer's megalomaniac assertion that no one present could touch him, including Sonnenblum himself. He bent an encouraging eye on Konrad.

"*Is* it as clear as daylight, Party Member Breitbach?"

"No," said Konrad. "A supporter of a movement is someone who professes himself in agreement with its aims; only someone determined to fight for them can be a member."

He had used yet another quotation, a quotation lifted almost verbatim from Hitler's trail-blazing work. Patzer had never even dipped into it, far less felt inclined to, because he was already engaged, at least in spirit, on a mighty tome of his own. Provisionally entitled *Per Ardua ad Astra*, it would acquaint the world with the Teutonic dreams that haunted his nights of agonizing cogitation.

Still looking boyishly amiable, Konrad warmed to his theme. "Supporters," he went on, quoting again, "are passive elements who simply acknowledge an idea—in this case, ours. Members, who deliberately take an active stand, may be regarded as an elite. To every ten supporters, there will at most be one or two members. If it's any consolation to anyone, however, they all have to pay."

"Heil Hitler!" cried Stenz, fired with enthusiasm by the prospect of raking in ten times as much as he had originally hoped. He was beginning to develop a soft spot for Konrad, unlike Patzer, who was panic-stricken by the sensation that his high-priestly robes were drifting rapidly downstream. Even the ladies of the Movement, who usually lionized him, were avoiding his eye. Profoundly shaken by their gross betrayal, and not by theirs alone, he raised his voice in a trembling protest.

"But this is sheer lunacy!"

"Lunacy, is it?" Sonnenblum smiled at Keller and Stenz, then at the ladies. Patzer he ignored. "Party Member Breitbach, the assertion just made by Party Member Patzer calls for a fitting response."

Konrad needed no encouragement. He was looking as outraged as a fishmonger whose wares have just been declared unfit for human consumption. "The bulk of mankind are torpid and cowardly!" he proclaimed—another quotation which sowed still greater confusion in the ranks.

Patzer leaped like a rabid dog, snarling and snapping at everything in sight.

"Am I alone in condemning these mental aberrations—these absurd and disgraceful pronouncements? They're not only an insult to our intelligence, they're an affront to the Movement!"

"I can only tell you," said Konrad, more in sorrow than anger, "that I've not been expressing my personal sentiments alone. I took the liberty of quoting from that noble book, *Mein Kampf*, by our leader, Adolf Hitler. The passages in question may be found between pages six-fifteen and six-forty-five."

"Most impressive!" exclaimed Sonnenblum. "Bravo!" Keller chimed in. The ladies of the Movement nodded approvingly, and the treasurer emitted another resounding "Heil Hitler!"—which summed up all there was to say.

Patzer, who had gone deathly pale, shut his froglike eyes in torment. He opened them again to find his universe bedimmed by gathering storm clouds. "You misunderstand me," he said in a strangled voice. "I may have been overhasty—not wrong, but overhasty. These things happen."

"Of course they do," said Konrad, and promptly made his next point. "Theories are fine as long as they stand up in practice, but the people who know most about their practical application are our District Director and his Stormtroop Commander."

Sonnenblum felt flattered and Keller could not conceal his delight at this unexpected bouquet. Konrad was obviously his man!

After sitting far into the night—the men were fortified with Königsberg beer and the ladies with sticky liqueurs—

94

the Gilgenrode branch of the NSDAP adopted the following "short-term plan of campaign."

1. Treasurer Stenz was to work out a scheme for financing special expenditure. This covered the procurement of uniforms for the SA, Hitler Youth and German Girls' League, the production of recruiting aids, financial assistance for needy Party members, the cultivation of *esprit de corps,* organization of festivities, and so on. This funding operation would be based on voluntary contributions from patriotic members of the public who would, in turn, be systematically encouraged to shell out by a team of qualified stormtroopers selected and supervised by their commanding officer.

Sonnenblum looked around the table. "Are we all agreed on this point?"

"Leave it to me," said Keller.

"Can we collect from outsiders?" Stenz asked brazenly. "Some of them are rolling in loot. Look at Sass!"

"Certainly not," ruled Sonnenblum, intent on observing the letter of the law. "Not directly," he added, and went on to quote a dictum from *Der Stürmer,* the Brownshirt newspaper renowned for pouring scorn on "the un-German spirit." This ran: "He who eats of the Jew, dies thereof."

2. On a provisional, probationary basis, Party Member Breitbach was to take over the functions of the existing Director of Propaganda, Party Member Patzer, who had unhappily ceased to be fully employable. Comrade Breitbach would ensure that the public were systematically enlightened, for example by leaflets, pamphlets, circulars, posters, banners, and personal discussion. "Beneficial contacts with the local press will also be maintained."

Konrad swiftly grasped the point of his District Director's edict. Nearly all the rest did too, and it tickled them. The summons to cultivate "contacts" was an oblique but official way of launching one Breitbach at another, or Konrad at Johannes.

The acting Director of Propaganda looked quite unconcerned. His only comment was, "Right, let's see what happens." Sonnenblum proceeded to the third plank in his program.

3. Intensified efforts would be made to neutralize certain persons whose attitude was incorrigibly hostile. These efforts would call for systematic cooperation by all branches of the Movement. "Concerted steps" would be taken under the District Director's personal supervision.

"Who gets it in the neck first?" asked Keller, hugely interested. "If you told us that, or dropped us a hint, we could channel our efforts in the right direction."

But Sonnenblum, eyes twinkling, preferred to set problems and allow his underlings to solve them. Keller assumed that Parson Bachus was to be given the Job treatment. To Treasurer Stenz, the only worthwhile target was Sass, the Jewish moneybags. Konrad, who knew that his father was first in line, merely smiled.

Items 4 and 5 called on the Party to polish its reputation, enlist public confidence and build up a reliable body of support. "To highlight the first part of this process," said Sonnenblum, "I propose to hold a 'German Day'—a public festival of great and wide-ranging importance, an occasion which our children and grandchildren will remember with joy and gratitude. Such is my wish and intention."

This announcement was loudly applauded by all present. They had an abiding love of festivals, so they hailed their leader's "German Day" with heartfelt enthusiasm. Joyfully, they visualized parades, brass-band concerts, communal singsongs, athletic contests, shooting matches, free refreshments in Market Square. . . .

The only dissenter was Stenz. "Jesus," he groaned, "what's it going to cost? Just think, anything up to a thousand people taking part, and one free beer a head?"

"Not just one," Sonnenblum ordained. "Schnapps too—jugs of it—and masses to eat. Meatballs, chops, sausages—the lot. It's time the people of this town realized how lucky they are to have us!"

Next morning, Johannes Breitbach paid another visit to 7 Market Square. He had been hoping for a private interview with Erika's father, but in vain. There was no one around but Beate Fischer.

Beate, who was bored, eyed him with interest. Though rather on the willowy side, Johannes had fine features and slender, well-proportioned hands. He also had exquisite manners, which impressed her greatly. She gave him one of her sunniest and most bewitching smiles.

"Herr Sonnenblum's out making history somewhere, and his mother's visiting Parson Bachus—he probably needs her spiritual guidance. Anything I can do?"

The plain truth was that Sonnenblum was still in bed, sleeping off the effects of last night's alcoholic and political self-indulgence, so the surgery was temporarily closed. Erika was teaching and Gertrude had gone shopping. Left to her own devices, Beate welcomed any form of distraction.

"You've got sensitive hands, Johannes," she purred. "Nice hands are a tremendous asset in a man, did you know that? Some women find them irresistible, but let's not pursue the subject—not here and now."

"I could return the compliment ten times over."

"I thought I didn't appeal to you."

"You're wrong!" he assured her eagerly. At this moment, the poet in him was far more active than the intellectual. He

97

was entranced by the picture Beate presented—by her dark but luminous coloring. "I've only seen you in the distance. You've always struck me as a very attractive person, but now we're so close—well, I can see just how lovely you are."

Beate struggled to conceal her pleasure. "All the same, I don't exactly look Wagnerian."

"Who cares?" This, Johannes thought, should be enough to convey that he was irked by the current craze for Nordic ideals of beauty. "You, my dear Fräulein, are the dark, mysterious, elfin type—you're an undine!"

Beate itched to ask what an undine was, but her experience of the opposite sex had taught her that brain-teasing questions could blight the atmosphere. She was always in the market for admirers, and this exquisitely polite, well-educated young man appealed to her immensely. He was just what she needed to fill a gap in her collection. Although she seemed to have made a promising start, she felt fractionally uneasy. Gilgenrode was a small place. People knew other people's business—or could if they chose to, and they usually did. That posed problems.

"I've read quite a few of your articles. They were very interesting." Beate gazed at Johannes admiringly. She had a talent for admiring glances, and he, like most men, rose to the bait. "Some of them were above my head, though. I'm not very well read."

"But you've got other advantages," he said quickly. "Beauty is as much a gift of God as intellect or physical strength. Nobody can have everything."

"Still," said Beate, "I do understand a lot of your stuff, and I like it. You love this part of the world. There's something very moving about the way you describe our countryside—which I don't really know in spite of living here. I've never met anyone capable of showing me what to look for."

Johannes didn't know whether to feel pleased or perturbed, but he certainly felt flattered. "If you'd really like to avail yourself of my services, Fräulein, I'd be honored—"

"Oh, thank you," she cried, like a child opening a Christmas present. "How sweet of you to offer! I accept, but I hope you won't get into trouble—with Erika, I mean."

"Of course not. The sole purpose of our meetings would be nature study and art appreciation. Nothing that passed between us could possibly affect the relations between me and my future bride."

Beate made no attempt to disillusion him. "We could even strike a bargain. You open my eyes to the beauties of my natural surroundings, and I'll do my best to talk Herr Sonnenblum into giving you a fair hearing. Does that sound reasonable?"

It certainly did. Johannes seized her hand but gallantly refrained from squeezing it too hard. He was not the first to mistake her for a fragile flower.

The township of Gilgenrode had a policeman named Kersten. All its pressure groups tried to ignore his existence, which was difficult in view of his height and girth.

As an inspector and chief of the Gilgenrode constabulary, Karl Kersten had three officers under him, but he made it his personal business to handle most of the problems that arose. He was also accused of indulging in a lawman's luxury; rashly, as some contended, he strove to see that justice prevailed on all sides—in other words, irrespective of rank or position, reputation or prestige, religious or political affiliations.

What earned Kersten local renown but soon branded him "extremely suspect" was his interference with various political meetings during the months preceding the Nazi takeover on January 30, 1933. He based his action on a decree issued by the Prussian Ministry of the Interior. This authorized the police to intervene if there were any "noticeable abuse of free speech" at a public gathering. It was left to the discretion of the police officer on the spot to decide whether any such abuse had occurred.

Kersten's first such "exercise of discretion" resulted in the premature dispersal of an election meeting held by the Social Democrats, Gilgenrode's smallest political party. He stepped in and broke it up after one speaker had sweepingly characterized the veterans of 1914–18 as "deluded dunderheads." For a few short weeks, Kersten rated as a staunch German Nationalist.

Then came the turn of the German Nationalist Party, headed by Richard Breitbach. When one of its speakers called the Social Democrats "unpatriotic Red scum," Kersten rose and marched to the rostrum. From there he loudly and firmly announced that the show was over.

Kersten was thereafter suspected of being an out-and-out Nazi, but this theory proved as short-lived as the rest. The very next political meeting, an NSDAP rally organized by Sonnenblum, had been in progress for only fifteen minutes when Kersten broke it up on account of "discriminating references to Jewish fellow citizens."

In short, Gilgenrode's police chief had an unwavering conception of where his duty lay and performed it to the exclusion of all else.

Off duty he was a loving husband to his gentle hippopotamus of a wife and a devoted father to his children, a trio of girls aged eight, ten and twelve. He enjoyed plain, ample meals and regularly drank a bottle of beer with his supper —two on Saturdays. Hard liquor he eschewed, just as he visited taverns only on official business.

When duty called, however, this massive man could tackle a case with dogged tenacity as well as an unswerving sense of fair play. Those who bore the brunt of his attentions found him ruthless, whereas others called him bold and courageous. This applied in particular to the "33 Ritterstrasse Case," which began in a relatively innocuous way but developed into a scandal fraught with disastrous political repercussions. It also claimed a life, but not Kersten's.

The root of the trouble was a cat aged three or four, white in color, with dark-brown flecks near the base of the tail—a long-haired creature whose docile, affectionate nature went hand in hand with extreme timidity and fear of strangers. She was no choice product of the breeder's art, merely one of Gilgenrode's several hundred strays that had been befriended by a lonely man. And this was the man who now called at the police station, cat in arms, and asked to speak to the officer in charge.

Kersten emerged from his office and gave the caller an appraising stare. He knew the man with the cat as Emil Spahn, usually referred to as "our Emil." Spahn was something of a character—wrinkled and ancient-looking, with a voice like broken glass and a vocabulary that suggested he was an educated man who had known better days. He had a reputation for making cryptic pronouncements whenever he got drunk—which was, to all appearances, very often indeed.

"Well, Herr Spahn," said Kersten, speaking with formal courtesy, "what can I do for you?"

Emil seemed unable to believe his ears. He shook his head like a horse plagued by flies. "Did you say *Herr* Spahn? Not just Emil, like everyone else—Emil the soak, Emil the loony, Emil the idiot? I'm not used to this sort of treatment, Inspector."

"Then you'd better get used to it from me, Herr Spahn. All men are equal before the law, and that's as it should be. I represent the law in this town, so please state your business."

Emil's disbelief lingered. He breathed heavily, wrestling with the realization that there was someone in Gilgenrode apart from Konrad Breitbach who did not deride, despise and abuse him—someone who seemed to take him seriously. A fact like that took time to digest. Tenderly and protectively, Emil extended his arms and held the cat under Kersten's nose so that he too could appreciate her feline charms.

"This," Emil said with a touch of pride, "is Susie. She scratched at my window a few months ago. Now she lives with me. We belong together; she's like a child to me. I'm her father and mother combined, and glad to be. Does that sound crazy, Inspector?"

"Not at all." Susie's large and lustrous eyes seemed to solicit Kersten's help and understanding. He regarded her intently. "A very handsome animal, Herr Spahn, but why bring her here?"

"Somebody's trying to murder her!"

Kersten didn't bat an eyelid. "I see," he said. "And what grounds do you have for such an allegation?"

"My Susie's being deliberately hounded. Stones have been thrown at her. Some of them hit her and others broke my basement window. Yesterday was even worse: somebody fired at her—seven or eight times, with a pistol!"

"Any idea who did it?"

"There's only one possible suspect: the lodger on the ground floor of the house where I live. Why should he, when I'm always so polite to the man and say such nice things about him? I even made a speech in his honor the other night—a public speech in the taproom of the Dog and Duck."

"I've heard about your hymns of praise to a certain party, Herr Spahn. Rather curious, from the sound of them."

"Curious, maybe, but why should he take offense? That trigger-happy swine is treating the house like a shooting gallery and Susie like a target. He hates the poor little thing!"

"So it's Keller."

"Precisely, Inspector. And now I suppose you'll shut your notebook before you've even opened it, eh?"

"You let me worry about that," Kersten said majestically. "Justice is indivisible, Herr Spahn, even where a cat's concerned. Besides, I like the look of your Susie—not that my personal likes and dislikes come into it."

The occupants of 33 Ritterstrasse, a dilapidated house behind Market Square, included SA Chief Keller, already a prominent and authoritative figure in the town, but destined before long—if all his wishes were granted—to become its supreme master.

Keller lodged with his sister Hermine, who was married to a municipal clerk, a sluggish and somnolent man of elephantine build and low intelligence. Keller occupied the largest room and enjoyed his sister's tender ministrations. Hermine loved her Hermann, and not just because he paid a decent rent.

What had lately made his presence even more welcome were the special donations—hampers of food, crates of beer, cases of schnapps—which arrived with gift cards bearing such cordial messages as "With warmest regards to our distinguished Stormtroop Commander, in the hope of continuing and profitable cooperation."

They could all—Keller, his loving sister and even his lard tub of a brother-in-law from the revenue office—have lived in harmony and comfort, but for one thing. Schiller says that no man, however devout, can dwell in peace if an evil neighbor wills otherwise, and 33 Ritterstrasse housed just such a one. Dwelling under the same roof as Hermann Keller—the very same roof, mark you!—was a semiimbecile named Emil Spahn, who talked to himself and was permanently drunk. To someone of Keller's ultra-German principles, the very sight of him was a constant provocation.

"Good day to you, Herr Keller!" the slobbering fool would cry when passing him in the hall or street. "Alternatively, a hearty Heil Hitler to you, Stormtroop Commander—take your pick!"

"Button your lip, you drunken halfwit!" Keller would retort. "I won't be pestered by a crack-brained idiot like you!"

Emil would cackle gleefully at his victim's attempted rebuffs. "What am I? A halfwit, a crack-brained idiot? Why, just because I gave you a Hitler salute?"

This lousy rotten drunk was an affront to the sensibilities of a populace which was becoming increasingly conscious of its racial superiority, the more so because he was lately said to be broadcasting statements of an insidious and subversive nature. Besides, he always carried that frightful cat around or ensured that it crossed his, Keller's, path. It usually slunk off at the sight of him, trembling with fear and respect—sensing his authority. So far, so good, but of late the wretched beast had dared to hiss defiance at him with back arched and fur bristling; indeed, if the creature could have spat fire it would have done so. Of that Keller had no doubt.

"Piss off, you mangy brute!" he would bellow in a commanding tone. "Get lost, unless you want me to wring your neck or kick you into next week!"

But Susie seemed bent on ambushing him, and each time she hissed more defiantly. No man of Keller's breed could stomach that, least of all from the familiar of a racial degenerate like Emil, and their feud culminated in the events which were officially filed under the heading "Cat Susie, attempts to kill same."

Inspector Kersten paid a formal visit to 33 Ritterstrasse, where he encountered some preliminary obstruction from Keller's sister Hermine.

"I think my brother's asleep."

"Then kindly wake him up, I want a word with him. It's police business."

A few minutes later, Kersten was ushered into the SA chieftain's lair. Crates, cartons and boxes littered the floor. Keller himself was sprawled across the bed in uniform with his collar unbuttoned. He peered sleepily at the all too familiar face of Gilgenrode's avenging angel.

"I want to ask you a few questions," said Kersten. "You've got some explaining to do."

"Do you know who you're speaking to?" Keller seemed eager for official confirmation of his exalted status, even from Kersten. "I carry a lot of weight around here, in case you hadn't heard."

"I know who you are," the policeman said stolidly, "and it doesn't have the slightest bearing on the matter I have to raise with you."

"In my official capacity?"

"No, Herr Keller. I'm simply questioning you in your capacity as an occupant of these premises. Someone has filed a complaint."

"Against me? Nobody but a complete asshole would dare do that."

Kersten, who could juggle with raw eggs when he had

to, looked quite unperturbed. "The complaint alleges an attempt on the life of a cat, in the course of which substantial damage to property was inflicted. I have to follow it up."

"Don't make me laugh!" Keller gave a hoot of derision. "Animals are things. You can do what you like to them."

"I'm afraid you're right, as the law stands. However, only the owner of an animal is entitled to decide its fate, and the cat in question doesn't belong to you."

"So what? The filthy brute's still alive and kicking."

"As I already mentioned," said Kersten, speaking with the persistence of a steady drizzle, "these alleged attempts on its life resulted in subsidiary damage to property. Several basement windows were smashed and wall surfaces damaged by bullets from a firearm."

Such presumption was too much for Keller's self-control. "Good God, man, this is nothing but a load of gossip! You don't seriously think you'll find any witnesses to back the story, do you? There isn't a soul in town who'd cross me without wetting himself. Emil might, but everyone knows he's off his head."

"I'm not so sure about that," Kersten said crisply. "There may be a case to answer here, Herr Keller. Perhaps you can produce a convincing explanation."

"You bet I can! Take those basement windows. Some youngsters had been chucking stones at one another in the street. I accidentally kicked them aside while passing, and they smashed a couple of panes. It could happen to anyone."

"And how do you justify the use of a firearm?"

"Rats. I saw some on the landing and tried to polish them off. There's your explanation, so put that in your pipe."

But the policeman was undeterred. "That leaves one

106

more question. Do you hold a license? Are you entitled to keep a gun, let alone use one?"

"Christ Almighty!" Keller's voice rasped like a bandsaw. "This is a time of national emergency, hasn't it dawned on you yet?"

"Emergency or not, the law must be enforced."

"Sure, *our* law! Better make a note of that. The commander in chief of our outfit has issued firearms to us. Check with Berlin, if you've got the nerve."

"I will," Kersten said simply.

"You do that!" Keller retorted with an evil grin. "Our boys in Berlin'll be fascinated to hear who's trying to put a spoke in their wheel."

The Strong Man's Arms, a tavern restricted to SA personnel, was inaugurated the following Saturday. Kimminger, who had been so actively encouraged to sponsor the project, spared no expense.

Freshly tapped beer was a natural necessity, with extra casks arrayed in the background, but numerous stone jugs of corn liquor were stored, ready for use, in the cool cellar beneath the bar. Pea soup fortified with chunks of smoked bacon was also to hand, as was a steaming ten-gallon cauldron in which sausages fragrantly bobbed and swirled. "It's all on the house," Kimminger kept repeating. "Regard it as my own modest contribution to the development of *esprit de corps.*"

Chief participants in this solemn inaugural ceremony were the sixty-odd stalwarts of the Gilgenrode Storm Detachment, whose canteen this now was. They stood there stiff and silent, frozen-faced and iron-jawed, behind their three platoon commanders: "Mule" Müller, "Softy" Schulze, and "Muscles" Feinemann. In front of them all, gaz-

107

ing into space with visionary intensity, stood Hermann Keller.

Also present, of course, were the leading lights of the Party. District Director Sonnenblum surveyed his trusty Brownshirts with lofty benevolence. Treasurer Stenz, who had accompanied him, was in an equally mellow mood, because the establishment of this recreation center had not required him to disgorge any "loot."

Kimminger, who was privileged to stand on the District Director's right, contrived to look as humbly grateful as befitted a guest of honor on his own premises. Stationed just behind this group of bigwigs was Party Member Konrad Breitbach, stormtrooper and acting Director of Propaganda, with a book clamped beneath his left elbow.

To begin with, everyone took a moment to admire the solid German splendor of the room—rugged tables and massive chairs, deal floor boards and curtains adorned with Nordic motifs, and, dominating the entire scene, a bar bristling with glasses and liquor bottles. The beer tap whispered and gurgled merrily to itself.

Sonnenblum's inaugural address was suitably brief. His men were itching to eat and drink their fill. He not only knew this but welcomed it, because its only effect would be to reinforce the bonds of the Movement. Good-humoredly groping for the common touch, he made the following announcement:

"Men, we belong to a nation that knows how to enjoy itself. Like everything else in this country, our celebrations must be bigger and better. The Führer himself has passed some fitting comments on the subject. Would you mind, Party Member Breitbach?"

Konrad briskly stepped forward and opened his book at one of several passages marked with slips of paper.

"I take the liberty of quoting," he said. "The words you are about to hear may be found on page three-eleven of this, the most inspiring book of all time: 'There are truths so obvious that, for this very reason, ordinary people fail to see or at least recognize them. Columbus's eggs lie around by the hundreds of thousands, but Columbuses are encountered more rarely. Even the most superficial study discloses that Nature's restricted form of procreation and reproduction is an almost inflexible natural law. Every creature mates exclusively with a member of its own kind. Titmouse seeks titmouse, house mouse seeks house mouse, he-wolf seeks she-wolf, and so on!' "

"How true!" Sonnenblum cried fervently.

Konrad closed his book and looked up into a sea of uncomprehending faces. He was shrewd enough not to savor this spectacle for too long. Instead, he quickly developed his theme.

"So much, my dear Party Members and fellow Stormtroopers, for our Führer's pearls of wisdom. Although they need no amplifying in themselves, you may be wondering why I should have chosen to quote that particular passage. I shall be happy to enlighten you—with the District Director's permission."

Satisfied that his ideological seed was sprouting, Sonnenblum granted it at once. Keller, too, gave a nod of assent. Konrad's glance of deferential inquiry had included him, and Konrad was his man. . . .

"Comrades," said the acting Director of Propaganda, "we must look at it this way. Our Führer sees to the heart of things—he's a Columbus who knows how to stand any egg on its head. His meaning here is as follows: Nature ordains that like should consort with like, just as one Party member feels drawn toward another."

"There you have it!" Sonnenblum called in stirring tones. "Comradeship—blithe and unquestioning comradeship! What more need be said?"

"Nothing," said Kimminger, "so why not dig in?"

The Führer's elite needed no second bidding. With a gladsome lack of restraint, they flung themselves on all that was so amply provided, rejoicing in their privileged status and the opportunities it presented. Soon moist-eyed with liquor, they broke into maudlin ballads or potent war songs such as "When Jewish blood spurts from the knife . . ."

The singers embraced each other and exchanged fraternal slaps on the back or buttocks. Their inebriation developed with surprising speed into a mood of sublime exuberance.

Visibly stupefied by a mere two hours of this revelry, the District Director announced his intention of leaving and letting the Brownshirts celebrate in peace. He congratulated Keller once more on his recreation center.

"A splendid establishment, and well worthy of you and your men. May the spirit of comradeship always prevail here!"

Treasurer Stenz also insisted on leaving rather than succumb to a dangerous weakness—when drunk, he became what he never was when sober, namely, openhanded. Stenz found it safer to drink at home. Kimminger too had a long night ahead of him and was determined to make the most of it: a certain Frau Schulze was waiting for him in the German Eagle's bridal suite.

Tempered by a thousand drill parades, Keller's steely word of command sliced the air.

"Atten . . . shun! Brace those thighs, men! Chins in, chests out, eyes on the senior officer present!"

His men did their best, some gently swaying, others stiff as concrete. Almost every eye was glazed with ecstasy.

110

"Comrades," cried Keller, "we thank our District Director for attending. Unfortunately, he has other duties to perform for our Movement before the day is done. We therefore bid him farewell with a triple *Sieg heil!*"

This called forth such a mighty, rhythmical roar that windowpanes rattled and beer glasses rang. Sonnenblum made a Hitlerian gesture of benediction before departing with Stenz and Kimminger. Konrad, now thoroughly accepted as one of the Brownshirt fold, was permitted to stay behind.

The patrons of the Strong Man's Arms waxed even more boisterous and exuberant than before. They drank beer by the tankard and schnapps by the tumbler, all without turning a hair. Many of them gulped down a late-night snack of pea soup and sausages. Soon afterward, several of them sealed the bonds of comradeship by vomiting in unison into the washroom basins. A glorious bender was nearing its climax.

"There's no getting away from it," Keller observed approvingly to Konrad, who was sitting beside him. "The Party's really going places."

"You bet," said Konrad, trying to guess which wassailer would be the next to fall headlong. He himself had not drunk much—nor, so far, had Keller. The two of them sat there like first-nighters in a box, almost deafened by the performance in progress a few feet away.

"Our comrades' standard of training is tip-top," Konrad went on. He had to shout to make himself heard. "So is their level of political indoctrination, thanks to you, Stormtroop Commander. The District Director said so only the other day."

"Did he, now!" Keller gave a complacent smirk. "He could hardly say otherwise, could he?"

"Internally—if I followed his meaning—our unit is a

splendid body of men, close-knit and well-disciplined. However, it ought to demonstrate this to the outside world."

"How, Konrad? What do you think he was driving at?"

"I think he meant we should concentrate on unmasking public enemies—not small fry, mind you, but really big game."

"Are you talking about your old man?"

Konrad dismissed this idea with a look of mild regret. "He's right at the top of Sonnenblum's personal black list. We mustn't deprive our chief of his fun, but there *is* someone he wouldn't mind leaving to you. If my hunch is right, it's the parson."

Keller turned a meditative gaze on his men as they staggered around with arms linked, admirably relaxed and receptive. There was little he couldn't do with them—they were as putty in his hands. Did that apply to young Breitbach as well? He leaned toward Konrad and subjected him to a confidential blast of schnapps-laden breath.

"Bachus? But is he still a problem from the Party's point of view? The man's been trying to lick our boots for quite some time. Sonnenblum knows that as well as I do. Why doesn't he knock him into shape personally?"

"I've supplied him with suitable ammunition," Konrad said, choosing his words with care. "The Führer's ideological arguments are quite strong enough to floor a would-be nonconformist like Bachus and coax him off the fence, but there's a snag. Not even Sonnenblum can afford to ignore the human element. His mother's a fire-eater. To make matters worse, she's a regular churchgoer."

"I get you." Keller's voice rang with manly resolve. "Then we'll have to do the District Director's job for him the next chance we get."

"Tomorrow will do," Konrad said quickly. "Tomorrow's Sunday. We could lean on Bachus after morning service

112

and appeal to his better nature. He must have one, so let him prove it. Still, there's a long time to go till then. Let's make the most of it, shall we?"

Shortly before midnight, the Strong Man's Arms witnessed the start of a race between amateur jockeys mounted on chairs. The latter, ridden backwards, served as horses, and the course extended from the leading edge of the bar to the back of the room.

Preliminary heats of six were run, after which the successful entrants participated in intermediate heats whose winners went forward to the final. The supreme champion turned out to be "Softy" Schulze.

Streaming with honest sweat, Schulze proudly inclined his head as Keller presented him with an SA dirk which shone like solid silver. The victor was hailed with rousing applause. Immediately afterward, all present broke into song once more. Their voices rang out, resonant with love of friend and defiance of foe, in the words and music composed by their late lamented comrade Horst Wessel, whose dastardly murder by Communists had earned him immortality. The SA was marching in close order, banner on high. They sang the song as if already aware that it was destined to become their country's next national anthem.

Keller was stirred to the core. He draped his granite arm round Konrad's slender shoulders and hugged him possessively. "My God," he breathed, "we'll do it yet! I'll make it with your help. We'll make it together! What a night!"

113

If GILGENRODE on Saturday night and the small hours of
Sunday morning resembled a witch's cauldron, it should
be borne in mind that darkness had been preceded by a
spring day so exceptionally hot and sultry as to make the
blood boil. Streets and houses continued to bask in the sun's
heat until long after nightfall. Few people thought of
sleep, and most were parched with thirst.

Gilgenrode's thirty-or-so inns and taverns, many of them
diminutive, were packed. Their patrons drank beer (in
smallish glasses) and corn liquor (in far larger glasses than
were customary elsewhere). Conversation was of secondary
importance.

Occasional entertainment was provided by Emil Spahn,
who gave guest performances in no fewer than five bars this

Saturday night. His current text ran: "He who eats of the Jew, dies thereof!" This, he explained, was a motto favored by the town's esteemed dentist and district director. He then proceeded, on Konrad's instructions, to amuse the general public by lauding him to the skies.

Many people dawdled in Market Square, chatting amiably. Others lolled for hours on the benches outside their homes—none of which had more than two stories—or leaned square-shouldered out of open windows.

Although the street lighting was poor, lynx-eyed observers kept watch on the social scene. Careful note was taken of any incident that could whet the imagination. On a hot night like this, enough conversational fuel was gathered to last the rest of the year.

Some hours before Keller's men started galloping wildly round their new canteen on chairs, Richard Breitbach met Beate Fischer at the German Eagle. As on most Saturdays, he had invited her to join him for dinner.

"Lovely to see you, sweetheart." Breitbach bent to kiss her hand. Though imperfectly executed, the gesture was gallantly intended. He straightened up and studied her face. "You're looking depressed, though. What's the matter?"

She shrugged. "I'm feeling low, that's all."

"Low, sweetheart?" he asked, radiating sympathy. "Nothing to do with me, I hope?"

"It's a whole combination of things." Beate was using her plaintive, little-girl-lost voice. She toyed with her crab soup as though she had lost her appetite. "For a start, there's Sonnenblum. He hates it when I go out with you—he might even fire me. Then what would I do?"

"No problem. I'd take you on."

"But as what?" She gazed at him with wide, childlike

116

eyes. "I'm a trained dental nurse. What good is that to you? Besides, he pays me well."

"I could easily outbid him."

She returned to the attack when the second course—ultratender saddle of venison with sour-cream gravy—was served. "Everyone keeps trying to buy me like a pair of shoes. It's humiliating, Richard—it sickens me!"

"I'd even be prepared—" Breitbach paused, slightly aghast at his own impetuosity. "I'll marry you, if you insist—I mean, if that's what you really want."

"Sweet of you." She brushed the corner of his mouth with her moist lips—she knew he liked that. "But we mustn't rush things. I'm completely at sixes and sevens at the moment. It isn't just Sonnenblum—though he's becoming more and more of a handful. There's my poor dear sister and her sick child. Her husband's an utter swine. I have to help her as much as I can. She doesn't have anyone else to turn to. You do understand, don't you?"

"Of course, sweetheart," he said quickly. Far be it from him to seem possessive or treat her like an article of merchandise. He mustn't try to force her hand. That—or so she had strongly implied—was his only chance of keeping her to himself.

Johannes Breitbach, poet and intellectual, diligent chronicler of the world of Gilgenrode and a man of unquestionably liberal and optimistic disposition, was privileged to undergo several rare experiences within the space of a single evening. The first was an opportunity to date Erika Sonnenblum.

This happened unbeknown to her father but with the express consent of her forthright grandmother. "You've got two or three hours," she told them. "Better get moving."

117

Johannes did so after his own manner. With Erika clinging to his arm, he took her for a walk to the castle whose crumbling but still formidable battlements looked particularly imposing in the twilight. He discoursed on the remarkable interaction between humanism, the tide of history and the aberrations of mankind. Erika, who was wise enough to receive his remarks in long-suffering silence, registered awe and attention.

Next they visited the only cinema in town, where *Came the Dawn* was showing. This epoch-making screen epic, every last foot of which was unadulteratedly German, recounted how a U-boat commander—one of the noblest, needless to say—looked certain death in the eye with sovereign calm and the benign approval of his wonderful white-haired mother.

Any such movie required sitting-through with total commitment and a stiff upper lip. Toward the end, when a fiercely gurgling influx of sea water claimed its heroic victims, Erika groped for Johannes's hand and squeezed it hard—a gesture that lasted for several minutes but was not inspired by any very loverlike emotion.

They emerged into the afterglow of the warm spring dusk. Still holding his hand, Erika said, "Should that have left me feeling uplifted? Depressed would be a better word. What are we meant to believe—that a man can only live for his country by dying for it as soon as possible?"

"My dear Erika, this world of ours contains the most varied and diverse forms of life—heroes and intellectuals, liberals and authoritarians, artists and administrators. They all have a perfect right to coexist. We must be free to go our own way, that's the essential thing."

"Which way would you go, if you could choose?"

"Back to the land, I suppose. I preach devotion to the soil we spring from, love of the creatures we live with, human and animal. Why? Don't you think I'm aiming high enough?"

They were still debating this question when they reached 7 Market Square. Grandmother Gertrude, who was leaning out the window, waved them inside.

"Come in, you can have the living-room to yourselves. It's a lovely warm night. I'm going to sit outside and enjoy it. I may be there for the best part of an hour, so don't waste time."

They tried to follow her advice, but in vain.

At 33 Ritterstrasse, Emil Spahn, drunkard and town jester, was calling his cat. His hoarse voice rose to a wail of desperate entreaty.

"Susie, my poppet, where are you? Come out, my little beauty. Don't be frightened, Emil's here. Show yourself, you queen among cats!"

But all that appeared was Hermine, Keller's sister, swathed in a floral bathrobe. "You, there!" she called angrily. "Stop that yelling! Don't you know what time it is, you—you creature?"

"Your pardon, ma'am." Emil bowed deeply and swept off an imaginary hat. "I never yell, it isn't my style—yelling I leave to others. I was calling my cat, that's all."

Hermine retied her bathrobe with a jerk, as though mentally garroting him. "You're causing a disturbance, and that's a criminal offense."

"Ma'am," said Emil, even more unctuously, "who am I supposed to be disturbing? Surely not you? You look wide awake to me, the way you do every Saturday night, when your worthy husband goes bowling with his friends and your beloved brother makes political history. That leaves you free to play with that nice young nephew of yours—play cards, I mean."

119

Hermine uttered a scream of fury. "You filthy brute! What are you suggesting?"

"Ma'am," Emil pursued with drunken dignity, "your honored brother is a great man. You're a lady of superior station and can behave as the spirit moves you. I, on the other hand, lead a very humble existence, but my cat forms part of it."

"Yes, and it went and crapped in the passage again— right outside our door, where we can't get rid of the stench. Well, we're not going to put up with it any longer!"

"My Susie is an animal of admirably clean habits, I assure you. If she did have an accident in the wrong place, as you claim, it can only have been because someone deliberately scared the poor little thing. Who was it, I wonder?"

"You're bringing tears to my eyes," sneered Hermine. "Get lost, you halfwit!"

"Certainly, ma'am—with pleasure, ma'am. All I ask of you and your brother is a chance to live in peace with my cat, nothing more."

So saying, Emil turned away and resumed his search. His plaintive cries remained unanswered.

Richard Breitbach was sitting in the restaurant of the German Eagle, gazing mournfully into an invisible fog bank.

Beate had walked out on him. Before him lay their untouched dessert—fruit encased in puff pastry and piled with whipped cream. The ice bucket beside him contained a bottle of Hoehl, a German sparkling wine that had once been popular in the officers' messes of the Imperial Army.

Before long, Kimminger sidled up and expressed delight at this opportunity to welcome one of his most honored patrons. "Please let me charge your wine to my own account—to celebrate the occasion, as it were."

Breitbach frowned at him. "What's there to celebrate? I hear you've just fixed up the Brownshirts with a home away from home. I'm surprised at you, Kimminger. I always thought you were a kindred spirit."

"So I am, Herr Breitbach." Kimminger's tone was ingratiating. "But put yourself in my place. Keller and a contingent of his greedy, ruthless thugs marched into my main establishment and tried to take it over. They'd have ruined me."

"They'll ruin us all in the end."

"Perhaps, but don't get me wrong. If I've given these goons a stamping ground of their own, it's partly to keep an eye on them. The manager's a hundred percent on my side—our side, I mean. He'll keep us regularly informed of what goes on."

"Glad to hear it." Breitbach forgot the gloom into which Beate had plunged him, albeit only temporarily. "In that case, I'll take you up on your original offer."

"With pleasure." Kimminger opened the bottle and poured two glasses. "Your very good health—and mine. We need all the luck we can get. When I think of your son joining that bunch of bruisers . . ."

Breitbach sipped his sparkling wine. "A remarkable boy, Konrad. Who'd have thought it of him? I wouldn't, would you?"

Kimminger, who felt satisfied that he had taken out an extra insurance policy, was enjoying himself. He lingered, even though Frau Schulze had been waiting upstairs for an hour. In his experience, keeping a woman on tenterhooks only intensified her self-abandon. He refilled their glasses and leaned forward confidentially.

121

"Your son and I were in school together, starting in primary school and ending up at the Kaiser Wilhelm secondary. There was quite an age gap between us, but Konrad wasn't the type you could ignore, if only because he made such a point of hiding his light under a bushel. Still Waters, we used to call him."

"I can imagine," said Breitbach. "Still Waters, eh? Who'd have suspected they ran so deep?"

Kimminger shrugged. "He didn't care two hoots about making friends or playing up to the staff, you could tell that a mile off. He always had his nose buried in some book or other, even during break. He knew everything about anything, but you had to ask him point blank or he wouldn't say a word. I found him a little bit creepy, to be frank. Still, who am I to judge? You're his father."

"That's a laugh. How many parents really know their children?"

Peter Patzer was in torment. He felt that he had been mercilessly disowned—trampled underfoot by power-crazed megalomaniacs and ruthless self-seekers. They had mocked, reviled and abused him in a way that could not fail to cut his sensitive soul to the quick.

He sat huddled in his rented room, staring through a veil of tears at the almost empty desk. All that reposed on it was a single sheet of paper. He feebly shook his head as though incapable of grasping what had been done to him—him, whose one desire had been to love and defend what merited his love; the true quintessence of all that was German.

It had always delighted him to study edifying pictures in the naturalistic style, wallow in romantic poetry or declaim verses that spoke of silver moonbeams, starry skies and the play of light on ripples in the water. He was particularly drawn to the magical darkness of the depths, the seductive whisper of water among reeds, the tug of swirling currents.

Peter Patzer's life might fairly have been described as harsh and austere. The last of five children, he had lost his mother at birth and been denied the protective touch of a father's hand. The man who had begotten him emigrated soon afterward and was never heard from again.

While still a baby, Patzer was adopted by a well-to-do aunt, who resolutely ministered to his every need. He was privileged to share her bed almost before he was in his teens. In return, she had financed his career as a humble primary-school teacher.

For as far back as he could remember, Patzer had been dominated by a yearning for someone to love. None of the objects of his passion seemed prepared to love him with the same selfless ardor, but he did not despair. He eventually went in search of God, the supreme being, and found him here on earth. From then on, he devoted himself to the service of Adolf Hitler with sacred zeal and absolute conviction.

But "they" wouldn't let him! "They" had poured scorn on his dearest beliefs, ignorantly spurned his store of hard-won principles, and finally thrown him out, kicking him in the process like some mangy cur.

By so doing, they had robbed him of the Party that had become his mother and deprived him of the Leader whom he regarded as the most consummate of all father figures. His life had lost its meaning. It was shattered and destroyed like a looking glass smashed by spiteful children.

He straightened up and brushed away the tears that were blinding him. If only for the last time, he needed to see clearly—needed to see the sheet of paper in front of him. Pulling an ink well toward him, he dipped his pen in it— No. 1 Nib (Very Fine)—and wrote in a trembling hand:

I, Peter Patzer, do hereby testify that I can no longer breathe the same air as the inhabitants of this town and the denizens of this planet. When my letter is found, I shall have ceased to exist. I have always striven to be a steadfast son of the Fatherland. I have loved and revered our Führer without question, and have, like him, yearned for the establishment of a Greater German Reich, for its everlasting supremacy and glorious exaltation of racial values. At the same time, I have encountered persons who are dominated by crude considerations of power. In them, true idealism has been replaced by the pursuit of profit.

And here, with due German candor, I must solemnly prefer charges against three named individuals: District Director Sonnenblum, Stormtroop Commander Keller, and Treasurer Stenz. Not only are these men incapable of responding to the clarion call of our heroic age; they dare to abuse its most hallowed beliefs. Profoundly materialistic by nature, they conduct themselves in a manner that imperils the moral foundations of our Movement. Their salient qualities are sordid hedonism, vain ambition, and personal avarice.

Their lamentably unidealistic life style is leading this town into a morass that threatens to engulf all that is noble and sublime. No true German can be expected to enter that morass. I shall therefore lay down my life rather than become the victim of such base, insidious and unscrupulous agents of corruption and perdition.

I trust that the above declaration of intent will sound a final note of warning.

After signing this document with his life's blood, as it were, Peter Patzer took an envelope and adorned it with the following inscription in bold capitals: "My Last Will and Political Testament. Concluding Observations on My Earthly Existence." Then he inserted the sheet of paper and deposited the envelope on his desk.

Like Parsifal going in quest of the Grail, he donned his Party uniform and bade farewell to the modest room that had been his home. Then he headed south toward the beckoning glint of Lake Gilgenrode. Mirrored in its waters, in all its soft and magically alluring splendor, was the moon.

Patzer was blind to his immediate surroundings. He did not notice the drunk vomiting noisily into a bush nor the couples entwined on the benches near by. Mesmerized by the moon's reflection, he doggedly tottered lakeward. Near the shore he tripped over two copulating figures, fell headlong in the moist sand, and laboriously picked himself up. The incident struck him as symbolic: in this world, flesh took precedence over spirit, and each man was intent on personal pleasure. Peter Patzer did not question the exalted purpose of his ultimate sacrifice. He waded into Lake Gilgenrode as if solemnly advancing on the Führer. "Heil Hitler!" he cried, and then he drowned.

Almost at the same time, or just before 10 P.M., Heinrich Sonnenblum sat waiting for Beate Fischer in a back room at the Fatherland Café. He had invited her to a *dîner à deux* after the opening of the Strong Man's Arms. That, in fact, had been his sole reason for leaving early, but Beate failed to appear at the appointed hour.

Sonnenblum became restless and drank several schnapps, but with little enjoyment. When Beate finally turned up, almost forty minutes late, he glanced accusingly at his watch.

He should have known better. Standing over him with arms akimbo, she gave him her most reproachful doe-eyed look.

"Is that all I mean to you—a receptionist who has to meet your schedule to the nearest minute? Please don't treat me like a serf, Heinrich, or I'll lose what's left of my appetite."

Beate had already dined once with Breitbach, but sparingly in view of her next date. Besides, the menu here was almost identical. Spooning up her soup with an indifference that wounded her ardent host, she casually repulsed the hand that crept along her thigh.

"Oh no you don't! I'm not a tramp."

Sonnenblum's normally pallid face turned still paler. He felt as if his blood pressure had dropped to zero. Waves of dizziness overcame him, and spots swam before his eyes.

"What are you doing to me?" he moaned.

Beate remained unmoved by this histrionic display. She was familiar with such outbursts, which seemed to be a peculiarity of the male sex. Man alternated between two roles: the adored hero and the poor, downtrodden wretch.

"You aren't the only person in my life. I do have other commitments, you know."

Sonnenblum gave a gasp of dismay. "Meaning what?"

"I've got a sister, and the poor girl's in a bad way. Her child's sick. She needs me. Even if I wanted to spend a bit longer with you tonight, I couldn't. Do you understand?"

"Of course," Sonnenblum assured her eagerly, clasping his left side with both hands. "There's nothing I wouldn't give up for your sake, Beate. I don't want to lose you."

"That's more like it. There may be hope for us yet." She sampled a little of her dessert, a chocolate layer cake steeped in honey and thickly topped with cream. "Too sickly," she announced, then pursed her lips and gave him a quick peck. "Thanks for being so understanding, Heinrich. It makes things a whole lot easier. But now, I'm afraid, I'll have to go."

Beate left her swain sitting alone over the debris of their

meal, looking forlorn but secretly feeling more than ready for bed.

It was just before midnight.

Also just before midnight, Felix Kimminger was at last able to retire to the bridal suite at the German Eagle, where Frau Schulze was waiting for him. The platoon commander's wife had already removed part of her clothing, either in response to climatic conditions or because of the extent to which she had applied herself to a bottle of eggnog provided by room service.

"You're late," she said reproachfully.

"It's never too late for what I've got in mind, sweetheart."

Kimminger was an expert at combining business with the maximum of pleasure. He never got involved with female employees or village virgins. Married women were his meat, preferably those with useful connections.

One was the mayor's wife, who expressed her gratitude by persuading her husband to help Kimminger in a mayoral capacity. Another was a schoolmaster's spouse who yearned for sex education but also possessed what Kimminger's commercial instinct told him was an invaluable asset: she was the only daughter of the local brewery magnate. More recently, he had taken up with various lady members of the Party, whose cultivation was, among other things, a form of political insurance.

Of these, Platoon Commander Schulze's wife seemed more than usually obliging—and experienced. "You're terrific!" she sighed happily. "You only have to tell me how you like it best and I'll do it."

"And you," panted Kimminger, "have got class. Does your husband know how lucky he is?"

"Oh, him!" She arched her body against his. "He's been

far too busy lately. There's only one thing he's after, and that's Keller's job."

Kimminger paused in his exertions; this shed a new and intriguing light on the situation. "With my connections," he mused, bending over her breasts, "I might be able to give him a boost. If you'd like me to, of course."

"That'd be great," she said quickly. "He'd owe you a lot of favors, and so would I. Besides, it would make things easier for you and me." She seemed thrilled at the prospect of queening it as a stormtroop commander's wife.

Kimminger realized this as clearly as he foresaw the possible advantages to himself. That swine Keller, with his increasingly brazen demands, was becoming a menace. His removal would solve a lot of problems.

"All right," he said, "let's work on it together."

They started right away.

On the south side of Market Square stood the White Hart Hotel. It was a conservative and respectable-looking establishment with faded paint work but a neat and dignified interior. The proprietor, Herr Georg Gernoth, went to great lengths to preserve a refined, genteel atmosphere.

This was the hotel patronized by local landowners on the occasions when they found it impossible to avoid contact with the authorities based in Gilgenrode. The teaching staff of the grammar school frequented it, as did senior municipal officials and respected members of the business community. The White Hart's cuisine had a Gallic bias, which some found slightly suspect. Favored guests had their culinary needs attended to by the proprietor in person.

Gernoth was particularly fond of cooking for Siegfried Sass, or "the Jew," as most Gilgenroders now called him. Sass and his lawyer, Dr. Breile, were dining very late this evening, as if to escape attention. Gernoth served them a special feather-light meal of artichoke hearts, grilled lamb cutlets, and fresh fruit salad. With it they drank a Franconian wine, whose heavy fragrance Sass tempered with mineral water.

When coffee arrived, the lawyer steeled himself against the inevitable by tipping a large glass of brandy into his cup. That done, he came brusquely to the point.

"Don't misconstrue your position, Herr Sass. You're a Jew. As things stand at present, that makes you a prime target for exploitation."

Sass parried this with a smile. "Whatever I own is the product of three generations of hard work. My grandfather traded in cattle and hides before he opened a provision store. My father built a mill, a dairy, and a clutch of apartment houses. I've done little more than keep my inheritance intact and treat the local inhabitants with a certain generosity."

"Everyone knows that, Herr Sass. Our orphanage would cease to exist without your support. You also finance the old folks' home, the nursery school and a home for stray animals. The Germania Rowing Club is dependent on your munificence, and so is the Athletic Club, to mention only a few of your good works. But that's just the point. A lot of people question your motives. The Jew's trying to buy himself insurance, they say; he's made a mint out of us, and now he's scattering a few thousand marks around to keep us quiet."

"All that governs my decisions is the world I was born into. I love East Prussia. I love its natural beauty, its wide open spaces, its air of peace and security." The old man sounded utterly sincere. "This is my native land. How can I ever leave it?"

Breile forced himself to remain ruthlessly matter-of-fact.

"You're not being realistic. Sell all you can, salt away the proceeds, and get out as soon as possible. Somewhere overseas would be safest."

"No," said Sass, without the slightest trace of cantankerous obstinacy. "Here I belong, and here I stay."

"It's a pleasure to work for you," Breile said slowly, impressed despite himself. "I enjoy it as much as my father enjoyed working for yours, but things were far simpler in those days."

Sass seemed quite unperturbed by the gathering storm. "You remember my asking you to make some inquiries about a woman named Fischer? Have you done so?"

"I have, and there's plenty to report. Forgive me, but I can't help wondering why you're so interested in her."

"I'll do my best to explain." The old man's eyes twinkled. "Not that you'll understand."

"I can try."

"Please do, my dear Herr Breile, even if all I can tell you is this: I've always had a weakness for the beautiful and unpredictable. Beate Fischer seems to qualify on both counts. Well, what about her?"

Breile had compiled quite a bulky file on his client's object of interest. He pushed it across the table. "Most of it amounts to hearsay. What on earth do you plan to do with it?"

Sass reached eagerly for the proffered papers. "Human nature," he said, "has always been a playground full of strange and wonderful surprises. I'd like to join in the game for once—in my own way."

At Beate's suggestion, Johannes had been waiting at the south entrance to Gilgenrode's lakeside promenade since midnight. The leafy branches of a weeping willow screened him like a curtain as his eyes drank in the scene that presented itself by the light of the full, round, radiant moon.

Luxuriant flower beds glowed with varying shades of dusky red. Beyond them, like the outskirts of a mighty forest, loomed some dense blue-green shrubs. Bordering the pale ribbons of sandy path that ran between these were benches on which, visible only in blurred outline, human figures sat, knelt or lay, while other figures sprawled on the fragrant grass. Gilgenrode was having a more than usually procreative night.

Johannes continued to wait for Beate as arranged. Not really knowing what she expected of him, he had a sneaking hope that she wouldn't show up. On the other hand, she might be useful. Beate wielded considerable influence in an area of special concern to him—Erika's home—so he supposed he would have to be patient. He decided to give her at least half an hour.

Beate turned up forty-five minutes late. Johannes extricated himself from the weeping willow and hurried toward her. "We're in luck," he said, politely shaking hands. The pressure of her fingers surprised him. "It's a glorious night—absolutely perfect for showing off the beauties of our natural surroundings."

"Fine, let's get started right away."

He suggested a stroll along the path from Lake Gilgenrode to the Bismarck Tower. The inn there held a well-attended dance every Saturday night, complete with brass band.

Tower and inn were less than two miles away and could easily be reached in half an hour. The picturesque route was flanked by towering poplars and drooping willows. On the left shimmered the silver lake, on the right stretched an expanse of lush meadowland.

"How very, very beautiful!" sighed Beate, skillfully injecting a note of childlike wonderment into her voice. "Romantic, too." She took his arm as though seeking protection.

Johannes gallantly tolerated this intimate gesture. Striding along at her side, head erect, he launched into a dissertation with poetic undertones.

"Ours is a land of lakes and forests and pastures. It has remained almost unchanged for centuries, despite periodic visitations by a wide variety of human types—Slavs, Masurians, Poles, Teutonic Knights, political and social outcasts. All these people have left their mark on East Prussia and welded it into a geographical unit. That's why we offer so little scope for the rigid racial theorist—if you don't mind my saying so."

"Mind, Johannes? Why should I?" Beate had nestled against him and was listening intently. "Do you often come walking here with Erika—your future bride, isn't that what you called her?"

"No," he said truthfully. "I don't rush blindly into things, Fräulein Fischer. I'm not impetuous by nature, as I'm sure you've noticed. My father's quite different, and so is my brother Konrad. Nothing seems to daunt them, whereas I—"

"If I can ever help you in that way, Johannes, you need only ask."

"Thank you!" He seized her hands in a sudden fit of gratitude, and Beate surrendered them gladly. The moon overhead had now been obscured by gossamer clouds.

Parson Bachus, wearing an off-white nightshirt, was praying in his study on this most eventful of Gilgenrode nights. Bookshelves surrounded him like a stage set, but Bachus did little reading. He preferred to think of himself as a Christian man of action.

He was praying because he couldn't sleep, not just because of his wife, Esther, the daughter of a worthy Königsberg cleric who belonged to the anti-Nazi wing of the Protestant Church. Esther kept badgering him, kept urging him to be more like her revered father—in other words, strong in the faith and stoutly opposed to any compromise with the Nazi regime.

To make matters worse, Esther was considerably his junior, a fact that brought additional tribulations. "You claim you love and cherish me," she had told him in the privacy of their conjugal chamber, "but that's not good enough. Why don't you prove it?" As time went by, he found this increasingly difficult.

There were also the escapades of his under-age daughter, who was developing a taste for brawny peasants—even for Nazi stormtroopers.

But not even that exhausted the demands, doubts and depression that weighed him down. Now had come the letter on his desk, formally signed by the Acting Director of Propaganda, NSDAP District Branch, Gilgenrode. Its message was startlingly succinct:

> Remarks by our Führer Adolf Hitler, quoted from his book *Mein Kampf:*
> "1. To a political leader, the religious doctrines and institutions of his people must always be inviolable."
> See Page 127.

So far, so good. It would have sounded even more reassuring if it had not been immediately followed by another quotation. This ran:

> "Protestantism will always support the requirements of Germanism. These include inner purity, enhance-

ment of national awareness, defense of the German ethos, the German language, German liberty . . ."

Well, yes—why not? But what was the letter really getting at, and what did it require of him in practice? Although Bachus had a gift for interpreting the written word in his own way, he couldn't help being taken aback by the signature: "Heil Hitler! Konrad Breitbach."

The name stirred unpleasant memories. Konrad, he vividly recalled, had been the bane of his confirmation class. The boy had tried to discomfit him with an incessant stream of questions—questions posed in a quiet, friendly voice but with a persistence that defied the imagination.

Konrad was a born troublemaker, Bachus told himself. He was the smartest, shrewdest youngster he had ever come up against, and now, by God, their paths had crossed again.

Unwittingly, Bachus had almost put his finger on Konrad's ulterior motive. His aim was to prod the town's spiritual leader into a public profession of faith.

Inspector Kersten of the Gilgenrode constabulary felt no desire to engage in prayerful meditation. He was, after all, a practical man and the ever-observant eye of the law.

Kersten had long recognized that an alarming increase in criminal activities, and acts of violence in particular, occurred during the hours of darkness preceding every Sabbath.

Though not exactly low on other days, Gilgenrode's consumption of alcohol rose by more than a hundred percent on Saturdays, which inevitably led to arguments, insults and, ultimately, clashes of a physical nature. Injuries, even severe ones, were not uncommon, but fatalities seldom occurred. The local bone structure was robust and its resilience exceptional.

Apart from that, Kersten privately classified every Saturday as an "S" (for sex) day. He could, with tolerable accuracy, forecast the incidence of certain sex-related acts such as adultery, which was far from rare, or rape, which was usually a matter of allegation only. The beating of wives was regarded as a private affair of no concern to the police.

Other forms of criminal activity included the theft of motorcycles, purses and schnapps bottles (negligible) and the maltreatment of dogs, children and domestic servants (very few charges preferred). As for the few cases of arson that occurred, they nearly always turned out to be acts of simple revenge or childish self-indulgence. ("It made such a lovely blaze!")

Tonight, as Kersten watchfully roamed the streets of his little town, he felt more like a kindly Saint Bernard than a snarling Alsatian. In the middle of Market Square he came on a man relieving himself—not just anywhere, but up against the base of the war memorial.

It was none other than Richard Breitbach, patently drunk and grinning from ear to ear. He had downed the contents of several bottles in an attempt to forget Beate and her feline fits of temperament. In this he had clearly succeeded, so the sight of the policeman failed to quench his spirits.

"It's a fair catch," he said, without cutting his sacrilege short. "I couldn't restrain myself any longer. You can charge me if you like."

"No charges," said Kersten. "If there were any spectators, you might be accused of committing a public nuisance, but I don't count. As an officer of the law, I can only advise you to be more careful in your choice of target."

Breitbach scratched his head with one hand and buttoned his fly with the other. "What's this, a policeman who allows for human nature, even here in Gilgenrode?"

"Here or anywhere," Kersten replied politely, and he walked off.

His next port of call was the town's most recent watering-place, the Strong Man's Arms. A wall of sound hit him as he approached. Mingled with the dull thud of pounding boots and the clatter of chairs in violent motion were yells of delight, the tinkling of glass and the splintering of wood. As long as no neighbor complained that the Brownshirts were disturbing his night's repose, however, Kersten could not step in. Experience suggested that no one would be rash enough to do so.

The inspector continued his tour until he came to Ritterstrasse. Here, in the vicinity of Number 33, he was accosted by Emil Spahn, who darted out of the shadows and barred his path.

"It's me, Herr Kersten. You know me and I know you—at least, I hope I do. They aren't all like you, worse luck—far from it! Take that jumped-up sergeant who calls himself a stormtroop commander and orders everyone around. Know what he called me? A rotten, degenerate, antisocial parasite!"

"Is this a formal complaint? Do you have any witnesses to support your allegation?"

"Crazy I may be, Inspector, but I'm not as crazy as that. You expect me to take on Keller and his gorillas single-handed? It'd be like tackling a tank with a peashooter. No, I only want what's mine—the one thing that makes my life worth living. It's my cat: she's disappeared."

"She'll turn up, Herr Spahn. I'll gladly keep an eye open for her. Mind you, I can't make any promises."

Emil took Kersten by the sleeve of his tunic and drew him close, an act of lèse-majesté that the policeman indulgently tolerated. "Look, Herr Kersten, I know my life's a mess—rather like this country. I'm used to being kicked around, but even I refuse to give up the last thing I can still call my own. Nobody's going to deprive me of my cat—not my darling little Susie!"

"Take it easy," Kersten said soothingly. Years of police work had inured him to dealing with distraught members of the public. "I reckon your Susie's out on the town. Cats do these things. It wouldn't be so extraordinary—not on a fine night like this."

"You may be right. I hope so, but she never leaves my side for long. If something's happened to her—if someone's done away with her—I'll kill the man that did it!"

In the Strong Man's Arms, the Brownshirts had almost completed their process of systematic self-intoxication. They performed drunken dances, reeling around in circles with their arms linked and bawling wildly into each other's sweat-streaked faces. From time to time their voices soared in some stirring army ballad or marching song.

This apart, they were filled with joyful anticipation by the prospect of an event commonly known as the "Fire Drill." This, in the authoritative view of Stormtroop Commander Keller, was a custom in the best sergeants'-mess tradition and must never take place before midnight. It consisted of a male efficiency contest based on "hose pressure."

Keller marshaled his men into two ranks in the middle of the canteen, which had been cleared of furniture. His voice rang out in a series of commands.

"Front rank, about . . . face! Rear rank, three paces to the rear . . . march! Both ranks, hoses . . . out!"

Two rows of unsteady figures obediently took up "hosing"

positions, "nozzles" aimed at their opposite numbers. Then came the crucial order:

"Water . . . on!"

Some contestants had already relieved the pressure on their bladders and found it hard to get the distance. The majority produced little more than a trickle, though half a dozen managed to anoint their opponents' boots. "Increase pressure!" exhorted Keller, who had appointed himself referee and detailed Konrad to act as linesman.

And then came the unique achievement of which, as Keller's verbal tribute later phrased it, the victor's children and grandchildren would speak with awe and admiration. Alone among this elite, one Brownshirt managed to turn in a really sparkling performance. Such was his range that it encompassed his opponent's breeches, his tunic—almost his very face.

The performer of this brilliant feat was Platoon Commander Schulze, the man whose wife was even now improving his promotion prospects in a hotel bed with Felix Kimminger. Keller pronounced him a runaway winner and invested him with the time-honored title "King of the Urinoco."

Schulze was crowned with a laurel wreath ordered specially for the occasion—"in honor of your outstanding achievement"—whereupon the survivors of Fire Drill broke into a frenzied *zapateado,* satisfied that they were men, *real* men.

In all this roomful of revelers, most of whom continued to bawl, belch and cavort while the rest slept the sleep of the dead, only two men were fully alert. One was Keller, who prided himself on the vast amount of drink he could carry, and the other was Konrad, who had contrived to lessen the effect of his intake by secretly swilling water in the washroom. He did not recoil when Keller draped an arm around his shoulders and nodded at the seething throng.

"That's what I'm aiming at," the Stormtroop Commander roared happily. "Absolute obedience, total commitment! What about your favorite author, wouldn't he agree?"

"A hundred percent, in principle. Our Führer's glorious book *Mein Kampf* contains numerous appeals for absolute and unstinting self-sacrifice."

"That sounds promising, Konrad, and you won't lose by saying so. Just between us, old son, my platoon commanders are a willing trio, especially when it comes to piss-ups and peeing contests, but they're pretty short of gray matter. One or other of them'll have to go before long. Anyway, there's every chance I may have to take over a far bigger job myself in the near future. Can you think of a possible successor—eh, Konrad?"

Konrad got the picture, or most of it, but he was past being surprised by anything. He didn't even blink when the Brownshirts' drunken orgy was invaded by a uniformed policeman—one of Kersten's three subordinates. This one possessed something which put him under a special obligation: he carried a Party membership book, and he took his membership seriously.

Very confidentially, but loudly enough for Konrad to overhear, he whispered into Keller's receptive ear.

"They've found a stiff in the lake. Nothing so unusual about that, of course. It happens several times a summer, especially in Lake Gilgenrode—you know the old-wives' tale about water sprites—but this time the victim's a member of our district branch. It's Peter Patzer. I thought you'd like to know."

"Stupid asshole," said Keller. He scowled, thinking hard. There was no mistaking his uneasiness at this highly unwelcome news. "Patzer never was a shining example to the Movement, and this proves it. Plenty of good intentions but no guts."

"I see," said the constable. "So you think it was suicide."

"Why come to me about it?" asked Keller, still trying to dodge the issue. "You should have gone to see the District Director."

"I tried to, but his mother says he's ill in bed. That's why I'm here."

Keller struggled to reach a decision. Konrad sat there digesting the latest turn of events. Tragic or not, he seemed to be relishing it.

"Fair enough, Comrade," Keller said eventually. "I'm the one who counts here after Sonnenblum. You were right to tell me, but what's all this crap about suicide? Patzer may have gone for a midnight dip and drowned. Maybe he went for a boat ride and sank."

"In Party uniform?"

"In white tie and tails—who cares?" Having once decided on the best policy, Keller pursued it with vigor. "No fuss, that's the main thing—nothing that could harm the Movement. Every responsible Party member has a duty to avoid that."

The constable promptly agreed, but added, "It won't be too easy to convince the Inspector, though. Kersten can be pretty obstinate."

"Sooner or later," Keller said firmly, "everyone in this town will see the light, even Kersten. You'd better make sure he does if you want to go places, understand?"

"I'll do my best." Keller was not alone in nursing lofty ambitions. The card-carrying constable, who had his eye on Kersten's job, saluted smartly and hurried out.

Unabashed by Konrad's attentive gaze, Keller belched

loud and long. "That silly cunt Patzer! I always said he
was useless but nobody took any notice. Anyway, we're rid
of him at last. Let's have another drink to celebrate. Dead
men don't talk, thank God!"

Konrad looked less sanguine. "If it really was suicide,
there's something worth bearing in mind. People who kill
themselves usually like to have the last word. They tend
to leave a farewell letter explaining the whys and where-
fores."

"Goddammit!" growled Keller, clearly alarmed. "I
wouldn't put it past him, the conniving bastard!"

"And that could drop a few people in the shit. You, for
instance, or me—not to mention some others I could name.
We ought to do something, Comrade Keller. The question
is, what?"

The Stormtroop Commander's immediate reaction was
to bellow for a large schnapps.

Konrad emerged from the Strong Man's Arms just as
sunlight was flooding the streets with gold. Staggering along
in his wake came a group of brown-shirted comrades, some
still bawling merrily, others green with nausea. Beside him,
stiff as a ramrod and deep in thought, strode Stormtroop
Commander Keller.

They had been joined by Platoon Commander Schulze,
whose brow was adorned with the laurel wreath that identified him as King of the Urinoco. He wore it proudly
cocked over one eye.

"Cheer up, Comrade Keller," Schulze called brightly.
"That was a night to remember. You ought to be feeling
on top of the world."

Keller glared irritably at him. "My job calls for more
than a strong bladder," he snapped.

141

Schulze, who took this as a grave insult, looked aggrieved and sheered off, muttering angrily. Keller ignored him and turned to Konrad.

"If that idiot Patzer really did write a farewell note, would he have had it on him when he took the plunge? If he did, the police must have it by now."

"I doubt it." Konrad had carefully considered this point. "He was a schoolmaster, remember, and schoolmasters like to keep things neat and tidy. Patzer wouldn't have let a little matter like suicide change his habit patterns. My guess is, he left the note at home, in a prominent place."

Keller gave him an approving slap on the back. "Good thinking! That means I'd better get hold of his love letter before anyone else does."

He walked off. Schulze, who had been dawdling in the background, caught Konrad up. His eyes were alight with comradely concern.

"What's up with Keller, jumping down my throat like that? He turns every little fart into a thunderstorm, that man. It doesn't exactly make for team spirit."

Konrad had no hesitation in coming down on Schulze's side, at least outwardly. "Keller's methods don't appeal to you, Comrade, and you aren't alone. Still, he is our commanding officer."

"He may be now," snarled Schulze, "but it needn't be permanent. Keller isn't the only man for the job. There are others—better ones. Heads'll have to roll, of course. Speaking for myself, I'll be ready when the time comes."

Inspector Kersten completed his long nocturnal patrol and returned to police headquarters, which occupied a suite of offices in one wing of the town hall. Here he listened to his subordinates' accounts of their own night's work.

His faint air of boredom vanished in a flash when the card-carrying constable made his report.

"A case of drowning, sir. The man's body was washed up near the municipal gardens. He couldn't have been in the water long, from the look of him. That makes three this year. Pure routine, I'd say."

"Has he been identified?"

"The name's Patzer, Peter Patzer. Accidental death, no doubt about it."

"Don't jump to conclusions," Kersten said sharply. "Our job is to establish the facts, not make unsupported statements. Let's see what you've got in the way of solid evidence."

The evidence was duly submitted: incident report complete with sketch map, preliminary medical report, personal particulars, inventory of deceased's clothing and personal effects. Kersten studied these details closely and unhurriedly. Before long he gave a series of disapproving grunts and wagged his bullet head, which was more square than round.

"Haven't I taught you anything? Have all my little lectures been a complete waste of time? Accidental death? This case reeks of suicide, can't you see?"

The card-carrying constable looked discomfited. "You may be right, Inspector, but . . ." His tone became almost imploring. "There's something you should know. The deceased was a Party official. I'd take that into account if I were you. It makes a difference."

"Not to me it doesn't," said Kersten.

143

THAT SAME bright and vernal Sunday morning, Inspector Kersten went into action with a ritual solemnity unusual even for him. After completing his study of the Patzer file, he informed his subordinates that he intended to clinch the case by conducting some personal inquiries.

The few people out and about at this early hour stared at Kersten as he made his stately way across Market Square. Instead of the peaked cap that normally adorned his head, he was wearing a tall, helmetlike contraption known as a police shako. This headgear was reserved for special occasions such as national holidays, public ceremonies and proceedings of a very formal nature. His present mission appeared to fall into the last category.

Kersten began by calling at 33 Ritterstrasse and asking

for Keller. This provoked a clash with Keller's sister Hermine.

"You can't see him," she said. "It's impossible."

"But essential," Kersten persisted. "I'm here on official business."

"My brother's had a tiring night, also on official business, and he told me not to wake him till eleven. After that he's going to church. Come back later."

Kersten retreated a couple of steps. He couldn't bring too much pressure to bear. There was no formal justification for it, so he saluted stiffly and marched off.

A few minutes later he knocked at the door of 7 Market Square and was admitted by Gertrude Sonnenblum. She eyed her early-morning visitor quizzically.

"You look a proper treat in that helmet of yours—just like a dashing young cavalry officer."

"If you mean the shako," Kersten told her gravely, "it's part of parade dress. I felt the occasion warranted it."

Gertrude gave him a beaming smile. "Lord, I hope you aren't all dressed up for my sake. Have I done something illegal? I've wanted to, lots of times, but I never seem to manage it."

"I'm here to see your son, Frau Sonnenblum."

"He's sleeping it off. It's a regular Sunday habit of his—must be something to do with his official responsibilities. You won't get any sense out of him. He's feeling as sick as a dog."

"I understand." Once again, Kersten could see no alternative but to withdraw gracefully. He could hardly interview Sonnenblum by main force. "I'd better come back later."

"Not so fast, young man," Gertrude called after him. "From the look of you, I'd say you've got a nasty surprise up your sleeve for my Heinrich. If so, he's welcome to it—that and any other kind of shock treatment. Am I right?"

A gleam had come into Kersten's eyes. "You could be."

Gertrude disappeared into her son's bedroom. Sonnenblum lay muffled in his blankets, streaming with sweat and snoring loudly. He was probably in the throes of some nightmare about Beate. Gertrude whipped away the bedclothes and emptied a jug of water over him.

Sonnenblum's eyes opened with a jerk. He propped himself unsteadily on one elbow. Though drugged with sleep, he quickly groped for the dignity proper to a senior Party official.

"Wha—what's the meaning of this!"

"You're wanted, Heinrich. It's urgent. The police are asking for you."

"The police?" Sonnenblum scowled. "Tell them to get lost!"

"You can tell them yourself," Gertrude said gleefully, "but you'd better hear what the inspector has to say first."

Laboriously, Sonnenblum pulled on a brown bathrobe and tottered into the living room. Here, in his mother's presence, he was informed that Patzer had been found drowned, and that inquiries into his death were in progress.

"Well," Kersten concluded, "may I have your comments?"

"My God, what do you expect me to say?" Sonnenblum covered his bloated face with both hands as though trying to hide his grief. Emotion would have been unworthy of a true man, especially a true German, and he was both!

His mother eyed him with a mixture of pity and amusement. "That's floored you, hasn't it?"

"Patzer dead?" Every inch the District Director, Sonnenblum stared at the floor with solemn mien. "He was one of our best men, if not *the* best. What a loss to the Movement! How did it happen? I can only assume it was a tragic accident."

"Accidental death can't be ruled out," said Kersten, "but it seems unlikely in view of the circumstances."

Gertrude blithely took the hint and enlarged on it. "So it wasn't an accident. Murder's out too, I imagine, or the inspector would be turning the town inside out, not paying social calls. That leaves suicide."

"You've put your finger on it, madam." Kersten gave the old woman a respectful little bow. "There are some pretty strong pointers in that direction—for instance, the behavior of certain individuals. Herr Keller, to name but one."

Sonnenblum looked bemused. "If he had something to do with it, why don't you pay him a visit?"

"I tried before coming here, but his sister refused to admit me. The door to his room was ajar—I suspect he was listening in. I had meant to question him along the following lines. Was he, that is to say, your stormtroop commander, prematurely informed of the deceased's death by one of my men, who happens to be a Party sympathizer? If so, did he then steal a march on the police by entering the deceased's place of residence? Not to mince matters, did he gain access by false pretenses?"

Sonnenblum looked even more confounded. "But—but why should he do that?"

"I've already ascertained that Herr Keller did, in fact, call on the deceased's landlady in his capacity as commander of your Storm Detachment. He informed her that the deceased's room might contain Party documents of a confidential or even secret nature, and that these must be transferred to a safe place. The suspicion logically arises,

148

could material evidence have been removed in the process? And that, Herr Sonnenblum, brings me to another point. Did you give Herr Keller any instructions or suggestions on the subject?"

"Certainly not. Why on earth should I?"

"Then I strongly advise you," said Kersten, "to clear the matter up. I suggest we have an immediate talk with Herr Keller—the two of us."

"Yes, Heinrich," said his mother, maliciously fanning the flames, "you'd better straighten things out right away, even if it costs the town a stormtroop commander—or a district director."

Now it was Sonnenblum's turn, clad in a brown civilian suit and closely escorted by Kersten, to call at 33 Ritterstrasse. This time, not even Hermine could concoct a plausible reason for refusing to summon her brother.

Keller mumbled something unfriendly under his breath. He climbed into his SA tunic and breeches before padding barefoot into his sister's front parlor. This room, whose main decorative features were pinewood, plush and cheap glass, owed its cleanliness to infrequent use. In one corner stood a sort of display cabinet, and in it reposed two books. Both were copies of Hitler's *Mein Kampf*, one of them presented to Keller on his appointment as stormtroop commander, the other a gift from his men.

Keller's hand shot out in a Nazi salute as soon as he saw Sonnenblum. He attached great importance to outward signs of political solidarity, even under circumstances like the present.

"Heil Hitler, District Director! What can I do for you?" Then he caught sight of the policeman hovering in the background. "What's *he* doing here?"

Sonnenblum edged in front of Kersten as though trying

to blot out the sight of him. "It has been alleged that you visited Patzer's lodgings after receiving news of his death. Is that true?"

"Certainly," said Keller, with devastating honesty. "And for a very good reason. I was protecting our interests."

"Your interests?" Kersten chimed in. "What sort of interests? Did you by any chance take possession of a suicide note, and did that note contain certain accusations? If so, .what form did they take and who were they leveled at?"

"That's no damned business of yours," Keller said truculently. "This is a Party matter, so kindly keep out of it."

Sonnenblum raised one hand in a magisterial rebuke. "Please, Comrade! Herr Kersten is only doing his duty. On the other hand, we owe a special duty to the state and our Movement. Before any more disagreeable misunderstandings arise, I suggest we clear the air in private."

Their interview, to which Kersten could hardly object, took place in Hermine's kitchen. She had brewed some coffee and filled two jugs. One she set before her brother and the District Director, the other she took to Kersten in the parlor. Her animosity toward the policeman seemed to have evaporated. She was all smiles now.

Back in the kitchen-cum-living-room, her excellent coffee went untouched. The District Director and his SA chief sat glaring at each other across the table. Sonnenblum, who spoke first, sounded grimly accusing.

"Is it true what that—that policeman says?"

Keller nodded. He might have been admitting that he had five fingers on each hand.

"You searched Patzer's room after his death?" Keller nodded again. "And you pocketed something? Good God, man, how could you be so foolish?"

"There'd have been hell to pay if I hadn't."

"What did you find?"

"Pretty much what he thinks I found, the uncooperative bastard—a so-called suicide note written by a notorious crackpot. Patzer was a traitor to the Movement. He couldn't fade quietly out of the picture—oh no! He took care to shit on us first. Your name headed the list."

"Curse the man!" wailed Sonnenblum. "Is *nothing* sacred! Here am I, the soul of generosity and consideration, slaving night and day for the good of others, and what do I get in return? Nothing but ingratitude, selfishness and obstruction!" This cry from the heart embraced Beate, whose behavior was preying on his mind. "May I see the letter?"

"Here, take it. I know it'll be safe with you." Keller had been prudent enough to make a copy, just in case. "Get a load of that—it'll knock you sideways."

Watching the District Director closely, Keller was gratified to see his hand shake and beads of sweat break out on his brow.

"Oh God," groaned Sonnenblum, "to think what might have happened if this vile rubbish had fallen into the wrong hands! But what do we do now? How do we extricate ourselves? How do we convince that officious policeman he's got the wrong end of the stick?"

"You're bound to think of something, District Director. If anyone around here can sell shit for shaving-cream, it's you."

The sale went ahead at once. Sonnenblum and Keller returned to the front room, which was gently bathed in morning sunlight.

Here Hermine poured the menfolk some brandy as a welcome complement to her strong brew of coffee. Although on duty, Kersten was in East Prussia, and no East Prussian lawman ever spurned an invigorating glass or two—if not three. The liquor did nothing to dull his senses, which

151

were now focused on Sonnenblum's fluent appeal for a sympathetic hearing.

"I think I've got to the bottom of this matter," he said. "It's absolutely true that our friend here entered the former home of Party Member Patzer—God rest his soul! However, he was not unnaturally afraid that important papers might be on the premises, secret documents belonging to our Movement. As he saw it, their recovery was in the national interest."

"Maybe, but a death has occurred." Keller's manner remained ominously official. "In such cases, no document or written material may be withheld from the investigating authority, least of all a suicide note."

"Nor was it," Sonnenblum assured him earnestly. "Herr Keller conducted a search in good faith, prompted by a laudable sense of responsibility, but he found nothing. He could not, therefore, have removed anything."

"It's the gospel truth," said Keller, raising his right hand like a witness taking the stand.

"Well?" Sonnenblum gave Kersten an encouraging smile. "Doesn't that set your mind at rest?"

"No," the policeman said flatly. He was looking as stubborn as a mule now, jaw jutting and arms folded. "If this was suicide, and everything points to it, there must be a farewell letter. That's the rule in at least nine cases out of ten."

"But not this time." Sonnenblum's assurance carried a menacing undertone. "Why should such a prominent and universally respected figure commit suicide? In the strictest confidence, my dear Inspector, Peter Patzer was destined for higher things—much higher things, and he knew it. In the event of my being appointed Regional Director, Patzer would have taken over the district branch. He didn't have the slightest reason to kill himself, don't you see?"

"No," said Kersten. "I can well understand why you'd welcome a verdict of accidental death, but this was no accident. Patzer's suicide note would prove that beyond doubt. Why not hand it over?"

"Because there isn't one," Sonnenblum insisted.

Kersten shrugged. "It'll turn up sometime. Then the fur will fly, you mark my words!"

So saying, he left, outwardly vanquished but inwardly hopeful that he had impaled Gilgenrode's brown-shirted potentates on the horns of a dilemma.

While Hermine was showing the policeman out, the District Director and Stormtroop Commander eyed each other with concern. They were both privy to a Party secret of the utmost significance.

"That dumb, pigheaded bastard!" fumed Keller. "He's a downright danger to the Movement."

Sonnenblum looked prophetic. "He'll have to play ball with us sooner or later. In the long run, nobody has any choice. It's just that he doesn't realize it yet."

"As far as we're concerned, what happened to Patzer was an accident. That's the official line and we'll stick to it like grim death, eh?"

"I'm sure it's the best solution. There can't be any suicides in our ranks, only heroes and martyrs. We'll give Patzer the funeral he deserves—that ought to banish any lingering misconceptions. Are you with me, Hermann?"

"All the way, District Director."

Parson Bachus was just preparing to conduct Sunday morning service when a contingent of Brownshirts paraded outside the austere, rugged edifice that served the town as a Protestant church. Twelve of them, including Konrad Breitbach, had mustered in uniform under the command of the man whose prodigious bladder power had won him such a famous victory the night before. They were waiting for Keller.

But there was no sign of him. The stormtroopers stood there at ease with pallid and impassive faces, trying to look sternly martial. Platoon Commander Schulze, on the other hand, seemed distinctly restive. To judge by their sidelong glances, the churchgoers who were streaming past regarded him as a species of fairground attraction.

Schulze's annoyance was intensified by the conduct of the sexton. That sanctimonious hypocrite in his gravy-stained cassock had been watching him and his men like an enemy scout. More than that, he had scuttled off to warn Bachus. Schulze caught a glimpse of the parson's pale moon face peering anxiously through the vestry window at the brown-shirted detachment drawn up outside his church.

Uneasily, Schulze turned to Konrad, who had contrived to stand just behind him. "All dressed up and nowhere to go," he grumbled. "What's the next move?"

"That's up to you," said Konrad. Schulze's mounting uneasiness delighted him. "You're in command till Keller turns up—if he does."

At that moment a boy appeared, a blue-eyed twelve-year-old with a confiding expression. He strongly resembled Keller and his sister Hermine, whose son he was, and he delivered the following message:

"The Stormtroop Commander says he's sorry, he can't make it. He's in conference with the District Director—it's very important. You're to carry on, he says."

Schulze turned to Konrad for some more advice. "Well, what do we do now?"

"Proceed according to plan," said Konrad, immensely heartened by the look of guileless stupidity on the Platoon Commander's bovine face. "In other words, we go to church.

154

You're in charge now—you give the orders and we'll obey them."

Schulze braced himself for a decision. He didn't have the remotest idea what Keller had in mind. Some kind of church parade, yes, but what was the object? A show of force, presumably. He squared his shoulders, called his men to attention and marched them inside.

Led by Schulze, twelve picked stormtroopers tramped rhythmically up the aisle. As though by right of conquest, they headed for the two front pews. The fact that several civilians were ejected with the aid of the sexton, who scurried on ahead, was a tribute to their status; they were only receiving their due.

As one man, they seated themselves in a compact, brown-uniformed mass. They did not gaze humbly at the ground but riveted their eyes on the altar like marksmen taking aim. Parson Bachus, who was already in position, clung hard to the edge of his stall to hide the tremor in his hands. Fighting down his initial panic, he spread his arms wide as though embracing the whole town, the whole of Germany, the whole universe. A Catholic might have been reminded of the Pope's Easter benediction.

In a quavering voice, Bachus invited the congregation to join him in the first verse of "A Mighty Fortress Is Our God." He launched himself into Luther's indubitably German and indubitably warlike hymn, and they all joined in —all of them! The Brownshirts sang too, with exceptional verve and vigor, a circumstance that dispelled the parson's fears and rekindled his Christian courage. He was further heartened by the sight of that odd young man Konrad Breitbach. Seated only a few feet away, Konrad gave him a cheerful smile—indeed, Bachus even thought he detected a nod of encouragement.

155

So, all was well after all. It seemed clear that the Party, here represented by its most potent and dynamic offshoot, attached definite importance to good relations with the Church. Added to this was the sympathetic response of his flock. He caught sight of old Frau Sonnenblum in a pew near the front, and she too gave him an encouraging nod— he was certain of it. Thus heartened, he embarked on a sermon notable for its patriotic and chauvinistic tenor. It was a long-established tradition, he said, that defenders of the Fatherland should visit the house of the Lord to pray for His blessing on their cause in time of war and peace. Weapons and regimental colors too were blessed, where possible, before each battle—a practice that had often proved efficacious.

"And now," Bachus intoned with rising fervor, "we see these splendid, forward-looking soldiers of the Führer united with us, shoulder to shoulder, in the house of God. If that isn't a heart-warming sight, what is?"

Schulze shuffled restlessly in his pew. "What's this," he muttered, "an act?"

"He's trying to soft-soap us," Konrad whispered back, "and his parishioners don't know what to make of it. Look at their faces! They're absolutely flummoxed."

"How do you think Keller would handle this?"

"No idea. It's your show, Platoon Commander."

"Do I have to swallow this trash," growled Schulze, "or do we make an ostentatious exit—or what?"

"A trained political activist must be able to grin and bear it: I guess that's what our District Director would say in your place. The one thing we can't afford is an unnecessary scene."

"You're right," said Schulze, gritting his teeth. "Who cares what goes on here, anyway?"

Superficially, he seemed to have a point. The church was

a small one, with room for only two hundred worshipers. Never crowded at the best of times, it had lately been more poorly attended than usual. Not, however, on this memorable Sunday morning, when a detachment of stormtroopers had marched in under the restive gaze of the faithful, to be welcomed like prodigal sons by the shepherd of the flock.

"And so it turns out yet again," cried Bachus, aflame with brotherly love, "that the ways of the Lord surpass all understanding!"

They certainly surpassed his own.

"May I have a nice cold beer, Mother?" Sonnenblum pleaded faintly.

"No." Gertrude was busy with her pots and pans, from one of which rose a beguiling aroma of sauerbraten. "Nothing alcoholic before lunch."

"But I'm not feeling well," he said, flopping onto a chair near the stove. "You've no idea how worried and depressed I am."

"So would I be, in your place. Your practice is going to pot—and no wonder, the way you've been neglecting it."

"I may give it up altogether," he confided, portentously knitting his brow. "If they appoint me Regional Director I'll have to devote all my time and energy to the Movement."

"And give up Fräulein Fischer too, eh?" Gertrude cackled merrily.

"What would you say, Mother," he asked in a slow, ponderous voice, "if I told you I intended to marry her?"

Gertrude stirred her pans and poked the wood-burning range beneath them. Sparks flew, bathing her strong and rather masculine features in an intermittent red glow. "I want you to have anything that'll make you happy," she said, "even a brown uniform, even Fräulein Fischer. But are you sure she'll have *you?*"

"If that's another reference to Breitbach, forget about him. Who cares if he *is* forcing his unwelcome attentions on her? Only the best is good enough for a girl like Beate, and that means me, not Breitbach."

"You can have that beer after all," Gertrude told him kindly. "You sound as if you need it badly."

Heinrich Sonnenblum pounced on the permitted bottle, which was cooling in the sink. He opened it and sucked with the avid concentration of a baby at its mother's breast. Gertrude watched him with mild concern. "I wasn't talking about Breitbach," she said. "I meant Keller."

"Keller?" Sonnenblum stared at her like a dachshund whose owner has thrown it a rubber bone instead of the genuine article. *"That* prize bull? Don't make me laugh!"

"Cows are partial to bulls, Heinrich."

"It's absurd!" Sonnenblum took another fierce swig at his bottle. "Keller's what I've made him—he owes me everything. He'd never dare meddle in my private life. Besides, he's crude. Haven't you ever noticed his grimy fingernails? Beate's a fastidious creature. That would be enough to put her off in itself."

"Really?" Gertrude gave a scornful laugh. "So he'd give her the creeps, would he? Then why are you trying to hand him your daughter on a plate?"

"It'll be a long time before Keller gets my blessing," he replied quickly. "I'll have him house-trained by then."

Gertrude carefully turned the sauerbraten in its stew pot. "Keller's been far busier than you seem to think, and not only with your girlfriend. His latest hobby is religion. Some of his Brownshirts came to church this morning. You've never heard singing like it. They bellowed like rutting stags at full moon. I could hardly believe my eyes and ears. Even Bachus choked up."

"What!" exclaimed Sonnenblum. "You're pulling my leg!"

"I'm only telling you what happened." Gertrude paused to savor his horror and disbelief. "Very impressive it was too, but hardly in line with Party policy."

He struck his brow. "Am I surrounded by idiots?"

"Quite possibly, but who cares what a handful of idiots get up to? You can find fools anywhere, any time, especially here and now—they're as common as cow chips in our part of the world. What matters is, who turned their heads and whose blood are they really after?"

"You're trying to poison my mind, Mother. Your suspicions are utterly ridiculous."

"Call them anything you like, but they're well founded—they're already coming true. You thought you were rearing a docile flock of sheep, didn't you? Well, now they want to act like wolves. It suits the age we live in."

District Director Sonnenblum telephoned Stormtroop Commander Keller and issued him an immediate summons to Party headquarters.

There he awaited him behind his directorial desk, on which stood a swastika flag stiffened with bent wire to suggest that it was fluttering in an eternal breeze. Sonnenblum himself looked cold and froglike, ready to jump at a moment's notice. He grasped the arms of his chair with hands that trembled slightly.

Keller marched in and performed a regulation salute. "Stormtroop Commander Keller reporting as instructed," he said, all blithe and unsuspecting. "Always at your service, District Director," he added.

159

"We can skip that sort of rigmarole, Keller. Solid achievement is all that counts with me."

Slightly unnerved by Sonnenblum's glacial reception, the SA chief reviewed his recent conduct and found it irreproachable. "What's up? I thought I handled the Patzer business pretty well."

"So you did, but what were your men doing meanwhile? Sitting in church—in uniform! Like a bunch of choirboys!" Sonnenblum shook his head. "I can hardly believe it."

"That's Schulze's fault—he must have blown a fuse. While you and I were conferring on a matter of national importance he took the bit between his teeth and marched his men into church, where that smarmy subversive of a parson walked all over them."

"Don't give me that! Schulze's one of your platoon commanders and his men belong to your unit. You're their commanding officer, which makes you responsible for them and this whole sorry business." Sonnenblum drew himself up, looking positively statuesque. "As if I didn't have enough problems on my plate, your men behave like bleating sheep."

"I'll clip their wool for them, never you fear!"

"Glad to hear it." Sonnenblum's gracious nod of approval was swiftly succeeded by a stern admonition. "Whenever they become unavoidable, disputes with the Church are my personal responsibility, remember? I can handle them without your help. You'd do better to concentrate on your main assignment—the one we discussed at our last Party meeting. Get me some donations, Keller. Donations so generous that every festival ever held in this town will pale into insignificance beside our German Day."

"Certainly, District Director," said Keller, earnestly but with evident relief. "Leave everything to me."

Konrad was indulging in what he considered to be a brief but essential interlude as a confusion-sowing propagandist. He drafted a number of "Confidential Memoranda," inserted them in buff envelopes, and distributed them around Gilgenrode like cuckoo's eggs. Most of them were culled from the Führer's store of wisdom.

German Girls' Leaguer Eva Schwarz received the following injunction: " 'Girl, be mindful of your duty to become a German mother!' See *Mein Kampf*, p. 10." Konrad's postscript: "Heartiest German greetings. Always at your service."

For Parson Bachus: " 'But he whose fervor fails and whose lips remain sealed—he has not been chosen by Heaven to proclaim its will.' *Mein Kampf*, p. 117." Konrad: "Do you know the will of Heaven? I sincerely hope so. . . ."

For Treasurer Stenz: " 'One should beware of thinking the masses more stupid than they are. In political matters, emotion often proves a better judge than reason.' See *Mein Kampf*, p. 190." Konrad's comment: "In other words, the masses are stupid. Mobilize their emotions and cash in quick."

Konrad took the next of his "Führer's findings" to Siegfried Sass, who gave him a warm welcome.

"There you are at last, my boy—or should I call you Party Member Breitbach?"

"Not unless you want me to turn around and walk straight out—I mean, not unless you're going to treat me to some Dundee cake, the way you always used to."

The old Jew made a sweeping gesture of invitation. "Help yourself. It's all ready to cut, and it's all for you and me."

Konrad munched away with obvious enjoyment. "Actually," he said through a mouthful of crumbs, "I half expected you to show me the door after my recent antics. Or haven't you heard?"

"You're the talk of the town, Konrad. Every sparrow in Gilgenrode sings your name from the roof tops. I was curious to see you again."

"To see if I had changed?"

"We've been sharing the occasional Dundee cake since you were five, my boy. You can get quite close to someone in twenty years. I think I know you well enough."

"I've learned a lot from you and your approach to life, Herr Sass. Talking to you, dipping into your books—well, it's left its mark. I'm probably half-Jewish under the skin."

"In this day and age? Jehovah preserve you, my boy!" The old man threw up his hands, then very slowly lowered them. He gave Konrad a searching stare. "Do you know how you look to me? Thoroughly un-Teutonic. That uniform looks incongruous on you."

"Glad to hear it. I told you, you've taught me a lot."

"Too much, I'm afraid. Your present behavior and future plans sound unmitigatedly Jewish—I use the term loosely, like a certain book you're fond of quoting."

"Thanks for the compliment."

"I meant it as a warning. I admire this escapade of yours, Konrad, but it's too much of a good thing. Overdo it, and you're almost bound to come to grief in the end. They'll call you a subversive—worse still, a Jew-infected subversive."

"That's another compliment," said Konrad, still munching.

"Be careful, dear boy," Sass said quietly. "I'd be sad if anything happened to you. I don't have any children or family, as you know, so I need some heirs—heirs of my own choosing. I've already earmarked two and you're one of them."

162

Konrad stopped chewing and stared at Sass with his lips slightly parted. After a lengthy pause for thought, he said, "Any conditions? Do you want me to give up my Party shenanigans?"

"No conditions, Konrad, least of all that."

"Then I'll earn your money with a vengeance." Konrad grinned happily to himself. "Let's see if I can manage to act like a full-blooded Aryan Jew."

Stormtroop Commander Keller fled his District Director's presence at top speed. An all-out clash might have led to a complete break between them, and that was a luxury he couldn't afford—not yet.

The seeds he had sown were still germinating. If he wanted to get anywhere—with the Movement, with Beate or anyone else—he would have to be patient. Well, he told himself, patience was one of his cardinal virtues, and he also had the bright ideas to go with it.

His first brainwave was a visit to the home of Gilgenrode's only market gardener and florist, who was already at lunch with his numerous family.

"Heil Hitler, Party Members all!" Keller cried. "Don't let me interrupt—carry on with your eating." He turned to the florist. "When you've finished stuffing yourself, don't take a nap right away. Make me a really high-class bouquet and have it delivered to Fräulein Erika Sonnenblum, with my compliments."

The florist gave a meaningful wink. "Yes, sir!"

"Don't jump to conclusions," Keller told him, winking back. "In the meantime, clear the decks for a big order. There's Party Member Patzer's funeral coming up, and it's got to be really impressive. I want dozens of wreaths with ribbons a yard long and big fat swastikas all over them. The Party's paying for the lot, so I'm sure you can write off the cost of my bouquet. Is it a deal? Fine! Then enjoy your meal, folks!"

A minute later, Keller ran his self-convicted flop of a platoon commander to earth in the middle of Market Square. "Urinoco" Schulze was standing beside the town-hall fountain, which took the form of a swan that seemed to pee with quiet persistence into an ornamental basin. The fountain had been presented by Siegfried Sass on the occasion of a postwar midsummer festival.

"What have you been up to, you blithering idiot?" snarled Keller. "Marching our men into church like Sunday-school kids! I'm responsible for you, so that makes me look like a political ignoramus. What the hell were you thinking of?"

Schulze strove to preserve the male dignity to which he and his circle always aspired. "My conscience is clear, Stormtroop Commander. It was my duty to stand in for you, and that's what I did. I'm one of your best men—you're always telling me so. Look at last night."

"That was last night. Since then you've behaved like a colossal asshole. I was planning a full-scale attack on the Church—even an imbecile could have seen that. It's a question of political maturity, Schulze, and you don't have it. You've fallen down on the job; you're a write-off."

"Nobody writes *me* off!" Schulze glared at Keller, bull-necked and bellicose, ready to charge. His lips were tightly compressed and his blue eyes shone with Germanic menace. "I was only doing my duty, damn it all!"

Keller was impressed by this signal display of obduracy: Schulze looked genuinely threatening. He could be ditched, but a better opportunity would present itself in due course. "Fair enough," he said soothingly. "Everyone

164

makes mistakes now and then. What matters is to acknowledge them and shoulder the blame. Are you ready to do that, Comrade?"

"Absolutely, Stormtroop Commander!"

"Excellent." What an abortion of a man, Keller thought, but he cloaked his contempt in bluff benevolence. "So, you're prepared to explain your men's hymn singing to the District Director and make it clear that I had no part in it. That sniveling priest is the real nigger in the woodpile. You'll have to show him what you're made of as soon as possible. There should be a chance in two or three days' time, when we bury our old friend Patzer. Bachus may make trouble over the funeral, the bigoted bastard, but we'll show him!"

"May I have the honor of dealing with him personally?"

"Request granted."

"Thank you, Stormtroop Commander." Schulze seemed deeply touched by this mark of renewed confidence. Mournfully, he confided, "I sometimes feel like an elephant ambushed by pygmies. When that happens, I go wild. I could trample on everyone and everything in sight. I'm like that."

Keller didn't dwell on this psychological revelation. He was seized with an urgent desire to be pleasantly diverted by the fair sex—Beate Fischer, to be precise.

Beate was spending the afternoon with her sister, as she did nearly every Sunday. Gretl was several years younger but looked rather worn—understandably, in view of her domestic commitments. Her household consisted of three children under school age, one of them a chronic invalid, a large Alsatian dog, and a husband.

The latter was a municipal employee responsible for

165

town planning, highway construction and building permits. He had an inflated sense of his own importance and claimed to be grossly overworked, hence his need for repose.

On Sundays he slept till noon, had lunch, and then returned to bed until his wife roused him with a pot of coffee and a slab of freshly baked almond cake. Of this he devoured several square feet a week, with consequent effects on his waistline.

"How do you bear it?" Beate asked Gretl, while her sick child whimpered and her husband snored with stolid, torpid contentment in the room next door.

Gretl's smile was bleakly resigned. "I don't have any choice. Men are like that. Even you'll get used to the idea sooner or later."

"Me? Never!" Beate spoke with absolute certainty. She was sitting beside the window in her bra and pants, reverently proffering her body to the sun. She was starved for air. Besides, a deep tan suited her dark coloring.

"If I get hitched, it won't be to just anyone. He'll have to have class."

"Class, here in Gilgenrode?"

"There's quite a range of possibilities, even in this one-horse town." Beate lay back in the armchair and stretched, girlish breasts jutting, womanly thighs slightly splayed. "I can have almost anything, right here on the doorstep: money, influence, muscle—even brains and sensitivity."

This was a quadruple allusion to Breitbach, Sonnenblum, Keller and, last but not least, Johannes. Beate yawned.

"The trouble is, I can't make up my mind."

"And meantime you're at it with all of them?"

"Not necessarily. You've been reading too many women's magazines, Gretl. What they call fulfillment usually turns

166

out to be the beginning of the end. Either the lucky lads get sick of you and drop out, or they start getting possessive and confine you to barracks. Never surrender, that's the secret, but there are all kinds of ways of keeping them on the boil, from handholding to brinkmanship. It's risky sometimes, but mostly it's fun. They go as soft as blancmange if you leave them to stew a while."

Gretl had been standing by the window during this dissertation, watching the world go by. Suddenly she stiffened.

"You've got a visitor. It's Keller—he's heading this way."

"Get rid of him," Beate said without a moment's hesitation. "We don't have a date, so tell him to get lost. I refuse to be pestered."

Gretl opened the front door to find Keller poised on the doorstep, looking cheerfully virile.

"Heil Hitler, ma'am. May I see your sister?"

"Sorry, she's asleep."

"Then wake her. Tell her I'm here. Tell her I'd like to take her for a stroll. Coffee and cakes or a glass of wine—anything she fancies."

"Herr Keller," said Gretl, "I know Beate likes you a lot, but I also know what she doesn't like, and that's a man who won't take no for an answer. Please stop pestering her."

"*What* did you say?" Keller demanded incredulously. He felt a prey to yet another of the misunderstandings that had lately been afflicting him like a plague of mosquitoes. "You call it pestering, when all I did was ask if she'd appreciate my company?"

"You don't have a date with her, so you aren't on her schedule. If I were you, Herr Keller, I'd cut my losses and leave."

The SA chief dropped his mask of courtesy and retired, fulminating. A string of unintelligible words escaped his lips, much as if he had hawked and spat. Their probable purport was that he wouldn't be treated this way—his self-respect forbade it.

Still in quest of relaxation, Keller headed eastward to the municipal gardens and knocked at the door of 14 Preussenstrasse, a rather shabby terrace house occupied by Platoon Commander Schulze and, thus, by Schulze's wife.

As Keller well knew, his subordinate spent every Sunday afternoon at the lakeside sand dunes, giving premilitary instruction to members of the Hitler Youth. This was why he had come, but the door remained obstinately shut. A woman neighbor bustled up.

"You wanted Frau Schulze?" she inquired, cooing like a delighted dove.

"No, her husband."

"He's hardly ever in. Nor is she. A very hard-working couple, the Schulzes. They're busy all around the clock, especially nights. Any message I can give if I do happen to see them?"

Keller shook his head and stomped off, emitting another series of furious grunts. Which, being interpreted, meant, "Bloody women! How dare they do this to me—*me!*"

Kersten, Gilgenrode's worthy police chief, took the view that an officer of the law should treat every case as impartially and unpolitically as possible. Lately, however, he had sometimes felt tempted to depart from this basic rule.

As, for instance, when the card-carrying constable burst into his modest office with an air of deep official concern.

"Trouble, sir," he announced with relish. "It's our Storm-troop Commander's sister. She's having a purple fit."

Kersten's expression was mildly attentive. His voice carried no harsh undertone, no hint of reprimand; he simply set the record straight.

"Herr Keller isn't 'our' stormtroop commander—or not mine, anyway. Policemen aren't stormtroopers, nor is an informant's status of primary importance. What's it all about?"

"The said lady has lodged a complaint against a person known to this department. It's Emil Spahn. She says he's been making a nuisance of himself."

"Really? In what way?"

"He lives in the same house—as Keller and his sister, I mean—and he's been turning it upside down, searching every nook and cranny from the basement to the attic. He's also been combing the neighborhood, and all on account of some cat or other."

"You mean he hasn't found it yet?" Kersten betrayed an almost personal interest in the news. "Poor man, I'm sorry."

He rose without bestowing another glance on his puzzled subordinate, buttoned the collar of his tunic, buckled on his belt and holster, picked up his cap and set it neatly on his head.

Then he strode out of his shabby office and into Gilgenrode. He was off to rescue a cat and its owner. But in vain.

Konrad sought out Schulze at the sand dunes, where the platoon commander was trying to drum the military virtues into a group of brown-shirted schoolboys. Object: supreme physical fitness. Method: utter physical exhaustion.

The youngsters were driven up the dunes and down again. They flung themselves flat, rolled sideways and crawled to and fro before digging in, barehanded, to escape imaginary bursts of machine-gun fire. All concerned, cattle and herdsman alike, were breathless but radiant with the knowledge that their underlying aim was lofty, if not sublime. The whole animated scene was bathed in buttercup-yellow sunlight.

169

Despite his exertions, Schulze quickly spotted the newcomer and gave him a friendly nod. He brought his toughening-up course to a temporary halt.

"Not bad, eh?"

"Very impressive, Comrade Platoon Commander. I admire your work immensely."

"That's nice to know." Schulze joined Konrad on a convenient boulder. "You obviously appreciate my efforts."

"So does nearly everyone else around here. The District Director said as much only the other day, off the record. 'Our Schulze's a hundred percenter,' he said. 'He knows the meaning of loyalty and devotion to duty.' "

"You bet I do. Sonnenblum's got brains. He knows real talent when he sees it. Others don't, dammit."

Konrad knew who he meant—Keller, of course—but he didn't utter the name or even hint at it. Hitler could supply all that required to be said on this subject. Like Schulze, the Führer was ever reliable.

" 'What matters it to a German oak,' " he quoted grandly, " 'if a wild boar brushes against its trunk?' That goes for you, Comrade, and it's time you woke up to the fact."

"I know, but how can I fight back—effectively, I mean?"

"Take your cue from the Führer. As he says on page three-two-seven of his book, 'Performance of duty means service to the community, not self-gratification.' "

"Performance of duty . . ." Schulze seemed to glow with a dark inner fire. "Service to the community, not self-gratification—sure, that's it, and I'll do it for anyone who stands between me and my duty."

"The Führer would be delighted with you," said Konrad. "Your attitude is perfectly in line with his own, as expressed on page three-two-one: 'The hammerblow of fate suddenly strikes steel; and, as the workaday husk disintegrates, the

170

previously hidden kernel lies exposed to the eyes of a wondering world!' So much for that quotation, Platoon Commander. I'm sure you find it quite as inspiring as I do."

"I might almost have said it myself," declared Schulze, whose sights were already set on higher things. "But what do you think it means in practice?"

"Our Führer makes that crystal clear, this time on page three-seven-nine; 'But he who is unequal to that responsibility . . . or too craven . . . is unfitted to be a leader. Only the hero is destined for that!' Are *you?*"

"I certainly am!"

"And are you ready to take on Keller if necessary?"

"Him and anyone," Schulze proclaimed with missionary zeal. The extent of Konrad's duplicity was lost on him. His eyes were firmly fixed on the future.

Keller had succumbed to the desire for total oblivion and blissful stupefaction; in other words, he proposed to get drunk. Making his way to the Fatherland Café, he flopped into a chair and sent for Kimminger, who appeared without delay.

"What can I do for you this time? You only have to say, Stormtroop Commander. I want you to feel at home here."

"Hogwash," said Keller. "Results are all I'm interested in. For a start, what about that bloody parson? It's time we settled his hash, but how? Let's have some ideas, Kimminger, and give 'em to me straight."

"How about girls?" Kimminger filled their glasses with champagne, taking care to give Keller the lion's share. "Choir girls, I mean. They say he gooses them in the vestry during extra tuition."

"Well, does he? Suspicions are no damned use."

"The police opened a file on him two or three years ago, so why didn't they start proceedings? Because the parish council hushed it up, that's why. Several of his victims were over sixteen, and they were browbeaten into saying they had led him on. Legally speaking, that let him off the hook."

"But he's married, the dirty old man!"

"You can say that again." Kimminger clicked his fingers for another bottle of champagne. "His wife's got hot pants, didn't you know? I can highly recommend the lady—she's still in peak condition and a mighty experienced performer. She'd even give Beate Fischer a run for her money."

But this allusion had an extremely unwelcome effect. "Leave her out of it," Keller snarled. "Are you suggesting you've—"

"Of course not, Herr Keller." Kimminger spotted his mistake and hurriedly changed tack. "Right you are, I'll see you get all the dope on Bachus, the choir girls, and his wife's goings-on. Anything else?"

Keller was still incensed by Kimminger's suggestive reference to Beate, the more so because he feared it might be based on personal experience. He too decided on a quick change of tack.

"From the sound of it, Kimminger, you're keen to stay on good terms with the Movement. The question is, how much is our good will worth to you? We ought to discuss that right away."

Kimminger's round and rather ingenuous-looking face— a successful form of commercial camouflage—turned pale and puce by turns. "What is it this time?"

"This time," said Keller, "I'm talking about a German Day—the biggest and best ever held here. Sonnenblum wants it to go down in the local annals, but it won't unless we get some really generous support from right-minded citizens like you. We're counting on you more than anyone."

172

"I'm honored," Kimminger assured him. "What figure did you have in mind? Would a thousand marks do?"

There was no mistaking Keller's dissatisfaction. His brows contracted in a leonine scowl. "Multiply that by ten and you'd be talking. We want this thing to go with a swing."

Kimminger flinched, but only for a moment. He did some rapid mental arithmetic, simultaneously fortifying himself with champagne. His hands closed on the glass as if it were a climber's handhold. At last he said, "It might be arranged. All right, count me in."

Keller's eyes twinkled. "But if I know you, Kimminger, you won't be doing this for love of the Führer or me. There's bound to be a bloody great catch in it somewhere. You want a quid pro quo, right?"

"In a manner of speaking," Kimminger replied blandly, sure of his ground and almost as sure of Keller's response. "My idea is a division of labor: I supply you with the necessary funds; you dispose of public enemies."

"I get you," said Keller. "Speaking of public enemies, do you have anyone special in mind?"

"Gernoth, of course." Kimminger's reference to his chief competitor carried burning conviction. "The White Hart's a hotbed of subversives. Gernoth mixes with shady characters—intellectuals, democrats, reactionaries, conservatives, civil servants, even that buffoon of a policeman, Kersten, who lays down the law around here. They all feed their faces at cut rates, shoot off their mouths about us, slander us behind our backs. And you know who Gernoth's best-heeled customer is? The Jew! Sass could buy us all up three times over. Do we have to stand for it?"

"No, Comrade, you're goddam right we don't!" Keller's fraternal form of address was quite spontaneous. They were

173

both in the same boat, it seemed—both borne along by the same current. They sealed the transaction by clinking glasses. The Party was richer by ten thousand marks—or as good as—and Kimminger could look forward to acquiring Gernoth's hotel. Everything had been settled in an atmosphere of true German harmony.

By the time dusk descended on this sun-drenched day in early summer 1933, Stormtroop Commander Keller felt satisfied that he had laid a series of explosive charges that would, if all went well, clear every obstacle in his path. The road to supreme power, at least in Gilgenrode, would soon be open.

Lolling over Kimminger's third free bottle of champagne, Keller downed its contents like water. Then he repaired to the washroom for a prolonged piss. As he stood there belching, deep in thought and filled with hope for the future, he chalked up the following points in his favor:

1. Patzer's suicide note would have inflicted grave damage on the Party. This he had averted by pocketing it. He had even made that self-important ass of a policeman look foolish in the process.

2. As a result, the District Director had no choice but to trust him implicitly and cooperate to the full. Sonnenblum was on the retreat. He had even offered Keller his anemic daughter.

3. The full cost of Gilgenrode's German Day would be met by Kimminger. This was due entirely to him, Keller. Money was flowing in from sources hitherto undreamed of.

4. Although a handful of his dumbest men had truckled to the Church under Schulze's command, this lamentable defeat had been largely wiped out. He would, however, deal with Bachus or have him dealt with—that much he

promised himself. No one could defy a man of Keller's stature and remain unscathed.

5. Conclusion: his star was definitely in the ascendant and his position was undeniably strong. It would provide a perfect springboard for all he was now determined to achieve under the auspices of Adolf Hitler, his revered Führer, who had recently stated in the *Völkischer Beobachter* that "the SA is our destiny!"

Keller emerged into the street and wove his way across Market Square, heading for home. Here he proposed to seek solace with his beloved Hermine and treat her to some of the fraternal companionship she always enjoyed so much.

Reaching 33 Ritterstrasse, he found her in bed with her husband—more precisely, astride him. The paunchy civil servant was showing the whites of his eyes and grunting like a stuck pig while his hands roamed frenziedly up and down Hermine's back. She turned to give her brother an imploring stare. Just another couple of minutes, it seemed to say, then I'll be through with him.

Keller retired, still swaying. A bitter laugh escaped his lips. He might have known it! His obese brother-in-law always took a Sunday afternoon nap, and this was its time-honored conclusion; this, week after week, was when he exercised his conjugal rights. However distasteful, it was a fact of life.

It was also a circumstance that whetted Keller's own appetite. He was overdue for the reward that belongs to any man at the top of the heap—ample satisfaction and complete fulfillment. His next attempt to seek out Frau Schulze proved as unsuccessful as the first—she was still out. Another rebuff awaited him at the home of Frau Bachus, the parson's wife, who informed him, with a trace of regret, that she was otherwise engaged.

It occurred to Keller, as he nursed his rage and frustration, that Beate Fischer might be home by now. He tottered off to 9 Market Square, which abutted Party headquarters and Sonnenblum's surgery, and trudged up the stairs to Beate's apartment—top floor, first right. Here he hammered on the door, loud, long and insistently. By now his body was on fire, as though it had been flailed with a bunch of stinging nettles.

Beate, wearing a sky-blue bathrobe, opened the door a couple of inches. "What are you doing here?" she demanded in an icy voice. "I don't like gate crashers, Herr Keller. You're being a nuisance."

"Come off it, girl!" Keller lurched drunkenly against the door, throwing her off balance. She retreated a step or two. "We're old enough to know the score. I've got plenty of what you need, so help yourself."

"No, thanks." Beate spoke sternly but soothingly, as a trainer pacifies a restive tiger. "It isn't that I find you unattractive, but—"

"So let's get cracking!"

"Nobody samples me like a box of candies—I thought I'd made that clear. What's more, you promised to respect my feelings. There are certain conventions to be observed."

"And there's an exception to every rule!" he bellowed like a bull in heat. "I'm feeling that way inclined."

"But I'm not."

Keller barged into the apartment, pawing at her. "Stop play-acting, girl. No need to put on airs, not with me. I know all about you and your goings-on. I know who you've been with, too, which is just what makes me so curious. Come on, let's cut the cackle. No one'll ever put it to you the way I can, you gorgeous little bitch."

Beate was trembling now, with rage as well as terror. She pushed him away, but he returned to the attack at once.

176

She looked at his sweaty, contorted face—the embodiment, so it seemed to her, of brutality and stupidity—and drove her fist into it.

Though not delivered with any great force, the blow was enough to halt him in his tracks. He stared at her open-mouthed.

"Who the hell do you think you are?" he snarled, "you —you rotten cow!"

His bloodshot eyes became even more suffused. Now it was his turn to lash out in a sudden access of destructive fury. He drew back his fist and aimed it at her face and mouth. There was a dry crack like a cigar box splintering.

Beate fell to the floor with blood streaming down her chin from a split upper lip. She crawled crabwise into a corner, gasping for breath. "You'll regret this," she muttered faintly.

Keller came and stood over her. "You had it coming, you whore!" And then, just before she passed out, she saw him spit at her.

DISTRICT DIRECTOR Sonnenblum stood poised with his back to the wall that bore Hitler's photographic likeness, presumably striving to resemble his Leader. He almost succeeded, and not only where stance and demeanor were concerned; the peremptory yelps that escaped his lips were also reminiscent of the Reich Chancellor.

"Party Members, Comrades!" he said. "I declare this meeting open. There's only one item on the agenda: the funeral of our late lamented friend and comrade, Peter Patzer. My slogan for the occasion consists of three words: big, dignified, impressive!"

Sonnenblum's face was as pale as goat's cheese, and his hands were shaking. Without a word of excuse or explanation, Beate had failed to turn up for work this Monday

179

morning. What was more, he had been consoling himself with the bottle. Stormtroop Commander Keller looked equally care-worn and hung over. Tensely studying Sonnenblum's every gesture and turn of phrase, he felt temporarily reassured; it was clear that his boss knew nothing of last night's incident.

The others looked grave and deferential. They were waiting for orders, directives and instructions.

"Party Member Patzer lost his life in a tragic accident," barked Sonnenblum. "We shall give him the send-off he deserves, but this will need organizing. To preface the ceremony, I've drafted an official Party communiqué. Be good enough to note its contents."

The man responsible for such matters was Party Member Breitbach, Acting Director of Propaganda. He distributed a number of mimeographed sheets, which were perused with care. The wording ran as follows:

> The Gilgenrode Branch of the National Socialist German Labor Party, together with its affiliated organizations and associations, is grieved but proud to announce the death in a tragic accident of one of its most popular and respected members,
>
> Party Member Peter Patzer.
>
> We shall escort him on his final journey with due ceremony, confident that the people of this town will wish to participate. Further details will be announced prior to the interment.
>
> Signed: Heinrich Sonnenblum,
>
> District Director.

There was a universal murmur of approval. Comments ranged from "Most impressive!" to "Dignified and effective!"

"Good." Sonnenblum was gratified to note this unanimous but not unexpected response. "Please get that published, Comrade Breitbach." He smiled grimly. "I'd like to meet the man who'd dare to spurn such a heartfelt appeal for public mourning."

This sally drew a brief burst of laughter in which Keller's hoarse guffaw could easily be distinguished. It was yet another demonstration of the solidarity that reigned among sworn confederates. Konrad was alone in expressing some discreet misgivings.

"Every funeral needs a graveyard," he said. "There's only one in town, and that belongs to the Protestant church. What if the parson refuses to admit our late lamented friend?"

"If he does," Keller said eagerly, thirsting for action, "we'll finish him. I and my men have only been waiting for the right moment."

"Not so fast." Sonnenblum silenced Keller with an upraised hand, then turned to Konrad. "What on earth do you mean?"

"Only this," said Konrad, doing his best to sound like the humblest of devil's advocates. "According to Inspector Kersten—and I suppose we've got to take his views into account—Patzer's death may have been suicide."

Sonnenblum irritably shook his throbbing head. He was finding it hard to think straight. "Who cares? There's a lot of gossip around, but how does that affect the issue?"

"It could make quite a difference, District Director. The Church's funeral regulations are centuries old. Where suicides are concerned, it tends to apply some very peculiar standards."

"Balls!" exclaimed Keller. "We won't stand for *that!*"

Treasurer Stenz injected a characteristically practical note. "The Church won't refuse anyone six feet of real estate if there's enough loot in store—cash, I mean—and we're

181

rolling. Don't worry, we'll buy old Patzer into that boneyard one way or another."

"Except," said Konrad, "that our comrade may find himself shoveled into a hole on the sidelines, without the rites of the Church." His tone was deliberately provocative, as it nearly always was when Bachus's name cropped up.

"Bachus would never dare!" roared Keller. "He needs a firecracker up his ass, that man. Want me to give him a dose of our special treatment, District Director?"

Sonnenblum massaged his throbbing head before reaching a decision. "This meeting is adjourned for fifteen minutes. I'm going to telephone the Regional Directorate and request an immediate ruling."

As soon as he had left the room, the others rose to stretch their legs and gird themselves for the fresh exploits that would soon, beyond all doubt, be demanded of them. This they did by generously availing themselves of the wide variety of bottles arrayed on a side table. Ceremoniously, they raised their glasses and drank.

Keller drank too, towing Konrad into a corner with his free hand. "What I said just now about that preacher and his church," he began, "I was right, wasn't I?"

Konrad nodded. "You precisely followed the Führer's line in *Mein Kampf,* where he ruthlessly condemns the sins, omissions and transgressions of our ecclesiastical institutions. He does, however, concede the existence of decent and responsible Christians—in other words, Christians who are German to the core."

"Unlike that pigheaded parson!" Keller sounded very sure of himself. "He needs a thorough working over. No half measures, no shilly-shallying, no dithering!" This was an unmistakable dig at Sonnenblum. "If a man can't make up his mind, he's asking for trouble."

182

"The same goes for women," Konrad said gravely. "Look what happened to Fräulein Fischer."

Keller gave a perceptible start. "Who's been talking?"

"News travels fast in a friendly little town like ours. People keep their eyes and ears open, and some of them are saying you roughed the lady up last night—their expression, not mine."

"It's a lousy lie!" snapped Keller. "I only appealed to her better nature."

"You must have appealed pretty hard—she needed medical treatment. That could be awkward."

Keller slumped against the nearest available wall. "It's all a misunderstanding. Second-raters love slinging mud at their betters, and this is a prime example. All that happened was, the girl tripped and hit her head. I tried to save her but I was too late."

"You do have a point in your favor, of course. No woman likes to admit she's been punched in the face. A thing like that could hurt her reputation."

"There you are, then." Keller looked immensely relieved. "It's going to be all right."

"Not necessarily—in my humble opinion." Having struck oil, Konrad busily exploited his find. "A full-blooded female like Beate Fischer doesn't take kindly to being manhandled. She may appear to swallow it now, but she'll never forgive or forget—especially as she knows there are three or four men who'd be only too happy to take her part without even being asked. That's worth bearing in mind too, Comrade."

Keller grunted disdainfully. "You're forgetting who I am. I speak the language these women understand best, but that's not all. I've also got sixty loyal men behind me, and you're one of them."

"Certainly, Stormtroop Commander. You can count on me." Konrad paused. "From every angle."

Heinrich Sonnenblum rejoined his select band of senior subordinates. His telephone conversation with the Regional Directorate—perhaps with the Regional Director himself—seemed to have put him in a dynamic mood. He surveyed the room with a masterful air, as though refreshed in spirit and strengthened in his personal views.

He had not, in fact, telephoned the Regional Directorate at all, merely swallowed two painkillers and dunked his buzzing, aching head in a basin of cold water. He had, however, reached some extremely fruitful conclusions, and these he proceeded to impart.

"Our old friend Patzer is assured of a plot in the churchyard because that can be purchased out of Party funds. As for the last rites, we shall organize those ourselves. Everything must be as solemn and dignified as we can make it. Torches will be lit, wreaths laid and flags flown at half-mast. The introductory music will, of course, be 'Once I Had a Comrade.' Then will come a reading of some appropriate passages selected from our Führer's *Mein Kampf,* followed by a stirring funeral oration in honor of the dear departed. That I shall deliver myself. Next, the 'Horst Wessel Song,' all verses, after which Patzer's coffin can be slowly lowered into the grave by our comrades in the SA. That should make an impact, don't you think?"

The Hitler Youth representative was moved to a spontaneous display of enthusiasm. "Bravo! It's time we emerged from the Middle Ages."

"Quite right," said Eva Schwarz, speaking on behalf of the German Girls' League. "There's a difference between the cross and the swastika. We must make that clear, once and for all."

Ilse Peller, widowed chieftainess of the National Socialist Women's Association, had a constructive suggestion to make. "Our members have formed a choir," she announced, "a choral society with a growing reputation for melodious and well-disciplined singing. *We* could introduce the ceremony with a song like 'Hail to Thee, O Vale of Silence'—or something similar. Our repertoire is almost inexhaustible."

This touched off another interruption from the progressive-minded Hitler Youth leader. "And we of the Gilgenrode detachment," he said, trembling with revolutionary ardor, "have our own corps of drums—drums with genuine calfskin and hardwood sticks. They make a solemn, muffled sound, thoroughly primeval but unmistakably Germanic. Our drummers could escort Patzer's coffin to the graveside."

"Fine." Sonnenblum radiated appreciation despite the lingering ache in his head. "Then that's the way we'll handle it—unless, of course, somebody has a better idea?"

Prompted by a glance from Konrad, his trusted confederate, Keller claimed the floor. "We must allow for every eventuality, District Director. I think Comrade Breitbach has another suggestion to make."

"Well, what is it?" snapped Sonnenblum, unpleasantly surprised.

Konrad clasped his copy of *Mein Kampf* in both hands, like a talisman. "To the extent that they deal with the Church and its dignitaries, our Führer's writings contain the following advice: 'Voluntary cooperation by potentially favorable elements in the Church, whether definite or only presumed, should always be benignly tolerated; any public head-on clash should as far as possible be avoided.' "

The District Director glanced sharply at Keller; then, rather more indulgently, at Konrad. He made a gesture of lordly dismissal.

"Of course I recall the passage, and I'm pretty sure I

know what the Führer was driving at. Our nation has been enslaved by the Church for hundreds of years. It isn't strong or enlightened enough to throw off the yoke overnight. There are too many ingrained prejudices to be broken down, and that will take time."

"In other words," snarled Keller, "the parson must be kicked into line if he won't cooperate."

Konrad cleared his throat. "His voluntary cooperation would make things far less complicated."

"Cheaper, too," said Treasurer Stenz.

"Why not enlist him as a Party auxiliary?" the Hitler Youth leader cried enthusiastically. "The results could be very beneficial."

This suggestion was well received, largely because Sonnenblum, on whom all eyes rested, had given an unmistakable nod—only one, but it signified assent. That clinched the matter. Even Keller hurriedly changed his tune.

"You only have to tell us what you want, District Director."

"My original plan for a purely Germanic funeral," Sonnenblum said smoothly, "was designed to cope with the possibility of obstruction by the Church authorities. If Bachus falls in with our arrangements, we shall naturally take our cue from the Führer, whose principles must be our sole guide. Are we all agreed?"

They were—all except Keller, who was downing hard liquor by the tumbler. He buttonholed Konrad and hissed in his ear.

"You really loused things up that time, man. I'm going to leave my boot up your ass the next chance I get."

The keenest of all the local platoon commanders, Erwin Schulze, continued to be widely known as "Urinoco"—just that—because tidings of his well-nigh superhuman prowess

186

during the inauguration of the Strong Man's Arms had quickly percolated the highways and byways of Gilgenrode. In the intervals between training sessions, classes of instruction and spells of guard duty, Schulze—like any true German male—felt a recurrent desire for the beloved spouse who always showed such a welcome readiness to tire him out in bed. He felt it again today, but a visit to his home revealed that she was out, so he inquired of her whereabouts from the woman next door.

"If there's anything I can do for you," she said in an inviting tone, "feel free. Why not step inside?"

Schulze lingered discreetly in the hallway. "I'm looking for my wife. Any idea where she is?"

"Oh yes, I've an *idea*." The next-door neighbor, whose name was Angelika, smiled at him. Her eyes were narrowed and her lips slightly parted in imitation of her favorite movie star. "I don't know for sure, of course, but I've got my suspicions—plenty of them."

"What sort of suspicions?" Schulze demanded. "You'd better explain, and quick!"

Angelika steered him into her living room, waved him on to the sofa, and sat down close beside him. Her eyes quickly widened as they roved over his broad shoulders, his stalwart legs and what lay between them.

"Care for a drink?"

She got up and filled two glasses from a bottle on the sideboard. It was a homemade liqueur, jaundice-yellow and thick as molasses. There must have been a dozen egg yolks whipped up in the high-proof spirit. Schulze drank it down like water.

Angelika edged a little closer. "Oh, go on, don't begrudge your wife a little fun. Everyone needs a change now and then. You could do with one too, and so could I. The way you look at me—well, it turns my knees to jelly!"

Schulze rose abruptly to his full height and stood glaring down at her with a face like thunder. "My dear madam," he said, as though dictating a letter of complaint, "I'm a man of principle—a man of honor. Loyalty means everything to me, and the same goes for my wife. I wouldn't advise anyone to doubt it."

"Maybe, but you're only human. You're a man, so why not act like one? With me you can, and welcome."

"Don't change the subject!" Schulze's voice was almost trembling now. "You've slandered my wife and insulted me —deeply! If you can't prove your filthy allegations, you're in trouble. Let's have some names!"

"Go on!" Angelika gave a raucous laugh. "What's all this about allegations? I never said a thing—you must have misheard." Spitefully, she added, "Far be it from me to spread stories about two fine men like Felix Kimminger and Hermann Keller."

Schulze felt as if he had been blinded by a dazzling desert sun—scorched by a fire-breathing dragon. His face turned gray and amorphous, like congealed lard.

"Did you say Kimminger?" he rasped. "Keller too? I just can't believe it."

"You don't have to. I picked their names out of the hat. No need to get so hot under the collar, love. When you've calmed down you can pay me another visit. The sooner the better."

Schulze uttered a howl of fury and dashed out of the house.

Stormtroop Commander Keller was determined to extend his sphere of influence. With this in mind, he left Party headquarters and headed south across Market Square toward the White Hart. Here, as Kimminger had suggested,

188

he proposed to engineer a clash with the enemies of the people.

Striding into the hotel, a sternly uniformed figure, he paused for a moment to glare at its stuffy, plushy, upper-class décor. The carpets were patterned with flowers, mostly roses. He marched contemptuously across them to the desk, noting as he did so that the curtains were made of pale, faded velvet—nice and inflammable—and that the furniture, which dated from the previous century, looked extremely fragile, like something out of a lady's boudoir. A few well-aimed kicks would easily reduce it to matchwood.

He brought his fist down hard on the bell and demanded to see the proprietor of this citadel of decay. Georg Gernoth was a short, suave, rather portly man with a round and rosy face. His cheeks lost some of their color when he saw who his visitor was, but his tone was professionally welcoming.

"What can I do for you, Herr Keller? A word in private, perhaps?"

The only response was a curt nod. They retired to Gernoth's office, where, undisturbed and unobserved, Keller got down to business—his business.

"You, Gernoth," he said bluntly, "are a foreign body, an alien element in this town. It's time you did something about it."

Gernoth blanched. His hands fluttered like frightened pigeons. "You obviously misjudge me, Stormtroop Commander," he said, gazing at Keller with abject submission. "I'm not a political animal, just a humble hotelier who devotes his life to the service of others. The doors of my establishment are open to all—you included, of course."

"You surely don't expect me or the District Director to use the same premises as a Jew like Sass! The very idea!"

"Permit me to explain, Herr Keller." Gernoth had begun

189

to wash his hands with imaginary soap and was stammering a little. "It's true, I admit it: Herr Sass does dine here sometimes, but usually in a private room. He's been a regular here for years, just as his father was in my father's time. One has to make certain allowances, don't you agree?"

Keller was provoked rather than appeased by this line of defense. "A private room, eh? So the old goat insists on being served by Aryan waitresses where nobody can catch him pinching their bottoms, does he? A Jewish parasite like him can afford big tips, I'll bet! And you have the gall to admit that this notorious subversive sits there feeding on kosher food prepared in a German kitchen? It's a disgrace!"

"Herr Sass is an elderly man," Gernoth retorted with sudden audacity. "He's also a very retiring person who lives quite modestly and would never do anything to offend public opinion. When he eats here, he's always served by one of our waiters."

"Ah-ha!" Keller remained implacably hostile. "That takes the cake! So the Jew's a fag as well, is he, and you stand for it?"

Bruised and battered by this relentless pressure, Gernoth gave up. "Just tell me what you expect me to do, Herr Keller. As soon as I know, I'll try to comply with your wishes."

Keller's spirits soared, eaglelike. He felt as if he, and he alone, were the Führer's local mouthpiece. "We have a proverb," he said curtly: " 'He who eats of the Jew, dies thereof.' Well, so does he who feeds them. Behavior like yours could whip the people of this town into a righteous fury and bring down their patriotic anger on your head. I mightn't be able to hold my men in check, and that could be risky—very risky. They wouldn't stop at a few sticks of furniture—blood might flow. Is that what you want, Gernoth?"

The hotelier gave an apathetic shrug. "You mean my days here are numbered."

"That's just about it. You've got some dangerous commitments and liabilities. Unload them—sell up and get out while you're still ahead. That'll dispose of all your worries."

"You want me to sell?" said Gernoth, pricking up his ears. "Who to?"

"You're bound to find a buyer."

"I understand." Even as he uttered these words, torn between fear of man and faith in the Almighty, Gernoth was struck by an idea. "But how would it be—and I hazard this suggestion with all due respect—if I requested your personal protection? Any help from you and your men would be worth a great deal to me."

"A great deal?" Keller pounced on the phrase. This unexpected proposal merited consideration. "All right, Gernoth, spit it out. What sort of figure did you have in mind? It's a purely hypothetical question, naturally."

It dawned on Gernoth that he might be able to hook a really big fish. It all depended on the bait. "Your help would be worth any figure you care to name, provided I could raise it. Let's say a lump sum of ten thousand marks —no, fifteen. Further installments would depend on the terms of our contract."

Now it was Keller's turn to look confounded. He was in something of a quandary, and the situation made him uneasy. At the same time, he began to glimpse its remarkable potentialities.

If he played his cards right, he could not only foot the bill for Sonnenblum's German Day, but stockpile further substantial sums for the benefit of the Movement. That would make him far and away the most influential man in town. No one would be able to hold a candle to him, not even Sonnenblum. Overwhelmed by this realization, he

191

gave an involuntary grunt of delight. Then, for tactical reasons, he looked stern.

"Your proposals have been noted. I'll think them over, but if you try and bilk me, Gernoth, I'll finish you. I'll have you publicly displayed in the square with a placard round your fat neck. 'I'm the biggest swine in town, I help the Yids to do you down. . . .' That's what it'll have on it!"

"No, please don't—anything but that! My offer's absolutely binding, believe me. I'll give you any guarantee you like."

Keller rose. "Good. You've obviously grasped the truth, Herr Gernoth. The way things stand, there are only two choices open to you and everyone else around here: do your patriotic duty, or start praying."

District Director Sonnenblum found Parson Bachus at work in his garden—snipping early roses, loosening the soil in his borders, fostering growth, encouraging flowers to bloom, anointing the earth with dung and liquid manure.

Bachus straightened up at the sight of Gilgenrode's Party boss. He raised one arm in greeting, though only the left one, and tried to strike a pleasantly informal note.

"Just between ourselves, Herr Sonnenblum, I sometimes think I've missed my vocation. I'd really like to have been a gardener."

"You still can be, especially if you persist in your present attitude. God Almighty, Bachus, why be so damned obstructive—to us, of all people?"

The parson wiped his hands on his gardening smock. "If you're talking about Patzer's funeral, District Director, I'm prepared to make almost any concession. However, burying suicides isn't one of them, I'm afraid. The rules of the Church leave me no option. Please try and put yourself in my place."

192

"So you're still being obstructive." Sonnenblum scowled. "Do you really want to make your life a misery?"

"I told you," Bachus said mournfully, "I've no choice. If I grant your request I'm bound to offend my parishioners and the Church authorities. If I don't, I'll be in hot water with you. What on earth can I do?"

"Are you really convinced it was suicide?"

"Inspector Kersten says so, and Kersten's an honest man —honest but troublesome, certainly in this case. Troublesome from both our points of view."

"I question that." Sonnenblum produced a sheet of paper and waved it like a flag beneath the parson's widening eyes. Konrad had handed it to him only minutes earlier. "Here's an official statement. Perhaps it'll make you see sense."

Bachus snatched at the document. It was headed "Memorandum," and it ran:

> According to information received this morning from Inspector Kersten, head of the Gilgenrode Constabulary, the circumstances relating to Peter Patzer's death are as follows:
>
> 1. Foul play can be ruled out.
> 2. Accidental death can also be virtually excluded.
> 3. The deceased may therefore be assumed to have committed suicide. This cannot, however, be proved beyond reasonable doubt.

"Which implies," Sonnenblum said triumphantly, "that Kersten's hypothetical suicide may never have occurred."

Bachus spread his hands in submission. "If you say so, I'll take your word for it. Very well, I'm prepared to give your deceased the last rites."

"But don't say a word out of place, Herr Bachus, or

193

you'll answer to the SA. They're itching to pin something on you, especially Keller. Don't let it come to that. They'd squash you like a bug, and I couldn't stop them."

Stormtroop Commander Hermann Keller had put in a strenuous but successful day's work. He decided to crown it by paying a semiofficial visit to his comrades in the Strong Man's Arms.

His arrival was joyously acclaimed. After decreeing his men a ten-gallon barrel of beer at Party expense, he delivered a brief address:

"Comrades, tomorrow is a red-letter day. Patzer's funeral will give us a chance to show this town what really counts, so build up your strength. Cheers!"

On this inspiring note, Keller departed to join his beloved sister, whose husband—he knew—was out bowling. When left to themselves, Hermann and Hermine were wont to intoxicate each other with visions of a German future ruled by genuinely National Socialist ideals. Tonight, though, their harmonious twosome was interrupted in the most unceremonious way.

A voice burst upon their ears, hoarse with despair and harsh with accusation. It belonged to Emil Spahn.

"Are you there, Keller?" Emil was shouting up the stairs. "Then show your face and look at what you've done!"

Keller dashed to the door, flung it open and leaned over the banisters. His barrack-square bellow rent the air.

"Pipe down, you half-wit! Shut your stupid trap or I'll plug it with my fist!"

"Isn't one murder enough for you, Keller? Are you going to kill me as well as my cat?"

After a lengthy search, Emil had finally found his pet in the trash can. He held its stiff, cold little body accusingly above his head.

"This is your doing, Keller. My Susie's been killed, beaten to death with a stone—either that, or someone smashed her skull against a wall, and you're the only possible suspect. Everyone else loved my Susie, but you hated her—that's why you killed her. You're a murderer!"

Keller's voice lost none of its commanding timbre. "How dare you accuse me of murder, you subhuman shower of shit? You belong in an institution, and that's where you'll go if you don't shut up."

Emil embraced his dead cat with infinite tenderness. His eyes were swimming with tears, but his words were like flung daggers.

"All right, Keller, all right—have me certified and stick me in an asylum, you murderer! Call me crazy, for all I care. Being crazy has its advantages. I can do just about anything I like—I can treat you the way you treated my cat."

"Piss off, you nut!" roared Keller, and he slammed the door. In a gloomily prophetic tone, he said, "We're surrounded by loonies, Hermine. I don't just mean that miserable creep Emil—he stands out a mile. There are plenty more, but don't worry. I'll root 'em out like weeds."

That night, Siegfried Sass was invited to dine at home rather than patronize the White Hart, as he had intended. Georg Gernoth had proposed this change of plan in a conspiratorial undertone.

"My dear Herr Sass, please allow me to serve you in your own home, as I have done on a few special occasions in the past. You host the party and I'll foot the bill, but I *would* like, with your permission, to invite a couple of guests: Dr. Breile and Herr Breitbach senior."

Sass's complimentary dinner began at eight on the dot. Breitbach and the lawyer turned up in good time, both of them with obvious alacrity. Gernoth had the meal carried across from his hotel in silver chafing dishes, lovingly put the finishing touches to it in Sass's kitchen, and then served it himself. First came a game pâté; next, saddle of lamb roasted in a charcoal-fired oven; and, finally, a heart-shaped marzipan pudding coated with the thinnest imaginable film of bitter chocolate. The accompanying champagne was a well-chilled Pommery.

"What an excellent meal!" Breitbach's enjoyment was as transparent as his curiosity. "Rather extravagant, though. Who's paying?" He surveyed the others with an apologetic smile. "I realize that's a crude question—quite as crude as the age we live in—but I'm sure we weren't invited just to revel in Herr Gernoth's cooking."

The hotelier folded his hands like a man at prayer. "I received a visit from Keller today. He made some undisguised threats. I'll spare you the distressing details, but what they amount to is this: either I sell my hotel at once or it goes up in smoke."

Breitbach nodded. "That sounds like Keller. Extortion is all in a day's work to him."

"From what I've heard on the legal grapevine," said Breile, "it's Kimminger who's planning to buy you up cheap. They say he's promised the Party a donation of ten thousand marks."

"If that's so," Gernoth exclaimed, "I went one better— it must have been intuition. I offered Keller fifteen thousand minimum."

"Splendid!" Breile looked thoroughly approving. "It seems these people not only have political principles— they've worked out a corresponding scale of charges. I find that interesting."

"Let's not beat about the bush, gentlemen," said Sass. "The root of the matter is money."

Gernoth stroked his chin for a moment. "I'll sell if I have to, but never to Kimminger. I'd sooner the place went to Herr Breitbach, but what would he do with it?"

"So you've promised the Party fifteen thousand in protection money plus more to come," Breile said. "Keller's people are bound to take the bait. The Brownshirts may be stupid, but even they can tell the difference between ten and fifteen."

"We must keep our eyes open, that's the main thing. Political hibernation can be fatal—we may never come out of it." Breitbach sounded truculent, as he always did when conversation turned to Sonnenblum and his cronies. "If the Nazis insist on acting like mad bulls, they deserve to be skewered."

Breile shook his head. "I'd favor a rather more subtle approach. In this case, I suggest that Herr Gernoth pay the promised fifteen thousand, but not out of his own pocket. He raises a loan instead."

"From Sass!" Breitbach cried in high delight. "Then, if we have to, we can prove that the Nazis are accepting cash from a Jew."

"What I have in mind," Breile pursued quietly, "is the establishment of a foundation funded by leading citizens of this town. Its aim would be to promote national values, patriotic endeavors, civic pride—and anything else of an equally nebulous nature."

"National reconstruction, social welfare, communal progress!" Breitbach chuckled heartily. "That always packs a punch, but what's it going to cost?"

"No names will be mentioned—modesty precludes their disclosure." The lawyer's eyes twinkled. "But we shall announce the sum subscribed: one hundred thousand marks! That ought to make people sit up. The capital will be pro-

197

vided by the four anonymous sponsors of the fund: Sass, Breitbach, Gernoth, and yours truly."

"Did you say a hundred thousand?" Breitbach had turned pale. "Split four ways, you mean?"

"Of course not. For obvious reasons, the major share must come from our Jewish fellow citizen. As for us three, I suggest we each invest a thousand. Herr Sass will put up the remaining ninety-seven thousand. Would you be prepared to do that, Herr Sass?"

The old man thought for a moment. "Let's say I wouldn't be averse. It mightn't buy me any life insurance, but it might buy a little good will. That's worth something." He shrugged. "Very well, gentlemen, make the necessary arrangements."

To Breitbach the future seemed radiant with promise. For a few short minutes he even forgot his growing uneasiness about Beate, who had been avoiding him lately. The thought of immediate action was a comfort.

"Now," he said, "I'm going to work on Sonnenblum."

By this he meant, first, that the dentist's rent would be doubled forthwith; second, that he would be requested to remove the slogans adorning his premises ("Germany Awake!" and "The Führer is Always Right!"); and third, that any plates beside the front door apart from the one bearing Sonnenblum's name and professional qualifications must be taken down at once. That included the plate inscribed "NSDAP Headquarters, Gilgenrode District," whose erection had not been approved by the landlord.

Breile gave these measures his expert approval. "You're quite entitled to insist on them," he said, "but I hope we can achieve a little more than that."

"My only fear," said Gernoth, "is that we'll have to pay and go on paying forever more."

"To me," Sass confided gravely, almost shamefaced at his relentless exposure to such an impulse, "all that matters is to be able to die in peace and, I hope, with a modicum of dignity, in the town where I was born and spent my life. No price would be too high to pay for that."

The funeral of Party Member Patzer took place on a day when the sun's rays seemed to transfix the ground like burning arrows and even the bleached gray headstones looked incandescent. The blazing heat dulled the senses and brought forth torrents of sweat. The mourners, somberly attired in dark suits or brown uniforms, thronged the churchyard in a mood of stolid resignation.

Word had spread of the compromise reached by Bachus and Sonnenblum: the Party was to sing and speechify, the Church to bless and pray. This arrangement embodied a perfect separation of powers under which harmony promised to reign supreme.

Patzer's coffin was borne to the graveside by four Brownshirts, among them Platoon Commander Schulze, whose air of grim solemnity was more than usually pronounced. When strong and exalted emotions prevailed, Schulze's capacity for self-commitment was infinite.

Just as the coffin, draped in swastika flags and almost obscured by lush green laurel wreaths sprayed with gold paint, was deposited beside the grave, the Women's Association choir, augmented by members of the Hitler Youth, broke into "Once I Had a Comrade." They sang with ear-splitting intensity and volume, providing a convenient opportunity for surreptitious conversation.

Keller, who had been strutting nervously to and fro, took advantage of the din to accost the District Director.

"Let's hope Bachus sticks to his end of the deal. I don't

like the look of him standing there like Martin Luther in person."

Sonnenblum frowned. "By all means keep him up to the mark, Keller, but watch your step. Be as tactful as you can."

"I get you," Keller said eagerly. "Tactful, but only as tactful as possible."

He sidled up to Bachus during the third verse of the hymn to comradeship and addressed him in a piercing whisper.

"It was an accident, don't forget. Make that clear, or else!"

So far, everything had gone according to plan. Sonnenblum was looking conciliatory and Bachus avoided the limelight. As for the mourners, they were happily swallowing all the platitudinous fare set before them. This was partly because every East Prussian interment was followed by a funeral feast of guaranteed magnitude: rivers of sustaining soup, mountains of roast meat and sausages, streams of beer and schnapps. It was a prospect worthy of a little endurance.

The District Director had, in his creative wisdom, supplemented Konrad's draft oration with some remarks of his own.

"Our beloved Peter Patzer," he declaimed, "who lies here before us, was a man of high ideals, a man deeply devoted to the Führer, Adolf Hitler. The incorrigible subversives in our midst could not and would not tolerate this fact. Their pernicious mentality rejected it, so they destroyed him just as they destroyed that other martyred hero of our Movement, Horst Wessel. Like him, however, Patzer will live on; like him, Patzer is assured of everlasting life."

These potent words were hurled at the apathetic, sweating throng like chunks of concrete. Even Johannes Breitbach was stung by their implied reproach and retired from

200

the scene. So, with a snort of contempt, did Gertrude Sonnenblum. Three other mourners discreetly joined them. Now came the moment for Bachus to deliver some concluding remarks and speed the deceased on his way with a benediction. He spoke of the Lord's mysterious ways. They were, he said, inscrutable and inexplicable, but truly wonderful nonetheless. They had to be accepted in a spirit of profound and heartfelt humility.

Keller, who was still hovering at the parson's elbow, whispered, "Stop hedging, man! Tell 'em it was an accident!"

While this clearly audible prompting was in progress near the grave, the sexton bustled up and tried to elbow his way between Keller and Bachus. The Stormtroop Commander responded to this presumptuous behavior by fending the sexton off so vigorously that he stumbled, lost his balance, and fell into the pit that by now contained Patzer's coffin. He landed on the lid with a muffled crash and lay there like an upturned beetle, legs thrashing helplessly.

"An occupational hazard," Konrad said under his breath. He knelt down and offered his hand to the fallen servant of God, who hauled himself erect and scrambled to the surface.

Bachus was so disconcerted that he gabbled a hurried prayer and took to his heels. The sexton hobbled after him.

The tormented priest had thus abandoned the field to Sonnenblum and his men. The Brownshirts stood there looking rather at a loss until their leader had a flash of inspiration.

"The 'Horst Wessel Song'!"

Voices rang out and shovels were diligently wielded under Keller's supervision. Once again, Platoon Commander Schulze demonstrated his exceptional zeal by bulldozing great mounds of sandy soil into the open grave.

"A great success, the whole thing," Sonnenblum murmured contentedly. His opinion was shared by others including Konrad, not that Konrad meant what they did.

On the evening of the same momentous day, Breitbach invited his sons to join him around the family dinner table. Kitchen and cellar were taxed to the limit in the hope of making this meal a victory celebration.

"Well," he said, "be honest—wasn't that a positively grotesque performance in the churchyard today? Those arrogant Brownshirts made real asses of themselves. No sense of proportion, that's their trouble. You ought to write a piece on it for your paper, Johannes."

Johannes frowned at an inoffensive slice of roast beef and pushed it aside. "Talk about the pot and the kettle! Sonnenblum isn't the only one who's making a fool of himself."

"Meaning what?"

"Meaning you and Beate Fischer."

"What about her?"

"She's far too young for you."

"What the devil do you mean?"

Konrad charitably absolved his brother from the need to reply. "Johannes is being his usual tactful self, Father. What he really means is, you're too old for her."

"Utter nonsense," snapped Breitbach, visibly piqued. "It's how old a man feels that matters."

"Beate's a sophisticated person," said Johannes. "She'll make her choice accordingly."

"But she won't find it easy," Konrad put in blandly. "Competition for her company is reaching the danger level. Have either of you seen her in the past two days?"

Johannes shook his head. Breitbach senior, who was looking uneasy, said, "No, but what does that signify?"

"Plenty, I'd say." Konrad maintained his bland, considerate tone. "If she's keeping out of sight it's because she doesn't want to be seen. She isn't looking her best—her face is cut and bruised in several places. Somebody beat her up, that's the story."

Breitbach and Johannes leaped to their feet. The table rocked.

"It can't be true!" Johannes cried in outrage.

"Who was it?" roared his father. "Tell me the bastard's name!"

Konrad shrugged. "If it wasn't one of you two, it must have been somebody else. Whoever it was, you'll find out sooner or later, but then what?"

The central flower bed in the municipal gardens beside Lake Gilgenrode was palely illumined by the moon. There, surrounded by park benches and early-flowering roses, Emil Spahn was using his hands to scoop out a grave for his cat.

"Goodbye, my darling," he said gently. He had wrapped Susie in a silk shawl which had belonged to his mother.

"Thank you for everything," he whispered to the diminutive corpse. He gave it a final embrace, cradling it tenderly against his heart. He was past weeping. "Thank you for being so soft and cuddlesome, so playful, so wonderfully affectionate. You brightened the last few months of my life."

He laid Susie in the little grave and started to cover her with earth. There was something benedictory about his movements. He took his time. It was as if he were alone in the world—as if the earth had ceased to revolve. Still kneeling, he bent low over the grave among the roses. When he got to his feet he was weeping again. His tears glistened in the moonlight.

"Are there any lengths these men won't go to?" he muttered, shaking his head. "Well, I'm a man too. . . ."

It was late when Parson Bachus paid another call on Siegfried Sass. He knocked discreetly and stepped back into the street, where the moonlight would reveal his identity. The old man came to the door himself, wearing a dark-blue dressing gown. His manner was straightforwardly hospitable. If there was any trace of uneasiness on his face, it was not on his own account. He had heard about the parson's tribulations in the churchyard and was beginning to feel sorry for him.

"Come in, Herr Bachus. I've just opened a good bottle of Burgundy, a Château Lafitte from the estate owned by Baron Rothschild—another Jew. Would you object to sharing it with me?"

"Herr Sass," the parson replied in a melodious voice that would have graced his pulpit, "the sole reason for my presence is to beg your forgiveness."

Sass was taken aback. He had been expecting a very different Bachus—a prophet misjudged, a reproachful defender of the faith, but here he was begging for forgiveness.

"A decent glass of Burgundy would do us both good," said Sass.

Bachus fortified himself before reverting to the object of his visit. "I'm here to ask your pardon, Herr Sass. Forgive me for being so obtuse, so presumptuous, so wrongheaded!"

"Please don't, Herr Bachus." Sass looked almost startled. "We all make mistakes. Say no more about it."

"But I must speak out, to you of all people. At our last meeting I offered you the protection of the Church. I offered to safeguard your property—even your life. I did so in good faith, fool that I was, but today the scales fell from my eyes. I now realize that I was deceiving myself and you, that my assurances were false—that I lied to you, albeit unwittingly. Can you ever forgive me?"

"There's nothing to forgive, Herr Bachus. It's all forgotten. Let's drink to that."

They did so, but the parson's agitation was slow to subside. "I always believed that everything in this country was more or less as it should be, but I was mistaken."

"Blame it on the Jews," Sass said wryly. "They're the root of all evil—it's down in black and white. Hitler's book says so."

"A work of the devil!" cried Bachus. "A heresy that is being deliberately propagated by Konrad Breitbach!"

"I know," said Sass, "he's been plying me with memoranda on the subject." He reached for some sheets of paper lying on a small table at his elbow. "Here, I'll give you a few samples. 'The greatest antithesis of the Aryan is the Jew.' That's on page three hundred and twenty-nine. 'Today, therefore, the Jew is the chief agitator in favor of Germany's utter ruin.' That's on page seven hundred and two. Now back to page three hundred and thirty: 'The Jew is guided by nothing but the naked egoism of the individual.' "

Bachus shook his large Lutheran head like a refractory horse. "That awful young man—his name keeps cropping up again and again. He fills me with a mixture of horror and amazement. What does he actually want?"

"To alert me to a development that he's as powerless to prevent as anyone. He realizes that words can kill, and he's using them himself rather than go to the wall—a fate that may yet overtake us both, Herr Bachus."

Platoon Commander Schulze rolled off his wife's inert body with a contented grunt. He had really put it to her

205

that time. If a job was worth doing, it was worth doing well.

She lay in blissful silence, but not for long. "You were terrific," she assured him. "You always are. There's no one to touch you."

"That's the way it should be." He stretched and rubbed his eyes, recalling a quotation from *Mein Kampf* that might have applied solely to him, Schulze: "Supreme importance attaches to the development of will power and determination, as well as to the cultivation of joy in responsibility." Konrad had copied it out for him.

"I was made for big things," he said, lying on his back now. "Some are, some aren't."

"That's what Kimminger says," his wife rejoined brightly. "And he packs quite a punch round here, doesn't he?"

Schulze propped himself on his elbows. "You know Kimminger? How come?"

"We met by accident." She nestled against his sweating flank. "I was sitting in the Fatherland Café with an old school friend the other afternoon, having coffee, when Kimminger came over and introduced himself. He hoped I didn't mind him asking, he said, but wasn't I married to Platoon Commander Schulze of the Brownshirts? He said he was a great admirer of yours—said you were the up-and-coming man in this town."

Schulze's expression conveyed that he thoroughly agreed but had still to be fully reassured. "And that's as far as it went?"

"What's that supposed to mean?" She drew away from him. "Are you accusing me, when I've always been faithful to you—when I've proved it over and over again?" She pouted. "Well, haven't I?"

"I'm sorry," he said. "I know you're a good and faithful

German wife, of course, but Kimminger's got a certain reputation. While we're on the subject, what about Keller?"

"Oh, *him*," she said darkly. "Let's not talk about Keller. He's no gentleman."

"You're telling me! Keller's behavior is thoroughly un-German. He doesn't have a spark of greatness in him. All that interests him is looking after number one."

"In every way," she agreed. "He keeps on making passes at me. Downright immoral, he is."

"What's that?" Schulze flared up like a bale of straw soaked in high-octane fuel. "Are you telling me he's made improper advances at you—you, the loyal wife of one of his own platoon commanders?"

"He didn't get anywhere, of course."

"Of course not!" Schulze said promptly. He rose, naked, from his matrimonial couch and started pacing tigerishly up and down the bedroom. "To think of that unscrupulous bastard lording it over the rest of us, here and now, in an age which belongs to the cream of humanity! I won't stand for it!"

"Then why not do something about it?" she purred.

"Come out here, Sonnenblum!" Richard Breitbach's voice shattered the tranquillity of the lilac-colored Gilgenrode night. He was standing outside the dentist's house with his legs planted firmly apart like an allegory of defiance.

A window opened and Gertrude Sonnenblum's head appeared. "Why, Richard, how nice of you to call. Come in!"

"Any time, Aunt Gertrude, but not when your son's at home. This isn't a social call. I've come here to have it out with him. Please don't be offended."

Gertrude nodded. A moment later, Sonnenblum's hoarse

voice became audible in the background. "Breitbach can go jump in the lake. Tell him that, Mother."

"Tell me yourself!" Breitbach yelled back. More windows opened near by. A number of Gilgenroders were hopefully manning their observation posts. "If you don't come out here this minute, I'll kick the door down."

"No need for that," Gertrude said serenely, "he'll come." She called back over her shoulder. "Heinrich, stir your stumps!"

"I'll call the police. I'll have him arrested for using insulting language and causing a breach of the peace!"

Gertrude clicked her tongue. "Now, now, don't forget you were boys together—you wrestled in the sandpit and raided my pantry more times than I can remember. That still counts for something, so get out there and see what he wants. Afterward I'll expect a full report from you. I want to know what this latest nonsense is all about."

Sonnenblum could hardly postpone the interview any longer. It took place beneath a lime tree on the edge of Market Square in an atmosphere that could only be described, despite the warm night air, as frosty. The two men frustrated would-be eavesdroppers by keeping their voices down.

"Why all the noise, Breitbach?" Sonnenblum's tone was studiously aloof and condescending. He even demonstrated his superiority by indulging in a grim jest. "Can't you wait to join the Party, or what?"

"I shit on your Party, Sonnenblum, you know that." Breitbach made it abundantly clear that he and the District Director had nothing left in common. "I'm going to ask you a straight question and I expect a straight answer. Did you hit Beate?"

Sonnenblum's jaw dropped. "Are you out of your mind? Me, hit Beate?"

208

"In the face."

Utterly aghast, Sonnenblum slumped against the lime tree and threw up his hands in horror. "How could you even think such a thing? You must be crazy."

"So it wasn't you," said Breitbach. "In that case, who was it?"

Sonnenblum looked as if he had been smitten with an attack of fever. "My God, what is all this? You say she's been beaten up? It's true I haven't seen her for a couple of days—she sent word she was sick—but . . ."

"So who was it?"

"I'd like to know that too!" Sonnenblum burst out. "I want the man's blood!"

"So do I, Sonnenblum, even if he's one of your Party faithfuls. No holds barred, all right?"

Sonnenblum mutely nodded.

During the early hours of the following morning. Stormtroop Commander Keller was found dead. His body was lying just inside the entrance of the house where he lived. He lay prone with his legs apart and his face cupped in his hands as though blotting out the world for ever.

Preliminary investigations revealed that he had been clubbed to death with a blunt instrument that had shattered the base of his skull. And now he lay there looking small and withered, as if he had never drawn breath.

Not that this was anything out of the ordinary. Experienced crime fighters know that the victims of violence often look shrunken and contorted, like worms sucked dry by ants. This was the state he was in when the police, represented by Inspector Kersten, took charge of his body.

Kersten's comment: "In this town, these days, anything's possible."

KERSTEN CORDONED off the scene of the crime, kept sight-
seers at bay and sent for Dr. Gensfleisch, a general prac-
titioner who doubled as medical examiner when required.
Gensfleisch examined the body and turned to the inspector.

"Probable time of death, around midnight. Cause of
death, injuries to the base of the skull inflicted by a single
blow delivered with a blunt instrument wielded with
considerable force. I'll be able to fill in the details when
I've taken him down to the morgue for a closer look—unless
you're thinking of calling in higher authority."

Kersten shook his head. "No, this is our body, and that's
the way it's staying. If my assessment of the situation is
correct, we can handle it ourselves."

He seemed to be right. At that moment, Keller's bereaved sister burst upon the scene towing a human scarecrow by the sleeve. She did not have to exert much force: Emil Spahn tottered quite meekly toward the scene of the crime.

Hermine's first inclination was to hurl herself on the corpse of her beloved brother with an anguished cry, but Kersten headed her off.

"I know how you must be feeling, madam, but I can't permit you to touch the deceased before his remains have been thoroughly examined."

The inspector pinned her firmly but gently against the nearest wall. Hermine sagged there, panting hard and gazing at her brother's lifeless form with tears streaming down her cheeks, but not for very long. She soon straightened up, shot out her right arm to its fullest extent, and leveled an accusing forefinger at Emil.

"It was him!" she screamed wildly, avid for revenge. *"He* did it!"

This happened early on the morning of yet another sunlit, scintillating day in spring. The trees still wore their freshest green attire, early roses were beginning to bloom, and a multitude of birds filled the air with song.

Kersten handed Keller's seething sister over to one of his men, who stationed himself defensively in front of her. The police chief then advanced on Emil Spahn. Emil eyed him with the docility of the blissfully inebriated.

"Herr Spahn"—Kersten said quietly, and the formal mode of address was like a friendly warning—"did you hear the grave allegation which has just been made against you? You needn't comment on it—in fact I'd advise you not to."

"Yes," muttered Emil. He said it again, this time distinctly, "Yes!"

"What do you mean?" Kersten asked. "What are you trying to say?"

"He's dead," said Emil, "and a good job too. He killed a poor, beautiful, defenseless creature. Anyone who can do that deserves to die."

"Is that an admission of guilt, Herr Spahn?" Sadly though Kersten put the question, he was quite prepared to take official note of an affirmative reply. "Do you confess to this man's murder?"

"Yes, yes!" Emil blurted out, leaden-tongued. "Somebody did it—somebody did this lousy world a favor, so why not me? Yes, I confess."

Kersten gave a resigned nod. "Then I'll have to arrest you, Herr Spahn. Kindly accompany me to the station."

Later that morning a conference was held in the District Director's office at 7 Market Square. The only item on the agenda was Keller's death.

Konrad, now fully established as Sonnenblum's confidential adviser, responded to a nod from his master.

"There's a certain amount of fluttering in the enemy dovecote," he announced. "Anti-Party elements are afraid they may be blamed for Keller's murder, if only indirectly, but Kersten seems to have the case sewn up. The chief suspect has confessed and been arrested."

This was welcome news indeed, Sonnenblum said promptly. He spoke with a touch of relief but did not for one moment forget to feign a sorrow and solemnity appropriate to the occasion.

"A terrible thing has occurred," he lamented in ringing tones, "but anything that fails to destroy us can only make us stronger—the Führer has said so himself. Our faith in the justice of our cause remains undimmed."

A certain disquiet invaded the gathering even so. The blame for this lay with the widowed president of the Women's Association, who actually had tears in her eyes and began to sob.

"Now, now, Comrade!" Sonnenblum said soothingly, masking his surprise with an effort. Could Ilse Peller have been another of the dead man's conquests? A closer look at her overripe Germanic visage suggested that this suspicion was absurd. "Let us mourn him by all means, but with dignity and composure."

"What an immeasurable loss!" she cried, bosom heaving. "What a man! We shall not see his like again."

"Nobody's indispensable," Schulze cut in. "He'll be replaced by somebody just as good if not better. The Movement isn't short of talent, thank God."

Ilse Peller's brimming eyes flashed fire in his direction. "Perhaps, but Keller was unique."

"Oh yes? In what way?"

She ignored the innuendo. "What I find so utterly incomprehensible," she said, clinging to her main preoccupation, "is that a subhuman creature like Spahn should have managed to fell such a superb specimen with a single blow."

Prompted by another glance from Sonnenblum, Konrad intervened. "Be that as it may," he said, "the police have a confession to that effect, and further inquiries have failed to yield any conflicting evidence."

"Pah!" Frau Peller angrily brushed this objection aside. "Policemen like Kersten have no sense of discrimination. Keller was a thoroughbred German of the highest caliber. He'd never have been beaten by a cretin like Spahn. Spahn kill Keller? Since when do stray cats kill German mastiffs?"

"Steady, steady!" Sonnenblum did his best to stem this elemental flood of womanly emotion. "We're dealing with a degenerate, don't forget, and degenerates are unpredictable."

"I suggest we take our cue from the District Director," said Konrad. "His instructions, if I interpret them correctly, are to avoid all unnecessary fuss and accept the official version of the facts."

"You're absolutely right," Sonnenblum confirmed. "No more complications, if you don't mind—we had quite enough of those in the Patzer case. Keller's dead and his murderer has been apprehended. Let's leave it at that."

Konrad assumed his most guileless and lamblike expression. "Which isn't to say," he put in, "that we won't have trouble with a few notorious subversives and politically contaminated dissidents. However, those we can deal with."

"Of course," Sonnenblum said firmly.

Platoon Commander Schulze squared his granite jaw, looking monumentally determined. "Anyone who makes trouble must be eliminated."

"Shown the error of his ways, you mean," Sonnenblum amended with mild approval. "Let's put it like that, shall we? The implication's clear enough."

This time, not even Johannes hesitated to man the intellectual barricades, spurred on by Konrad's allusion to Emil's predicament: "They're hounding an innocent man, Johannes. You must help to secure his release."

Johannes proceeded to publish a fiery article in the *Gilgenrode Observer*. This posed several important questions about Emil Spahn, the prime suspect and supposed culprit, who was being held in custody. Questions such as these:

Can a sick man be a criminal? Doesn't everyone possess the same legal rights? Isn't there an ever-present danger that prejudice may conduce to miscarriages of justice?

Enraged by these remarks, which were provocatively headed "Nip this evil in the bud," Schulze called at Sonnenblum's office.

"Have you read this crap, District Director? The man must be crazy. Shall I teach him a short sharp lesson, or would you like me to round up a squad of stormtroopers and pay his lousy rag a visit? No? Later, maybe? Good. Any time you say the word."

Sonnenblum promptly telephoned the proprietor, publisher and editor in chief of the *Gilgenrode Observer*.

"I wouldn't want to cramp your style, of course, but be warned! You can always count on my personal good will, but some of my stormtroopers are growing restive, not to say exasperated. About what? About the contamination of the press, about wishy-washy intellectuals and scribblers, subverters of public opinion, and so on. I'm trying to hold them in check, but I can't answer for their actions—especially as I share their doubts as to whether the whole thing was necessary in the first place. Was it?"

The editor's response came back pat. "I naturally believe in freedom of speech, District Director, but I never tolerate a wantonly subjective and biased approach to current affairs. I therefore regret this incident. The writer of the article will be put on ice at once. I propose to suspend him until further notice, possibly for good. I shall also counteract the effect of the original article by printing an instructive rejoinder. Any suggestions on your part will be received with gratitude and interest."

Written on behalf of his client Richard Breitbach, Dr. Breile's letter to Heinrich Sonnenblum opened on an extremely courteous note: "We greatly regret . . . owing to circumstances beyond our control . . . trusting that you will understand our position in this matter . . ."

Then, phrased with stark simplicity, came a number of demands relating to No. 7 Market Square. Herr Sonnenblum was requested to remove the slogan-adorned banners draped across the façade—purely on aesthetic grounds, of course, not political. He was likewise requested to take down the Party plate affixed to the door frame, this having been erected without the landlord's consent. Last but not least, "We respectfully advise you that your existing lease may be terminated in the near future. At the very least, a substantial increase in rent should be taken for granted."

Having read this communication with growing annoyance, Sonnenblum telephoned the lawyer to convey an unmistakable warning.

"Breile? How dare you send me this tripe! What the devil were you thinking of?"

"My dear Herr Sonnenblum, my personal views on this matter are entirely beside the point. I'm acting for a client whose legal rights are quite incontestable—as the law now stands. I do, however, concede that the former owner of the premises you occupy would never have dared to make such demands."

"The former owner?"

"Yes—Herr Sass."

"Did you say Sass? You mean I've been renting this house from a Jew?"

"Quite so, Herr Sonnenblum, and it would be child's play to prove it. Your former landlord made you a number of concessions in respect of rent and use of premises. They're all down in writing, and the relevant documents were conveyed to the new landlord when the property changed hands. I don't suppose you'd care to hear them read out in court."

"You lousy bastard!" yelled Sonnenblum, and slammed the receiver down. "I'm hemmed in by vermin, all drooling for their pound of flesh. Well, I'm no rotting carcass—I'm a lion among hyenas!"

"You're a big-mouth," his mother told him kindly. "On top of that, you surround yourself with enemies like Keller. You thought he was an obedient gun dog, when all the time he was a vicious mongrel."

"Please don't speak ill of the dead, Mother, it's bad form."

"Bah! Take your head out of the clouds and come down to earth. A few friendly words to Bachus and he'd eat out of your hand. Richard Breitbach used to be your friend. One quiet chat with him, for instance about your daughter's engagement to his son, and he'd come round in no time."

"Compromise with Breitbach? Really, Mother! We're worlds apart."

"What you mean is, you're both after Beate Fischer. Well, my boy, you've reached a dead end there. The sooner you two tomcats leave her free to choose the better —and she needn't pick either one of you, even if Keller has dropped out of the running."

But this was precisely the point on which Sonnenblum refused to see reason. "You can't understand—you're too insensitive!"

"And you're too unimaginative," his mother said blandly, like a nurse humoring a patient, "even for a town like ours. You know almost nothing about me and very little about Beate. Take my advice: forget your other ambitions and concentrate on pulling teeth."

For once without a copy of *Mein Kampf* under his arm, Konrad paid another call on Siegfried Sass.

"I've got a problem," he announced, "and it can't wait."

"How can I help?"

"Financially."

"So what's for sale this time?"

"Ever heard of Emil Spahn? My friends in the Party regard him as a pathological degenerate. Personally, I think he's one of the few worthwhile characters for miles around. He needs help, Herr Sass, and if anyone can supply it, it's you."

"I assume he needs an attorney, and attorneys cost money. Very well, Konrad, let's call in Dr. Breile. Breile's as dependable as anyone still can be, in this devil's kitchen."

The name of the man who descended on Gilgenrode in response to Dr. Breile's summons was Adelbert Runge. He trundled there from Königsberg in an ancient rattletrap of a Ford, which could raise the dust at all of forty-five miles an hour.

Runge's qualifications were as high as his fees. A defense counsel known throughout the profession for his daring but successful methods, he never made unnecessary allowances for the feelings of others, never hesitated to stamp on their corns or wound their German sensibilities.

Nothing about him was suggestive of brilliance as he pulled up in front of the White Hart Hotel and levered his elephantine frame through the door of his dusty roadster. His face might have been modeled in pale-gray sponge. He looked permanently exhausted, had mournful eyes and a surprisingly high-pitched treble voice. All in all, Adelbert Runge resembled a gargantuan child with a bad case of asthma.

Breile hurried out to meet him. "Ah, Counselor, good to see you again. If you feel like a rest after your trip, I've booked you a room with bath."

"Splendid idea," squeaked Runge. "I'll lie and soak while you fill in the gaps you left on the phone—that

219

sounds like a fair division of labor. I'm assuming it won't take more than a couple of hours to do what has to be done here—not that it'll affect the size of my fee."

Breile hastened to reassure him. "Of course not. The check's already made out."

"Mind you," the piping voice continued, "I'm only here to assist you at your personal request. Your client's identity doesn't concern me. I don't wish to know who you're acting for—you never told me, is that clear?"

"Quite clear. And now, what about that bath?"

Runge splashed happily around in the tub like an overgrown baby, while Breile enlarged on the situation. It seemed that the district attorney responsible for the Keller case had reluctantly granted Runge's request for permission to act on the suspect's behalf. The local police would have to be advised accordingly, but the first step was to persuade Emil Spahn to accept him, Runge, as his legal adviser.

"I'll get you in to see him," said Breile. "The rest is your pigeon."

In pursuit of his "pigeon," Adelbert Runge turned up at Gilgenrode police station and introduced himself to Inspector Kersten, whom he quickly recognized as a businesslike and imperturbable man.

"May I see your findings to date, Inspector?" he wheezed politely.

Far from objecting, Kersten surrendered the file without a murmur. Runge perused it for little more than half an hour, but his interest seemed to grow by leaps and bounds. Alone with Kersten in the latter's office, he turned to the policeman and looked him in the eye.

"Congratulations on a perfect job, Inspector. You ought

to be an attorney, though I'd sooner have you as a partner than an opponent." Runge tapped the file with a pudgy forefinger. "It all seems eminently clear and convincing, but I did spot one minor omission. Your collation of the evidence is extremely comprehensive and covers nearly thirty pages. There's only one thing missing, and that's a formal statement of your belief that the case would stand up in court."

Kersten did not reply.

"I think I know the reason. You're perched on a barrel of dynamite, Inspector, and you can't defuse it by yourself. You're dependent on assistance from higher up—in this case, from the competent district attorney—but you can't count on his backing. It's the modern epidemic: no one wants to stick his neck out. Well, never mind. I'm here now."

"Exactly, Counselor. Why *are* you here?"

"I've been briefed to get your suspect off the hook. By so doing, I shall relieve you of precisely the problem you're unable to solve without running a grave personal risk. Am I right?"

"Herr Runge," Kersten said candidly, "if things go on this way, it won't be long before I need an attorney myself —badly. In view of your fees, I'd better start saving right away."

The human hippo gave an infantile giggle. "I always offer special terms to anyone who operates on the same wavelength. First, though, I'm going to get Emil Spahn off your back in such a way that your superiors will think I've done so without your help—in spite of you, even. That'll leave you free to go after the right man, but tread carefully."

Kersten nodded. "The prisoner's all yours." Just for a moment, he dropped his formal manner and added, "So

221

try and do better than your colleague Dr. Breile. I mean, make that obstinate son of a bitch see reason."

To a man like Runge, this necessitated only three moves, all of which were completed in less than an hour. They passed off with little difficulty.

Phase One

The attorney visited Emil Spahn in his cell. Emil, whose face was a mask of gloomy resignation, looked thoroughly world-weary. Although he had been persuaded by Breile to take a look at the Königsberg heavyweight and consider him as a possible defense counsel, his first words were unencouraging.

"There's no point," he muttered.

"My dear Herr Spahn," said Runge, trying to fall in with his prospective client's mood, "I think I understand your attitude. To you, the dead man was a straightforward murderer—the killer of your beloved cat. If only for that reason, you feel no compulsion to mourn his death."

Emil's voice shook with sudden anger, like his hands. "Whoever brained him did a good night's work. Anyone who'd do that to a dumb animal is capable of doing the same to a human being. Keller's sort don't deserve to live."

Runge was unmoved by this indictment. He had come across plenty of queer fish in his many years as a defense counsel: conscientious killers, socially committed swindlers, and muddle-headed murderers of every known variety— murderers for honor's sake, for a sidelong glance or an incautious remark, for unrequited love, or simply for hunger. Nothing could surprise him now.

"I readily accept all you say, Herr Spahn, but the contrary holds good as well. Anyone incapable of killing an animal in cold blood is equally incapable of doing the same to a human being, and that applies to you. You couldn't have murdered Keller—it's not in your nature."

"But I've confessed," Emil said stubbornly. "I'd swear to it any time."

Phase Two

Runge became more direct. "You seem intent on self-destruction, Herr Spahn. May I ask why?"

"Because of Susie."

"You loved her, I know that. Somebody killed her. Then somebody killed Keller, but it certainly wasn't you. You're no murderer."

"Why go on about it? All I know is, whoever killed him did the world a favor."

"So you already said, but why should you insist on shouldering the real killer's responsibilities and suffering in his place? You aren't hankering after a martyr's crown, surely? It's quite conceivable that Keller was removed by someone of his own sort—someone with enough political ambition to stop at nothing, not even murder. Do you really want to shield him? Do you really want him to go scot-free?"

"Keller got what was coming to him, that's the main thing, and I've confessed. What are you going to do about it?"

"Well, Herr Spahn, since you're so insistent on your guilt, I shall have to clear you in spite of yourself."

Phase Three

There followed a series of well-tried courtroom maneuvers designed to confuse a witness and elicit the truth—

223

a procedure known in professional circles as the martyr's horse-cure.

In the presence of Inspector Kersten, who listened closely in the background, Runge took the prisoner apart.

"So you claim to have used a heavy object with sharp edges to strike the deceased in the middle of the forehead, as confirmed by the pathologist's findings?"

Unbeknown to Emil, they confirmed nothing of the kind. He promptly agreed, though the pathologist's report stated that Keller's death had been occasioned by a blow with a blunt, cylindrical object applied to the base of the skull.

"And you left the dead man lying there?"

"That's right," Emil said eagerly. "I left him just where he was." This also conflicted with the known facts. Keller had been killed outside in the street and then was dragged into the hallway.

It emerged from his replies to Runge's questions that Emil Spahn could not have been the killer of the suspected killer of his cat. Runge turned to Kersten.

"Is that the confirmation you needed, Inspector?"

Kersten could hardly conceal his delight at this swift denouement. "Yes, and even the district attorney will have to buy it. Herr Spahn's confession has been invalidated. I have no further grounds for holding him in custody."

"So you believe in the rule of law . . ." Runge ruefully shook his head. "You're a devotee of justice, Inspector. Very commendable of you, but do you really hope to uphold it against the present powers that be? If so, you've taken on a big job."

On that note, Runge pocketed his fee and departed.

Outwardly at least, all remained well with the little world of Gilgenrode. Nothing obtruded on the idyllic scene—no ugly modern buildings, no ostentatious statues of the great.

The townsfolk lived as though cocooned by the beauty of their untouched natural surroundings. Theirs was a world still innocent of concrete.

Cranes circled above the deep-blue lakes, of which there were many. Waterfowl nested on their shores in the shade of ancient trees. Game abounded in the broad tracts of forest, still unmenaced by those trigger-happy killers who call themselves sportsmen.

The nights in this peaceful expanse of East Prussia were filled with mysterious life. Here an owl hooted, there a bat flitted past, and everywhere myriad fireflies punctuated the gloom with their fitful light. Though rather on the solid, stolid side, the local strain of Homo sapiens was good-natured and fond of fun. Ever affable and helpful, albeit in a terse and monosyllabic way, the people of Gilgenrode were true children of the soil. Few of them guessed that their little world—and not theirs alone—was on the verge of extinction.

These people loved their native region. Each man's ambition was a cottage with a flower-filled garden, a shady tree—preferably a lime tree—and a friendly dog on the doorstep, breed immaterial. Two or three cats, too, no matter what their pedigree. Whatever lived here lived at peace with its neighbors.

Everything seemed immutably safe and sound, but an age was dawning—a new age—when all would be transformed.

After an absence of several days, Beate Fischer reappeared at Sonnenblum's clinic. She looked the same as ever, except that her dark and sensual charms were enhanced by some skillful paint work around the eyes.

Sonnenblum hurried over and clasped her in his trembling arms. "There you are at last!" he breathed; then he stepped back and examined her solicitously. "Would you like to talk about it?"

"I'd rather not," she replied with velvet-soft determination. "I'm sure you understand."

It was true: the thorny subject of Keller need never be raised again, and Sonnenblum was duly grateful. "You must rest, my darling. You must take care of yourself."

Now it was her turn to sound solicitous. "You're looking off color, Heinrich."

"I'm fit as a fiddle," he assured her. "Not that I don't have my worries."

"About me?"

"No, not now. The sight of you warms my heart—it always does. I couldn't be happier to see you again."

"I'm glad." She nestled so tenderly against him that his head swam. "In that case, we can get back to work."

"I don't know, sweetheart. I'm thinking of closing down the practice temporarily. It's a question of priorities, and the Party comes first. I must take steps to preserve its reputation."

"Take as many as you like." Beate's mild sarcasm was lost on him. "Meantime, I'll clear up here and wait for you."

Left alone in the office, Beate began by devoting herself to the dental concerns of Gilgenrode. First she brought the card index up to date, a task which bored her to tears. Then she flicked through the mail and discovered, to her surprise, that it contained some poetic effusions addressed to herself. There were three in all, personally composed by Johannes Breitbach.

The poems were dedicated to "B." Poem number 1 opened with the line: "When first mine eyes beheld your face . . ." Poem number 2: "Your gaze is like the rising sun . . ." Finally, Poem number 3: "Two minds that think, two hearts that beat, as one . . ."

Beate wondered what form the follow-up would take. There wasn't one, but she remained undaunted.

Platoon Commander Schulze was itching to win his spurs. In this he was encouraged by several of his subordinates and one in particular—the one he regarded as his staunchest supporter.

"All you have to do," Konrad had told him, "is comply with the wishes and intentions of our Führer as expressed in *Mein Kampf*. He strongly advocates the deliberate establishment of an elite. Feeble irresolution and craven prevarication, he says, are the root of all evil."

"You won't catch a man like me behaving like that," Schulze declared with grim self-assurance. "Anyone who thinks different better watch out."

Konrad was beginning to glimpse the platoon commander's potentialities. "Your moment has come," he said. "Make the most of it."

At that, Schulze marched off to see Sonnenblum. "Our Storm Detachment," he proudly announced, "is the Party's first line of defense. Keller's death has deprived it of responsible leadership." The speech sounded overrehearsed, but it carried conviction. "This is a dangerous and undesirable state of affairs, District Director. If it isn't put right soon, the town could relapse into democratic chaos."

Sonnenblum, who felt sorely tried, puffed and blew like a cardiac case being prodded up a mountain with a bayonet. With something of an effort, he conceded that, although the Party itself was the spearhead of the Movement, the SA was an auxiliary formation of vital importance.

"Personally, I consider it essential that our Storm De-

227

tachment be commanded by a man whose loyalty claims my absolute confidence. I have therefore recommended you to succeed our murdered comrade."

"Thank you, District Director!" Schulze barked the words with a back like a ramrod. "I and my men will regard it as our bounden duty to back you to the hilt. We shall eliminate anyone who stands in your way. The time has come to clean house once and for all."

Sonnenblum nodded, apparently in full agreement, but his thoughts had strayed to Beate and the tormenting uncertainty that surrounded their relationship.

What was the matter with her, he couldn't help wondering. Was she avoiding him? Was her ardor cooling, or was she simply trying to hook him? He would have to put a stop to these bewildering changes of tack—these jarring alternations between warm bath and cold shower. But how?

Sonnenblum was so deeply preoccupied with these nagging thoughts that he had stopped listening, not that he considered it necessary. "Urinoco" was a knucklehead; he was also his, Sonnenblum's, puppet. It didn't matter a row of beans what rubbish he talked.

"Keller may have had his good points," said Schulze, a little saliva forming at the corners of his mouth. "But all he did, when you come down to it, was try to join forces with the bourgeois capitalist elements in this town, and that's a definite violation of the Party's ideological code."

"I'm depending on you," Sonnenblum said wearily. His brain was still in turmoil, still dominated by thoughts of Beate. He felt as if his body temperature would burst the thermometer, and his eyes looked correspondingly feverish.

"In that case, District Director, I shall soon be giving

you a demonstration of the Storm Detachment's new and ultra-German *esprit de corps*. It'll take your breath away."

He was right.

Emil Spahn, amateur prophet and professional drunk, had received some measure of financial compensation from the special fund administered by Dr. Breile. It was generous enough to keep him in drink for a long time to come, with the result that torrents of verbiage descended on various local hostelries.

"*I* didn't kill Keller," Emil regretfully proclaimed. "That's official. But who did? Somebody must have, so who was it if it wasn't me?"

He paused to refresh himself.

"All right, I admit it: I'd gladly have wrung his neck for the sake of my cat. Many of you in this heaven-blessed country of ours will sympathize with my sentiments because we still regard animals as our dearest life's companions, even now."

Another pause for refreshment.

"But our world is threatened to its foundations. There are murderers among us, and birds of a feather flock together. That happens as soon as we accept cat-killers as a common phenomenon. It needn't be long before the manufacture of human corpses becomes just as common."

Emil's views earned scant applause—in fact he was banned from various bars for safety's sake. One landlord told him, "Drink as much as you like, Emil, but keep your trap shut." Another went so far as to threaten him with the police. Just before midnight, when Emil was on the verge of total inebriation in a third tavern, a gnarled old farmer named Gregor Griegoleit came in.

He had delivered a cartload of greens and had fed and

watered his horse. Now, with his equally ancient dog beside him, he was sitting over a beer and bockwurst. A taciturn figure with snow-white hair and a face like treebark, Griegoleit surprised everyone by making one of the longest speeches in his life.

"Emil, my lad, you sound like a crow cawing in a churchyard. God may not mind, but what about some others I could name?"

Sonnenblum was feeling persecuted. People were giving him no peace, and among those who cornered him in his office was Inspector Kersten.

He tried to imagine himself an ancient German chieftain sitting in judgment beneath an oak tree, but the illusion was hard to sustain from behind a crude pine desk. He would have preferred to picture himself ensconced amid the tempting profusion of soft, plump cushions on Beate's sofa. There being no question of this, he was more than usually irritated by the sight of Kersten standing over his desk like a graven image.

"You've let me down badly, Inspector. Your failure to solve this terrible crime is causing bad blood and communal unrest. It's got to stop."

"That's why I'm here, Herr Sonnenblum. It's my duty to warn you that I shall now have to widen the scope of my investigations into Keller's death. They may involve the Party, and the SA in particular."

Even Beate's image vanished at these words, if only briefly. Sonnenblum was quick to grasp the significance of Kersten's studiously dispassionate announcement. "This is absurd," he said hoarsely, "absurd and dangerous. It poses a threat to us all, yourself included. How dare you imply that one of our comrades may have murdered another in cold blood!"

230

"I'm not implying anything, just exploring every possible line of approach. If one of them leads to the SA, that's just too bad. I don't have any choice."

"If what you say is true, Inspector, I shall be forced to contact the Regional Director and formally request his help in averting a potential miscarriage of justice. Your departmental superiors would be called in at once. Do you really want it to come to that?"

"I'm simply doing my duty." Kersten sounded resigned but resolute. "No one can stop me doing that."

"I'm Konrad Breitbach. I know it's late, but I'm sure you won't mind. They say you're pretty unflappable, so I guess you won't be scared by me."

Beate peered at her late-night visitor with dawning interest. Through the apartment door, which she had opened a couple of inches, Konrad could see that she was wearing a sunflower-print housecoat over not much else.

"What do you want?"

"That's easy." Konrad blinked as though dazzled by her dark and radiant beauty. "I'm here to make your acquaintance and introduce myself—I mean, if it's all right with you."

"Be my guest." She opened the door wide.

Konrad walked in and surveyed the room with almost as much appreciation as he had bestowed on her person. It made a flowery, vernal impression and was unusually bright by Gilgenrode standards. On a small mosaic table lit by a lamp with a big shade covered in painted jungle blooms lay an open book.

Konrad sat down at the table uninvited, picked up the book and started leafing through it. He soon shook his head and smiled in a wondering way. It was a volume of nineteenth-century romantic poetry.

"Officially," he said, "I'm here to question you about Keller. His death is giving the Party a lot of headaches, so we need to be fully informed on the subject for safety's sake. However, I suppose you're going to clam up."

"You suppose right," Beate said firmly. "That concludes the official part of your mission. What now?"

"Now we get personal." Still holding the book, Konrad eyed her with boyish pleasure. "Just to avoid any misunderstandings, allow me to say you're far lovelier, not to say gorgeous, than I ever realized. That explains a lot, if not everything."

"Meaning what?"

"Something very important, for a start. As I see it, the local conventions don't apply to you. You're an absolute exception—a special case."

Her eyes narrowed. "They warned me about you and I'm beginning to see why. You obviously have a talent for telling people just what they want to hear."

"Curses!" he said theatrically. "You've seen through me."

"Know something?" She leaned toward him. "We're two of a kind at heart. You're fighting to stay afloat too, which means we could be friends. No use pretending, Konrad. You appeal to me."

"Likewise." His impish smile turned wry. "The trouble with this place is that it doesn't matter what you really are, only what other people take you for."

"Is that a dig at me?"

"Not a dig, just a friendly word of warning." Konrad stared at the book in his hand, looking more and more thoughtful. "You don't belong here—the place doesn't suit you, so why not get out while the going's good? That would be the best solution." He paused. "More's the pity."

Kimminger had requested the honor of Schulze's presence—his actual words—for lunch at the German Eagle, and Schulze had graciously accepted. Not, however, before loudly proclaiming his incorruptibility.

"Nobody buys me, Kimminger—certainly not for a meal and a couple of drinks. I've got my principles and I stick to them."

The hotelier galloped to meet him halfway. "But of course, that goes without saying!"

He was well versed in the new moral code. Schulze would be presented with a bill that covered only a small portion of the cost of his meal, but neither of them would flicker an eyelid. Appearances were all that mattered.

"What can I tempt you to, Stormtroop Commander?" asked Kimminger, instinctively promoting his guest. He went on to recommend the loin of beef plus kidneys or the shoulder of pork. Schulze rejected both suggestions in favor of something regional and sustaining like scrambled egg with boar and grilled chops.

"Don't overdo it, though. Not more than three chops and a few fried potatoes on the side."

"And what would you like to drink, Stormtroop Commander? A Burgundy, or some of the champagne your District Director appreciates so much?"

"I'm not the District Director or the Stormtroop Commander—yet," growled Schulze. "I'm an honest-to-God German. Bring me some good East Prussian beer."

This sounded like further confirmation of what Kimminger already knew: that he was dealing with a prime specimen of the German herd mentality. If only as regards the female of the species, he found the situation full of promise.

"I've been worried," he confided after a pause for refreshment, "by the way things are going."

233

"No need, Herr Kimminger." Schulze took a man-sized bite out of his third grilled chop. "I'm sailing the ship now, and I'm bang on course."

"I know," Kimminger said eagerly, "and it fills me with hope for the future. Far be it from me to cast aspersions on the dead, Herr Schulze, but I think you're much the better man. I hope you'll pardon the liberty."

"You're welcome."

"Speaking in the strictest confidence, I was alarmed by Keller's blatant failure to deal effectively with public enemies like Gernoth and Company. Things will be different now, I'm sure."

Schulze choked on a morsel of chop and swilled it down with beer. "Gernoth's a lackey of the Jews. He actually defied us—*us,* the SA!"

"And you aren't going to stand for it?"

"You bet I'm not. Anyone who gets in our way bites the dust, even if it's God Almighty."

The next outsider to visit Gilgenrode was a skinny, puny-looking little man who picked up his feet like an arthritic stork.

The occasion of his visit was an urgent telephone call from District Director Sonnenblum to the Party's Regional Directorate—or, more precisely, to the Regional Organizer, an enterprising character who went by the name of Fritz-Dietlof, Count von der Schulenburg.

"So you've got a skeleton in the closet," said Schulenburg. "Well, it happens in the best-regulated families. You can't get rid of it so you're unloading it on us, right?"

Sonnenblum cleared his throat. "I'm merely requesting interdepartmental assistance."

"Same thing. Luckily for you, we employ a troubleshooter to handle cases like yours. He's capable of anything, especially when it comes to skeletons—for those he's got a sixth sense. Let's hope your hands are clean."

"I had nothing whatever to do with the Stormtroop Commander's death, Regional Organizer, I can assure you of that."

"Fine, then you can look forward to our man's arrival with an easy mind. He's a detective superintendent named Tantau. If your conscience is clear, he'll let you sleep sweet. If not, you could have nightmares for the rest of your life."

Superintendent Tantau looked like an oversized dwarf. His dark-brown suit flapped loosely about him as though concealing nothing but skin and bone. Nobody would have taken such a shabby little scarecrow for a detective, still less for a homicide expert of unrivaled efficiency, but Tantau set store by his unprepossessing exterior.

Casually swinging a small suitcase, he sauntered from the station to police headquarters, where he asked for Kersten. Ever on the *qui vive*, Kersten ushered the visitor into his office.

"What can I do for you?"

The little man's opening words were stiff and formal. "Tantau, Detective Superintendent, here on special assignment. I should like to examine the Keller file."

It was handed over at once. Sitting there tensely beside him as he studied its contents, Kersten got the impression that Tantau had stopped breathing. He sensed that a storm was about to break over Gilgenrode.

Then Tantau sat back. He gave the inspector a long, almost impersonal stare, as though reading a book. At last he said quietly, "I congratulate you, Inspector."

"Why?" Kersten retorted with an edge to his voice. "Because I've got a line on the real killer, or because I'm being slow to nab him? There are plenty of moral cowards around these days. I suppose you think I'm one of them."

"Not necessarily, Inspector." Tantau laughed as if he had made a joke. "Whom does a good policeman work for? For his bosses, of course. I happen to be a policeman who specializes in garbage disposal, a member of the legal sanitation department, but it doesn't mean I'm a coolie."

Kersten vainly strove to follow the superintendent's train of thought. "I take it you'll tell me what you want me to do?"

Tantau nodded. "I'm counting on your cooperation. In practice, that means you'll pull in anyone I consider it necessary to interview. We'll then exert some combined pressure. When we nail our man, as I suspect we will, you can take your pick. Either I leave him to you, in which case you can enhance your professional reputation by marching him off yourself—"

"Or what?"

"Or you can unload the responsibility on me—my shoulders are broader than they look. I gather you've already been offered that escape route by Counselor Runge."

"You know him?"

"Distantly, as one lighthouse knows another by flashes in a stormy sky. But don't pin too many hopes on that. At the end of the day, everyone in this country will have to ride out the storm alone—or sink, unless he learns how to swim in mud."

9

"RIGHT. IF we want to reap the whirlwind we'd better sow
some wind." Tantau chuckled companionably at Kersten.
"Or, to use another metaphor, let's pick all the brains in
sight and see what comes out." He briskly rubbed his
hands as though the glorious spring day had turned chilly.
"How's your shorthand and typing?"

"Rusty but adequate."

"Good, that makes us a well-balanced team. I'll ask the
questions and you take notes. We'll start with Herr Sonnenblum."

Kersten raised his eyebrows. "Wouldn't it be wiser to
call at his office? He is the District Director—"

"*Our* status is all that matters. We aren't his underlings,
we're policemen. Does that reassure you?"

"Superintendent," Kersten said stiffly, "I hope I know

the meaning of an order, but it doesn't prevent me from questioning its wisdom. This is Gilgenrode, not Königsberg. Size counts for a lot."

"Wrong again, Inspector. We're dealing with an attempt to impose conformity on a gigantic scale. From that angle, there's little material difference between Berlin and the backwoods. The whole sky can be reflected in a raindrop, know what I mean?"

Kersten shrugged. "Very well, I'll send for him."

"But there's no need to threaten compulsion, if that's any comfort. Persuade your District Director to demonstrate his faith in German justice and set the community a good example. It's bound to be catching, and that's what matters. As soon as this so-called big-shot obeys the call, the rest will flock here like sheep. Off you go!"

The interviews that followed took the form of friendly chats conducted by Tantau and recorded by Kersten. Target number 1 was District Director Sonnenblum, who came under protest.

"Is this necessary?"

"We have a common problem," Tantau said courteously, "you in your capacity as the Party's senior local representative, I as a representative of the Regional Directorate. Our task is to discover whether members of the Party or its affiliated organizations—the SA, for example—may have been implicated in Keller's death."

Sonnenblum's jaw muscles tightened. "I find it presumptuous of you even to hint at such a thing. I can only regard it as a threat to the Party—possibly, even, to myself."

"Please, District Director!" Tantau looked shocked. "Don't jump to conclusions, I beg you. You're very highly thought of at the Regional Directorate. What's more, your conscience is clear—or so my instinct tells me. I sincerely hope I'm right."

Sonnenblum was followed by Richard Breitbach, looking cheerful and relaxed.

"I hardly knew Keller, Superintendent—I only met him a few times. If you're interested, I didn't take to him. The less we had to do with each other, the better I liked it."

"That accords with my existing information," Tantau said, smiling amiably. "You were on opposite sides of the political fence."

"Put it any way you like, my dear sir, but I'm not the sort of person who consigns a man to eternity for his political beliefs, however perverse they are."

The next to be summoned to police headquarters was Felix Kimminger, whose manner toward Tantau and Kersten was that of a fellow conspirator.

"Nobody deplores Keller's death more than I, Superintendent. He was an outstanding man. I valued him highly."

"It seems you valued him at ten thousand marks," Tantau said, very quietly, "not to mention other donations and contributions—or however you choose to describe them."

Kimminger was characteristically unabashed. "I was only doing my bit for the Movement. You wouldn't object to that, surely?"

Then came Hermine, the murdered hero's sister. She gave Kersten a withering glare before turning to Tantau.

"I've said it all before. Emil Spahn did it. Put him behind bars and release my brother's body. I want him decently buried."

"Here?" asked Kersten. "Just before German Day?"

Hermine didn't deign to answer. Without so much as a glance in his direction, she addressed her remarks to Tantau alone.

"My brother will be buried in his native village, next to our beloved mother. Herr Sonnenblum has been kind enough to arrange the whole thing, so do your duty and be quick about it."

The ensuing talk with Parson Bachus turned out to be a barren interlude. The churchman spoke without prompting.

"Well, yes—Herr Keller caused me a certain amount of trouble, but I forgive him. He couldn't help himself. He was a misguided man, like several others I could mention. I don't mean you, Herr Tantau, and certainly not the worthy Inspector here. I shall pray for the success of your joint endeavors."

The next object of interrogation was Beate Fischer. Tantau greeted her with polished courtesy. He was visibly charmed by her dark allure, graceful movements and dazzling smile.

"You're just as I imagined, Fräulein. I'm delighted to make your acquaintance."

"The pleasure's mutual," Beate replied, instinctively drawn to the strange little detective. "Most of the men I meet are on the make. Something tells me I'll be safe with you."

"You will." Tantau gave her a sympathetic grin. "But not because I'm past it or handicapped by my personal appearance. Appearances aren't everything, as I'm sure you'll agree, but I've no intention of joining the scramble for your favors. Bees are attracted by honey, but so is the occasional bear."

"That's my position in a nutshell, Herr Tantau. It gets pretty difficult sometimes."

"You probably haven't grasped the full extent of its difficulties. What some men call love can take the strangest forms. It can even lead to acts of violence like this one."

"I never meant it to happen."

"Your intentions are beside the point. All that matters is your effect on the opposite sex. In this case, if my arithmetic is correct, you were juggling with four men at once. My dear young lady, isn't that carrying things a little far?"

"They didn't need any encouragement, Herr Tantau. Keller was one of them, but it doesn't mean he was murdered on my account."

Tantau gazed benignly into her big green eyes. "You're a smart girl. I'm sure this won't be our last little chat."

"It's beyond me." Inspector Kersten was puzzled by Tantau's unmistakable air of satisfaction. "You've spent four or five hours swapping small talk with a dozen people, and nothing's come to light in the way of new material evidence."

"Be patient, Inspector. Every thriller needs a plot, and every plot has to thicken for a while."

"But you've only been talking to the extras."

"Yes, if you like to call them that, but they're an integral part of the production. We can't bring on the star till they're all in position."

"And where are we going to find *him?* Somewhere quite different, if you ask me. What about Sass and his attorney, or Schulze and his thugs? Konrad Breitbach could bear watching, too—he's got a finger in all sorts of pies. Then there's the White Hart Hotel set, who are said to be anti-Party. Finally, there's Emil Spahn, who's suddenly struck it rich."

"All in good time, Inspector. Let's sleep on it first, you in the bosom of the family and me in the hotel you just mentioned. Let's hope we both have an uneventful night, but stay tuned."

The White Hart, where Tantau had booked in, was an oasis of calm and security that evening—a haven of East Prussian hospitality. The dinner menu's *pièce de résistance,* braised duck with apple sauce, turned out to be a resounding success. An almost palpable sense of well-being pervaded the hotel restaurant.

Several extremely solid-looking citizens were dining with a gusto that was visible but seldom audible—a business executive, two municipal councilors, a school inspector, three master craftsmen and a prosperous farmer. Most were with their wives but all looked quite content.

A figure with snow-white hair flitted from table to table. It was Georg Gernoth, the proprietor, whose manner combined deference with dignity. He bade his patrons an urbane good evening, made an eagle-eyed inventory of their plates, cutlery and glasses, and ensured that his waiters observed the refinements of their calling. Eventually he padded up to Tantau, who was sitting by himself.

"I trust you're enjoying your meal, sir?"

"No reason why not. You keep an excellent table, and your regulars obviously feel at home here. So do I. You, on the other hand, are looking ever so slightly apprehensive—almost as if this harmonious atmosphere is too good to last. Is it?"

"Who can tell what the future holds in store?" Gernoth gave a fatalistic shrug, but his friendly smile persisted. "As long as my guests are satisfied, nothing else matters. The duck is a speciality of the house, incidentally. I hope you find it to your taste."

"I do indeed. It has a faint but unmistakable flavor of wild herbs."

"You have a discriminating palate, sir. These birds breed in the moorland north of the town. They live in the wild state, but their diet is supplemented with concentrates. That fattens them without spoiling their natural flavor." Gernoth bowed. "Permit me to wish you *bon appétit.*"

The springtime idyl continued. The restaurant buzzed with cheerful conversation, but the happy diners never raised their voices except in laughter or when exchanging toasts between tables. This they did with brimming glasses and the twinkling eyes of those united by bonds of good-fellowship. Then they continued to eat with quiet reverence, as if nothing in the world could shatter their contentment.

Until the Brownshirts appeared.

Schulze, who could already feel the touch of Keller's mantle on his shoulders, was out to prove his mettle with the maximum of speed and efficiency. To this end he had formed a few of his most trusted minions into a combat-ready flying squad for systematic deployment against the White Hart.

Two of his men had been posted at the main entrance and two more in the courtyard, guarding the rear exit. "Seal the place off," he adjured them. "Not a bedbug goes in or out till we've cleaned up this nest of subversives."

Then, flanked by two uniformed Brownshirts, he tramped into the restaurant. The trio halted and stood there like statues, legs slightly spread, bodies erect, muscular hands gripping heavy truncheons. The Stormtroop Commander designate was armed with an eight-millimeter automatic in a shiny leather holster. He tapped this menacingly while shooting off his mouth.

"Keep calm and carry on eating! This is an official raid. Anyone who gets in our way won't live to regret it, understand? We aren't interested in *you,* not this time. This time it's *his* turn!"

So saying, the uncrowned king of the Brownshirts shot out his right arm, but not in a Hitler salute. His forefinger was leveled accusingly at Gernoth, who had turned pale.

"At your service, sir," Gernoth quavered. "Might I suggest a word in private?"

This idea met with grudging acceptance. Gernoth scurried on ahead while Schulze marched along in his wake. The other Brownshirts remained on guard, toying with their truncheons and grinning balefully.

The diners had stopped eating. Conversation died and nobody dared to exchange a glance. Only one person seemed unperturbed by these proceedings and intent on his wild duck, though he kept a watchful eye on all that was happening around him.

That was why Tantau spotted what Schulze's thugs did not: one of his fellow diners had surreptitiously gone to work. Seated at a corner table and screened by a pillar, he scribbled a few words on a menu—possibly a name, a telephone number and a brief set of instructions. Then he pushed the menu toward a waiter standing near by. The waiter took it and backed stealthily through the door to the kitchen.

Tantau gave no sign of having noticed, but his curiosity grew by leaps and bounds.

Meanwhile, the acting Stormtroop Commander and the White Hart's proprietor had retired to the latter's office. Here they stood facing one another, Schulze like an avenging angel, Gernoth with an air of abject entreaty. Between them was a desk, bare except for a japanned cashbox. Gernoth picked up the box and clutched it to him.

"This is it, you scum," snarled Schulze. "I'm going to show you up for the Jew-lover you are, but first I want a written confession from you. Sentence will be carried out on the spot, understand?"

"Allow me to point out, with the utmost respect, my dear sir, that I had a firm verbal agreement with your late lamented predecessor—"

"He's shuffled off," Schulze said brutally. "Lucky he did too, or you and your Yiddisher cronies would have had him in your pocket. It won't happen to me. I represent the Führer around here, get it?"

"Of course, but . . ." Gernoth opened the cashbox with trembling fingers. A thick wad of bank notes came to light. "Fifteen thousand marks exactly. For you—I mean, the Party. Regard it as an interim payment."

Schulze snorted like a nervous stallion, impressed despite himself by the sight of so much ready cash. He struggled to preserve his Hitlerian detachment.

"A donation, eh? What's the catch?"

"No catch, I assure you."

Schulze reached for the bundle fast. He half sniffed it for a moment before dividing it between the pockets of his riding breeches. "All right, your donation is accepted—that's to say, taken into Party custody. We'll call it a first installment."

"What more do you want?"

"Your fifteen thousand marks are a definite admission of guilt, but I still want a confession. In writing, here and now."

"But I thought . . . Do you really think it's essential?" Gernoth was wringing his hands now. "What sort of confession, anyway?"

"Don't play dumb!" Schulze's voice was razor-sharp. "You'll confess to being involved with Jews and other public enemies. You regret it, you'll say, and you're ready to accept the consequences."

"Would it help if I increased my donation? What if I doubled it?"

"I wouldn't say no, as long as it's all right with the Party." Presumably he meant Sonnenblum. "But don't try and stop me doing my duty. If you're hoping for a miracle, forget it."

Gernoth cherished no such hope, but something of the kind occurred: Konrad Breitbach entered the restaurant with a book under his arm—a well-thumbed, dog-eared copy of *Mein Kampf*, without a dust jacket.

He disappeared into the hotelier's office without being stopped by the SA sentries, who were still on guard, thirsting for action. They merely raised their truncheons, rather in the manner of a salute, and gave Konrad a friendly grin. He was, after all, one of them.

Tantau had closely observed the arrival of this nimble-footed, boyish-looking *deus ex machina*. Now that he had finished his duck, he could restrain his curiosity no longer. Half crouching to escape attention, he tiptoed over to the man who had sent the message a few minutes earlier.

"May I introduce myself?" he asked politely.

"Please sit down," came the no less courteous reply. "I know who you are, Herr Tantau. Your presence in our little town has not gone unnoticed. I also know why you're here. My name's Breile, by the way—I'm sure it appears in your records."

Tantau nodded. "Delighted to meet you so soon, Herr Breile. I should have called on you in any case, tomorrow at latest."

"Or asked me to call on you?"

"Not now I've seen you in action. I'm thoroughly intrigued, I don't mind admitting. It didn't escape me that you smuggled a note to someone. The police—that was my immediate thought, but then *he* turned up."

"So you spotted my little maneuver." The lawyer's tone was half admiring, half wary. "Congratulations, but why should I have sent for the police? They were already on the spot, represented by yourself, but you let things ride and did nothing. Isn't this a clear case of trespass, apart from anything else?"

"Not necessarily. Before trespass can be proved, as you're naturally aware, the owner of the relevant premises has to file a formal complaint alleging unauthorized entry. Herr Gernoth didn't protest. He took the whole thing in his stride."

"You've got a point." Breile began to sense—and appreciate—his companion's dangerous subtlety. He had yet to discover its true dimensions.

"So you didn't send for the police," Tantau went on. "In order to contain the situation, you obviously thought it sufficient to alert that young man. Who exactly is he?"

"Konrad Breitbach. I'm sure you have his name on file too. Konrad's a man of many parts. He even has a capacity for logical thought."

"Mm," said Tantau. "That's something of a luxury these days. You think his logic's equal to the present situation? Will it produce results?"

It certainly seemed to, because the restaurant was emptied of Brownshirts within minutes. Schulze stormed out of Gernoth's office, grim-faced, and curtly beckoned to his occupying forces.

Then Gernoth appeared. Though pale with strain, he quickly remembered his gastronomic duties.

"Back to your posts," he told his waiters. "Brandy and liqueurs all around—on the house."

Konrad brushed past him with Hitler's magnum opus under his arm. He walked briskly over to Breile's table, de-

247

posited the book on a chair, and perched on it uninvited.

"Makes me look taller," he explained, and signified his desire for a beer. "I need one. Who knows, maybe I've earned one."

"You certainly have," said Breile.

"I'm most impressed," Tantau chimed in. "You silenced the lion in mid-roar. How did you manage it?"

Breile's prompt interjection was worthy of a good attorney. "Before you answer that, Konrad, you ought to know who you're dealing with."

"I already do, and so does everyone else in this dump. Herr Tantau's here to catch a killer."

Tantau nodded. "Quite so, but there's something else you should know. I never try to deceive people. In fact, I tend to put them on their guard against me. I'm also insatiably curious, Herr Breitbach. That's why I'm so keen to know what went on inside there just now."

"He simply cleared the air, I imagine," said Breile, still on a warning note.

"That's one way of putting it." Konrad picked up his beer, which had now arrived, and took a long pull. "You have to be up on the current ideology, Herr Tantau, and the best key to that is our Führer's literary masterpiece." He tapped the volume under his backside. "I not only know it inside out, I'm generous enough to share my knowledge with others."

"Is that all?" Tantau looked genuinely surprised. "You quoted a few passages from that book and they worked?"

"Like a charm. Mind you, I prefaced them by pointing out that the District Director thinks just like the Führer and expects all his underlings to do likewise. That did the trick."

"Splendid," said Tantau. His next words were startlingly to the point. "I suspect you know who killed Keller.

I do too, of course, but I don't have definite proof. Perhaps we could team up."

Breile made another warning noise in his throat.

"Not after one little beer." Konrad soothed the lawyer with a smile. "Maybe after two, if I'm not being greedy."

Tantau's first call of the following day was on Sonnenblum, who was still in his pajamas and gave the detective a surly reception.

"Last night, by the merest chance, I happened to be present when some of your stormtroopers raided the White Hart Hotel. A debatable proceeding, if you don't mind my saying so."

"First-class men under first-class leadership," said Sonnenblum. "Mistakes do happen, I freely admit, but they can always be put right."

"In this case, one of your troubleshooters stepped in just in time. Was he acting on your instructions?"

"In line with my general policy, yes. And now you must forgive me, Superintendent. For your information, the true National Socialist never looks back: he keeps his eyes firmly focused on the future. Our next and most important objective is Gilgenrode's German Day. I intend it to be a really memorable occasion, epitomized by some such slogan as 'Final Victory is Ours!' "

With this pronouncement ringing in his ears, Tantau left the Party boss and paid a call on Sass, who had just received Dr. Breile.

Tantau, who was not surprised or disconcerted by the lawyer's presence, made himself at home in one of Sass's comfortable armchairs.

"I'm not here to question anyone, or anything of that kind. I merely came to offer a little advice and information."

Breile frowned. "About what?"

"About the woman in the case—the eternal female, if you prefer."

"Beate Fischer," the lawyer said quietly. "Is that who you mean?"

"Precisely. A remarkable young lady, and one who occupies something of a key position in this affair. If she could be induced to leave the scene, it might disperse a few of the local fog banks."

Sass said nothing but did not seem averse to the idea. Breile spoke for him. "In the light of your investigations to date, Herr Tantau, how much importance do you attach to that suggestion?"

"I know this is a male-dominated society," said Tantau, "but let's take a lesson from the ancient Greek—or was he a Roman?—who pointed out that what one woman's hand can conceal between her thighs is enough to send whole empires tumbling."

"That may have been so in Athens or Rome," said Sass, looking faintly amused. "This is Gilgenrode."

"Where's the difference?" Tantau chuckled like a mischievous elf. "I don't see any. Period and place have little bearing on human foibles. There's a striking similarity between them the world over."

Sass had turned thoughtful. "I see you've discovered my Achilles' heel, Superintendent. It's true—I'm not indifferent to the lady's fate."

"Neither am I. Fräulein Fischer is a charming and desirable young woman, but she's also a threat to peace and good order, or as much of it as still survives here. Breitbach and Sonnenblum are permanently at each other's throats over her, and they aren't the only contenders. If she weren't here it would solve a number of problems—for her, among others."

"I know," said Sass. "She doesn't belong here. She deserves a different kind of life in different surroundings, and if I'm any judge she'd go like a shot. Personally, I'd welcome her departure from the bottom of my heart. It would give me the greatest pleasure to get her out of this place." "Delighted to hear it," said Tantau. "How about you, Herr Sass? Will you also be depriving us of your presence?" Sass shook his head. "You can't transplant an old tree."

Just forty-eight hours before German Day, Gilgenrode's answer to the Nuremberg rally, a final top-level conference took place in Sonnenblum's office. It was a momentous and uplifting occasion. The District Director's machine was running flat out.

The Women's Association had been fully mobilized, and the Hitler Youth and German Girls' League representatives reported the completion of their assigned tasks. Even Treasurer Stenz showed signs of satisfaction because all expenses were to be met by "donations" and would necessitate no dipping in Party funds. As for the SA, Schulze was able to announce that all security measures had been taken.

Sonnenblum was highly gratified. Beate receded from his thoughts yet again, though not for long. Misgivings of a different kind revived when Konrad requested a word in private.

"Well," he said uneasily, "what is it? Something unpleasant, from the look on your face."

"It's just that I don't want anything to cast a shadow over this magnificent festival of yours, District Director. To make absolutely sure, I suggest we clear the air with Schulze."

Sonnenblum's uneasiness persisted. "All right, Konrad. If we must, so be it."

Platoon Commander Schulze was summoned to the inner

office, scenting promotion. He was all the more taken aback when Konrad, with an amiable grin, said flatly, "Tantau thinks you murdered Keller. Did you know?"

"Who the hell do you think you are!" Schulze bellowed furiously. "How dare you repeat such a rotten, stinking pack of lies! I demand satisfaction, District Director. Tantau's got to go. You must give the man his marching orders."

"Unfortunately," said Konrad in response to an imploring glance from Sonnenblum, "the District Director isn't in a position to grant your request. Tantau happens to be here on assignment from the Regional Directorate."

"Balls to that!" roared Schulze. "Anyone who fails to put his country first can get screwed. You can't make an omelette without breaking eggs, so it's time the police stopped butting in. Aren't I right, District Director?"

Sonnenblum shuffled his feet. "Perfectly, in principle. The situation could turn sour—it might even cast a blight on our German Day, and that we can't allow."

"Then it's time that busybody buttoned his lip," snapped Schulze. "As for Konrad, he should stop spreading rumors about me. I don't like it. What's more, I don't intend to stand for it."

On that note he returned to the outer office, where the rest of the Party notables were plying themselves with drink. Still glowering, he raised his glass.

"To Germany," he said grimly. "Nothing else matters."

Left alone together, Konrad and Sonnenblum exchanged a long, appraising stare. At last the District Director mournfully shook his head.

"My dear boy, did you *have* to? Schulze will never forgive you for that—never."

252

"I'll survive."

"Oh God," said Sonnenblum, "if it isn't one thing, it's another. What have I done to deserve these everlasting problems?"

"They're inevitable," Konrad said dryly. "In a great age like the one we're privileged to live in, headaches never come singly—and they aren't confined to our public lives."

Predictably, Sonnenblum stiffened. "What are you driving at? Is that an allusion to Fräulein Fischer?" He sounded positively greedy for information. "What's the matter with her? What do you know about her?"

"Not as much as I'd like, but I do know one thing: she won't be played around with, any-which way. To that extent, District Director, I think you ought to be prepared for a few surprises."

Dr. Breile's invitation to call at his office was couched in the politest language. Beate turned up promptly, feeling more than a little curious, and was shown in at once. Though flattered by her royal reception, she did not drop her guard.

"I might hear something to my advantage, Dr. Breile— that's what you told me on the phone."

"Very much. so. You're being offered a large sum of money."

She gave him the searching, wide-eyed gaze of an expert on the opposite sex. Breile was a lawyer, not a lover, but he would—like any man—need careful handling.

"This offer—" she said, sounding wary but not dismissive, "what's the catch? Nobody doles out something for nothing. People will wonder what the payoff is—which is what I'm wondering myself."

"Look at it like this, Fräulein Fischer. A man's money is

his own to dispose of as he pleases. He can drink it away, gamble it away, spend it on an old folks' home, a home for stray dogs—even on the Party. Why not on you?"

Beate snuggled up in her chair, catlike. Her eyes were just as feline: iridescently green and slumberously alert. "You're talking about Herr Sass, aren't you?"

"I wouldn't worry about that," Breile said quickly. "You don't know Herr Sass. You've never even met him— as anyone here can testify. You're total strangers."

"But he wants to buy me out of here." Beate's curiosity was running riot. "Why?"

"I'd advise you to regard the matter in the following light. A client of mine is extremely anxious to enable you to start a new life elsewhere. Your choice of abode is up to you. Paris, London—even New York, which might be the safest bet. Everything would be financed on a lavish scale."

"But why should he go to so much expense? We've never exchanged a word, so he can't have had an old man's crush on me. What's at the back of it all?"

Breile gave a discreet little cough. "How much do you know about your mother?"

"Very little, to be frank." There was a brief, pensive silence. "She died when I was very young."

"I know, but before you were born Herr Sass employed her as a housekeeper. Are you beginning to see the connection?"

Beate blinked hard. "You mean that Herr Sass and my mother—that I'm . . ."

"I didn't say that. I'm merely saying that Herr Sass feels a duty to your mother's memory. She was almost like one of the family."

"I've almost forgotten her. She died giving birth to my sister."

"But Herr Sass remembers her well. His gratitude toward

her has left him with an enduring sense of obligation. He has now transferred it to you."

"In return for what?"

"Herr Sass has no children or close relations, no direct heirs. He can therefore choose his own heirs—which is what he has done. There's one other beneficiary, but my client's means are more than sufficient to provide for you both. The sole condition is that you should leave Germany. Are you willing to do so?"

Beate thought for a moment. Competition for her favors was getting out of hand. Quite suddenly, the prospect of escape seemed too good to miss.

"Why not? I'll pack my bags and leave tomorrow—for Paris, let's say. Would that be acceptable?"

"Perfectly. We're agreed, then. I shall confirm the arrangement in writing." The lawyer sounded as if he were congratulating Beate on her decision—but also himself for having engineered it.

Detective Superintendent Tantau was packing too, though his suitcase was a small one. He did not interrupt his labors when Konrad turned up and lolled in the doorway of his hotel room, grinning benignly.

"I hope this is my first and last visit, Konrad, for your sake as much as anyone's. You're obviously enjoying this small-town circus. In fact you've even started training a few acts of your own."

"It's a question of self-preservation, not inclination."

"Go on, you've tasted blood and you like it. I hear you had the nerve to pin Keller's death on that pathetic creature Schulze. What made you quote me?"

Konrad looked ingenuous. "I thought the suggestion came from you, Superintendent."

"From me?" Tantau slammed the lid of his suitcase

shut. "So it did, damn you!" He cackled unashamedly. "You're a crafty little beggar."

"Living here makes you crafty, but you can also have some fun at the same time. You enjoy a bit of fun yourself, if I'm not much mistaken."

"I'm afraid you're right. I play as many tricks as the climate in this country still allows."

"So let's make the most of the time that's left." Konrad's face clouded for a moment. "Are you going to take Schulze off our hands?"

"I'd like nothing better, but I'm only a troubleshooter, not an arresting officer. I'm the Regional Director's paper tiger."

"So you're giving up?"

"Not exactly. I've been clearing the field of fire for somebody who carries a lot more guns than I do."

"Meaning who?"

"The Party's regional organizer at Königsberg. Schulenburg's the name—Count von der Schulenburg. A hell of a fellow, in spite of his aristocratic tag. You can expect him here as soon as I've submitted my report. It'll be guaranteed to bring him running."

"And he'll nail our man?"

"Certainly, as long as our spadework proves adequate—which it ought to. After all, we've shoved so many firecrackers under Schulze's murdering backside he's bound to come clean sooner or later. To whom, though? That's the point to watch, my lad."

So saying, Tantau picked up his shabby suitcase and left Gilgenrode forthwith. Konrad felt strangely bereft as the train pulled out, leaving him alone on the platform.

Heinrich Sonnenblum sat brooding in his office, weighed down by innumerable cares. His breathing was stertorous, his gaze lackluster, his brain befogged by the gloom that threatened to engulf him. Beate was leaving. His pulse raced, and sweat broke out all over his body, armpits first, then chest. Before long, his entire face glistened as if it had been sprayed with oil. He was in torment, though periodic swigs of corn liquor helped to ease the pain.

Sonnenblum felt like a latter-day Job, but the full force of this simile escaped him even when his secretary announced that Platoon Commander Schulze insisted on seeing him at once.

Having swallowed an assortment of painkillers and patent cold-cure tablets and washed them down with schnapps, he did his best to deal as swiftly and effectively as possible with the man who loomed over his desk, stiff as a poker but glowing with self-esteem.

"I want to thank you, District Director. You've backed me all along the line."

"That's only as it should be," said Sonnenblum, fortified by a farewell telephone call from Tantau, who had intimated that there was no firm evidence against his acting Stormtroop Commander. "You're one of my best men."

"True." Schulze's manner was solemn but exultant. His eyes seemed to be focused on some infinitely distant Nazi-brown horizon. "It's because I'm so conscious of your approval and appreciation, District Director, that I can now claim responsibility for everything—everything! I do so with a clear conscience."

Sonnenblum gaped at him like a yokel staring at a fairground freak. "What exactly do you mean?"

"I did it." Schulze stood there imitating a granite statue of the unknown soldier. "Somebody had to."

Sonnenblum's trembling hands fastened on the edge of his desk. The hope in his eyes evaporated as doubt gave way to horrific certainty.

"So it was you!"

"Yes, I rid our community of a parasite. Keller wasn't just a bad National Socialist—his morals were a downright disgrace. He not only had the gall to pursue Fräulein Fischer, District Director. He even pestered my wife and your daughter, and who knows how many other fine examples of German womanhood. We couldn't let him get away with it, could we?"

"My God," groaned Sonnenblum, "what have I done to deserve this?"

Schulze blithely misunderstood him. "You don't know anything officially, of course. No need to pat me on the back in public, as long as we both know how much you appreciate the loyalty and devotion of the SA—under my command. Heil Hitler!"

Count von der Schulenburg's appearance in Gilgenrode was quite as prompt as Tantau had predicted. He turned up on the eve of German Day, a slim, agile man with thoroughbred-horsy features and eyes that seemed to ask a thousand questions.

Schulenburg had hardly booked into the German Eagle when he sent for Konrad Breitbach. He received Konrad in his underpants, sluicing his face in the washbasin.

"Ah, there you are," he called briskly. "I always like to give the right impression from the start. Like this, you see me as I really am: a civilian in fancy dress."

Konrad matched his flippant tone. "As far as I'm concerned, uniforms are transparent anyway."

Two minutes later the count donned his official trappings, beginning with a pair of brown Party breeches that flapped grotesquely round his thighs. The count wasn't designed for uniform—Konrad saw that at once. He later noticed that Schulenburg tended to fan himself with his peaked cap, loosen his tie and casually roll up his sleeves when the heat became too much for him.

"So *you're* Tantau's blue-eyed boy," he drawled.

Konrad raised his eyebrows. "That's news to me."

"Oh, but you are. I spent half yesterday and most of last night with him. He tells me you're a smart lad—almost as smart as me. We're two of a kind, he says."

"Except for a few minor differences—like you're a count, and I'm a tradesman's son; you're a VIP from the Regional Directorate, and I'm a humble Party member; you pack a big political punch, and all I can lay claim to is a little imagination."

"A little imagination goes a long way. Tantau's an expert talent scout, and his opinion's good enough for me. He says you're a youthful idealist. Well, that makes two of us, even if I am a bit longer in the tooth."

"What do you plan to do?"

"Shake this place up; and you're going to help me. By the way, we had better observe Brownshirt conventions and use the familiar form of address."

"No need to be familiar with me, Count. I'll help you all I can without that."

"To be honest, Herr Breitbach, this ridiculous band-of-brothers stuff doesn't come easy to me either, mainly because it's always the biggest assholes who insist on it. It's what they call comradeship. Personally, if I meet a kindred spirit—which doesn't happen often—I *prefer* to use Christian names. This is a case in point, so please let me call you Konrad. I'm Fritz-Dietlof—Fritz'll do. What do you say?"

"Fair enough, Fritz," Konrad replied warily. "You say you're going to give this place a shake-up. Where do you propose to begin?"

"In the logical place. Your present District Director's

pretty half-baked, even if he does mean well. Political dupes can be dangerous. It's gullible types like Sonnenblum who promote the toughs and killers in their ranks."

"And that doesn't suit the Party?"

"No, Konrad, it doesn't suit *me*. As long as I still carry some weight around here, and as long as I can still make it felt one way or another, your way included, I'll at least try to prevent the Party from degenerating into a complete free-for-all."

"You mean it's halfway there already?"

Schulenburg gave a rueful laugh. "You don't miss much, do you? What it boils down to is this: I'm trying to fill as many key posts as possible with smart but humane Party members. That's why Sonnenblum must be replaced."

"But who by? Sonnenblum's the best of a bad bunch. Do you plan to bring in somebody from outside?"

"That would be a tactical error. We'll have to find a replacement here in Gilgenrode. Tantau thinks he knows a suitable candidate."

Konrad winced as if he had been jabbed with a red-hot poker, then hooted with laughter. "You said you were smart, Fritz. You didn't say you were a comedian as well."

"Sometimes I manage to be both."

"What about tomorrow's jamboree?"

"It's still on."

"So the party games continue as before?"

"Yes, and you'd better join in quick. Give Sonnenblum an immediate report on our conversation, and don't forget to insert plenty of sinister and alarming remarks about me. I want him to think I'm out for his blood."

Konrad grinned. "Aren't you?"

That Sunday morning, when Gilgenrode's historic German Day received its official inauguration, the little town sweltered beneath a sky of luminous East Prussian blue. The temperature in the shade was 70 degrees, and it was rising rapidly.

In Market Square, level with the town hall but concentrating their efforts on Number 7, the District Director's residence, some four score members of the local choirs, male voice and mixed, had mustered to grace the festive occasion with song.

Drawing upon the most Teutonic items in the German choral repertoire, they sang with earsplitting fervor. Their jubilant voices rang around the square until even the roof tiles seemed to rattle in joyous communion.

Although the District Director rewarded his male and female choristers with a succession of appreciative nods, he found it hard to conceal his feverish disquiet. Again and again his eyes strayed to Konrad—or, rather, to the man beside him: the dread inquisitor from the Regional Directorate.

Schulenburg's greeting that German morning had been noticeably brusque and accompanied by an ominous smirk. "I don't wish to intrude, Party Member Sonnenblum— you'll very soon know when I do. For the moment, I intend to keep my eyes and ears open."

Sonnenblum too had been struck by the count's baggy, ill-pressed uniform. He wore his cap at a rakish angle and his aristocratically equine features were set in a mask of boredom. He also looked fatigued, presumably by last night's overindulgence in champagne. Rumor had it that Kimminger's cellar had taken quite a beating.

"What a stirring performance," he drawled, suppressing a cavernous yawn. He sidled over to Sonnenblum. "Tell me something, District Director. What's the exact purpose of this organized caterwauling?"

Without quite knowing why, Sonnenblum felt called on

to defend himself. His response was almost vehement. "Community spirit, sir—that's what we're trying to cultivate here, and choral singing is a recognized means to that end."

The count waved this airily aside. "But my dear Party Member, you're simply trying to curry favor with the reactionary sections of the population. Why no marching songs, why no heroic German battle hymns? All these choral tributes to the birds and bees are a sheer waste of time."

"Permit me to stress the importance of our German love of nature," Sonnenblum retorted stiffly. "I refer to a quality which some call romanticism. One can't afford to ignore it."

"I see," said Schulenburg. "Your views are highly symptomatic of the policy you've been pursuing here. I don't say they're necessarily mistaken. Not *necessarily,* mark you— I never jump to premature conclusions. Very well, what's next on your list of communal activities?"

These remarks—and those that followed them—all formed part of a systematic verbal bombardment. Unheard by anyone but their target, they were designed to maneuver him as far as possible from the firing line. This was not only necessary but desirable from his own point of view. Where ways and means were concerned, the count from Königsberg and the young saddler from Gilgenrode had much in common.

As for Sonnenblum, he felt thoroughly incensed by what he saw as Schulenburg's brazen interference. Having been well briefed by Konrad on the count's dangerously inquisitorial tendencies, however, he strove to treat him with some semblance of courtesy. He did not find it easy, but that was yet another of the many sacrifices demanded by his public position. Once again, his thoughts veered wildly to the subject of Beate and the chaos that reigned in his private life.

Sonnenblum pulled himself together with an effort. To

the uninitiated eye he presented a convincing picture of Party togetherness as he and the Regional Organizer strode across Market Square with Konrad ambling at their heels like a friendly pup.

The next item on the program was imminent. This, Sonnenblum explained, would be a communal service in the Protestant church. Nearly ninety percent of Gilgenrode's inhabitants were of the Protestant persuasion, another fact that had to be allowed for. It was proposed to dedicate a flag belonging to the local veterans' association, most of whose members had fought in the trenches and were strongly attracted to National Socialism. "A welcome trend," Sonnenblum concluded, "and one that deserves the fullest encouragement."

Schulenburg spun round and came to a full stop in the middle of Market Square, confronting Sonnenblum with his back to the war memorial. Though dovelike and mild no longer, his eyes did not exactly fix their prey like an eagle's —that stage had yet to come. He laughed in the District Director's face.

"You must be joking, my dear fellow. You actually propose to hold a church service for the Party and its affiliated organizations? Haven't you read the Regional Director's guidelines?"

"Of course," said Sonnenblum, radiating political zeal, "but every branch office has to make allowances for local conditions."

"Herr Sonnenblum! Those guidelines were issued by the Regional Director in consultation with National Headquarters. Most of them were drafted by me personally. They aren't open to random interpretation by individuals."

"But the special relationship between the Party and the Church—"

"Has been clearly defined. Our guidelines urge the

avoidance of all unnecessary disputes and differences of opinion—for the time being. Practically speaking, that means no peeing in church. Any Party member can attend a service if he insists, but only as a private citizen, never officially or in uniform—even if his mother does belong to the parish council."

Even Schulenburg felt a little surprised at the extent of his deliberate campaign to intimidate the hapless District Director. Wryly, he realized that it had been inspired by his strange new acquaintance, Konrad Breitbach. Well, he thought, why not? Nothing was straightforward these days. An objective could only be reached, if at all, by roundabout means.

Sonnenblum, who had turned scarlet, bowed his head. "You mean I've made an error of judgment?"

"To put it mildly—though a better word springs to mind. Fortunately, there's still time to put things right. The church service is canceled. What else do you have in store for us?"

Sonnenblum's dismay was all too evident. He continued to register ideological enthusiasm, but with little success. The count's gaze, which he studiously avoided, was becoming more and more eaglelike.

They were still beside the war memorial. This was topped by a clumsily sculpted soldier who, though clearly at his last gasp, was brandishing a tattered flag aloft in a final paroxysm of valor. Sonnenblum's courage and strength revived at this heroic spectacle.

"To fortify people and put them in the mood for this afternoon's festivities, Count, we've organized a communal repast of pea soup, salt pork and smoked sausage, to be served by a field kitchen and washed down with free beer."

"That's more like it." Schulenburg grinned broadly. "Who's paying?"

264

"The expense will be met out of donations. Our fellow citizens have been extremely generous."

"I trust you'll be able to account for these donations in full, District Director. We must have a chat about them later."

"My conscience is clear, Count."

"I sincerely hope so, in view of the rumors I've heard. They say there's Jewish money involved."

"I wouldn't know anything about that."

"Or don't wish to know! So who's running this celebration?"

"Our Women's Association, assisted by other sections of the local Movement. It's a joint creative endeavor on the part of all our most public-spirited organizations."

Whether because of the sun's increasing strength or his mounting agony of mind, Sonnenblum's perspiring countenance had regained its oily sheen. He didn't know which made him feel sicker, the loss of his beloved Beate or the obtrusive presence of this sinister Nazi aristocrat.

"Your stormtroopers are also taking part," drawled Schulenburg, lingering over the words. "Commanded, I presume, by one Erwin Schulze, sometimes known as Urinoco. I gather he owes his job to your personal recommendation."

"I submitted his name in good faith, Count. I was genuinely convinced of his suitability."

"And now?"

"Now—" Sonnenblum gulped. "Now I'm not so sure."

"You mean you recommend his immediate dismissal? If so, I'll gladly transmit your request to the Regional Director in person."

"I don't know anything any more," Sonnenblum replied in a strangled voice. He wished himself miles away in the heart of the East Prussian forests, a lonely hermit dwelling in perfect solitude, but the dream was a vain one.

"If I understand you correctly, District Director, you're no longer willing to vouch for this man. You don't exclude the possibility that he murdered his predecessor, is that it?"

"Yes," said Sonnenblum, shivering like a man with malaria. It was a confession, an admission of guilt, connivance and failure—of utter gullibility. With simple resignation, he added hoarsely, "I'm sorry, I suppose I've fallen down on the job. I'm ready to take the consequences."

The count waxed positively sympathetic. "Why, you're looking quite pale, my dear fellow—you must be sickening for something. Come, let's refresh ourselves at the Regional Directorate's expense."

Impulsively, Schulenburg took Sonnenblum's arm and steered him toward the German Eagle. It was a fraternal scene staged for the benefit of an admiring throng: count and dentist, Regional Organizer and District Director, united in intimate communion.

Little was said during the main course. Schulenburg ordered knuckle of pork with pease pudding and sauerkraut for both of them. It was not until the dessert arrived —a creamy lemon mousse—that he turned on the charm and compassion.

"Anyone can make mistakes, my friend. They usually pass unnoticed, but not this time. You weren't directly to blame for what happened here, I'm sure, but it occurred in your sphere of responsibility. I couldn't hush it up even if I wanted to. It's too late for that, so let's cut our losses."

Sonnenblum nodded apathetically and swallowed the contents of his glass, a tangy Franconian wine, with no perceptible pleasure. "What do you suggest?"

"It's really quite simple. All you do is resign your various posts—voluntarily. No official prompting, no compulsion.

Well, how does that strike you?" Schulenburg paused. "Pretty generous, eh?"

Sonnenblum felt helpless and forlorn. He was ready to surrender. He had lost Beate, and it now seemed likely that he would lose his leader, Adolf Hitler, into the bargain. His Adam's apple rose and fell.

"All right," he said. "I'll resign, but on what grounds?"

"I can think of several—ill health; overwork; a wish to devote more time to your practice. The Movement would continue to benefit from your services as an ordinary Party member, of course—I can formally guarantee that. We'd also issue a statement emphasizing what an immense loss your resignation represents to the Party."

"And who—" the Adam's apple bobbed again—"who's to succeed me?"

"I don't know yet, but you've given me an idea—one that could earn you a great deal of credit. I suggest you pick your own successor, and I can think of one recommendation we'd be happy to endorse."

"Who's that?"

"Party Member Breitbach."

"Konrad?" Sonnenblum blinked convulsively and shut his eyes.

"Who better? From what I've seen of him, he's shrewd and resourceful enough to handle anyone from a parson to a suicide squad like your Storm Detachment."

"Mightn't he be shrewd enough to turn the appointment down?"

"Nobody's that shrewd when an influential job's at stake." Schulenburg sounded very sure of his ground. Presumably he was speaking from personal experience. "Just you leave him to me."

———

Schulenburg wasted no time. He officially summoned Konrad to a private interview and tackled him at once.

"Well, this is it. The District Director has resigned. I now have to appoint a successor, and that means you."

Konrad gave him an indulgent smile. "I was expecting something of the kind after Tantau's spadework and your steamroller tactics, but I didn't think it would happen so soon."

"It can't wait, my boy."

"May I make a point, Fritz? In *Mein Kampf*, page seventy-one, Hitler states that no man should engage in public political activity before he's thirty, quote unquote."

"Can it, Party Member Breitbach. I'm familiar with your habit of making capital out of German literature's noblest living exponent, thanks to Tantau, but I also know my way around his extremely useful book. Your quotation from page seventy-one is incomplete. Our Führer qualifies it by adding that his thirty-year rule doesn't apply to men of exceptional talent, and that covers you."

"So you plan to turn our town into a Nazi showplace with me as stage manager. Correct me if I'm wrong."

"Let's give each other credit for a little subtlety, Konrad. The whole thing will look quite aboveboard. Sonnenblum will resign, preferably for reasons of ill-health, and personally recommend you to succeed him. I shall bestow my official blessing and leave you holding the baby."

Konrad shook his head admiringly. "Subtlety isn't the word, Fritz! You not only get rid of Sonnenblum, but you make him responsible for picking his own successor. That leaves you in the clear whatever happens."

"If I know you, Konrad, you'll take out some insurance of your own." Schulenburg grinned. "With a little help from me."

"All I really wanted was to help my brother marry the

girl he loves, and where has it left me? Up to my neck in sewage, that's where. There's something very symbolic about the color of this uniform."

"Much the same thing happened to me, my friend. They called me 'the Red Count' because I flirted with socialism and ended up a National Socialist. As Goethe so aptly puts it: 'Man errs for as long as he strives.' "

"And now you've stopped doing either?"

"I'm like you, Konrad—I'm a professional survivor."

"So you insist I take the job?"

"Let's say I strongly advise it. I want to be able to assure the Regional Director that everything in this lovely little town is going like clockwork. Is it a deal?"

Seemingly, it was.

Problems notwithstanding, Gilgenrode's German Day was proceeding on schedule. Almost without exception, the townspeople were taking full advantage of the various delights on offer.

Children hopped along in sacks, scrambled over tree trunks and raced across the turf clutching egg-laden spoons. Wives trailed after husbands with infants in tow, steam rose from field kitchens, beer frothed from casks, and nearly a thousand pairs of jaws chomped happily in unison.

The inhabitants of the little town strolled leisurely back and forth between the central cornucopia of food and drink in Market Square and the lakeside sand dunes, where field sports, lotteries and a marksmanship contest were being held. From there they streamed back to the place of communal refreshment to brace themselves for further exertions.

Dancing on the large expanse of greensward in the municipal park and a firework display on the promenade would be followed by a grand climactic binge in every bar and tavern in town—and that, to judge from past experience, would not end before sunrise.

Sonnenblum was not unduly missed on this, his final day as District Director, even by those whom he had regarded as his staunchest Party liegemen. They readily construed his absence as a considerate gesture—a welcome reluctance to intrude. Public festivities always went with more of a swing when the Party boss was not around.

The Brownshirts were equally unmoved by the absence of their commander designate. Konrad had informed them that Schulze had been called away on urgent official business. The gallant stormtroopers would not be told until the morrow that Inspector Kersten had, with the greatest of pleasure, escorted him in handcuffs to the remand center at Allenstein. They steadfastly applied themselves to quenching their thirst, which was as intense as ever.

Thus Gilgenrode wallowed in a treacly brew of communal harmony. Its inhabitants sweated, swayed and sang, linking arms or exchanging slaps on the back. Their voices rent the air throughout the evening and far into the night.

Now a simple dentist, Heinrich Sonnenblum arrived home early. He was pale, perspiring and rather unsteady on his feet. His mother greeted him with an anxiety that only sharpened the reproach in her voice.

"What's all this? Don't tell me you're drunk again!"

"Just tired," he said, edging past her. "Dog-tired. I'm going off to change." He scuttled into his bedroom and slammed the door.

Stiffly, as though half paralyzed, he stared at his reflection in the mirror on the wardrobe door. Seconds dragged by. Then, with a mixture of anguish and derision, he burst out laughing.

He began to tear off his District Director's uniform, tugging fiercely at its component parts and hurling them at random around the room. Panting hard, he removed his boots and flung them at the mirror, which broke. As he stood there in his underpants, staring at the mess, his mother's cheerful voice broke the spell.

"You look a lot more human like that than you do in that fancy-dress costume of yours. Have you taken it off for good? If so, my prayers have been answered."

"All I need is rest." His plea was a cry from the heart. "Bring me something to drink and then let me sleep. Only for a couple of hours."

Gertrude reacted with characteristic speed and decision. "If you're as done in as you look, perhaps you'll listen to reason at last. What about Erika's wedding plans?"

"All right, all right, if you insist. I just want to be left in peace. Let her get engaged to anyone she likes, even the Breitbach boy."

"Which one, Johannes or Konrad?"

"The woolly-minded poet or the political hatchet man? I find them both equally repellent. Please yourself."

"I will. You know you can rely on your old mother to do what's best for everyone. Have a few hours' sleep, but then we're going to celebrate two things at once: your daughter's engagement and your own resurrection—as a dentist."

Count von der Schulenburg was bidding farewell to Konrad and Gilgenrode.

"Here are four phone numbers for you, two of mine and two of Tantau's—one office and one private line apiece. Let us know at once if you run into trouble."

"How long before you expect me to call, Fritz, days or weeks?"

"A few months, probably. Not many people in this country seem to know what's really going on and where it may lead. We do, and that puts us under an obligation. The Führer says so himself."

Konrad chuckled. "Trying to beat me at my own game?"

"Why not? Here, put this in your pipe—you'll find it on page three-nine-nine: 'Anyone who knows a thing, is aware of a given danger, and can see a chance to remedy it with his own eyes, has a bounden duty to resist the evil and champion its cure quite openly.' There you have it, straight from the horse's mouth. We've got *carte blanche*."

"In that case, Heil Hitler! Let's hope it's ages before we see each other again, Fritz. Take care."

Gertrude Sonnenblum had swiftly and deftly concocted a dinner fit for a royal betrothal: eel in dill sauce and roast pork with dumplings followed by marzipan pastries and a strawberry flan, the latter heaped with whipped cream. All these delicacies took shape while field kitchens continued to steam outside in the square and the festive hubbub increased.

Although the table in the Sonnenblums' dining room was laid for six, the master of the house failed to take this in. All he noticed when he entered in a dark-blue civilian suit, still pale but somewhat rested and considerably less agitated, was that the happy couple were seated side by side, holding hands and whispering. The sight of him brought them politely to their feet.

He walked over with solemn deliberation, every inch the paterfamilias, and folded his daughter in a heartfelt embrace. "If this is what you really want, who am I to stand in your way? Be happy, my darling girl."

Erika, glowing like a summer rose, gave him a grateful hug. Sonnenblum turned and held out his hand to Johannes, who shook it. "My boy," he said graciously, "Erika is very

272

dear to me. Give her the happiness she deserves, that's all I ask. Good. Now for some food."

"Not yet," Gertrude decreed from the doorway. "The party isn't complete. We're still two short."

One of the missing guests, Parson Bachus, arrived a moment later. He began by paying homage, in tones of pastoral affection, to his "dear, devout and esteemed Frau Gertrude." That done, he strode briskly over to Sonnenblum.

"I bear you no grudge. You are, after all, the son of a lady who enjoys my deepest respect. My only regret is that you and your men missed church today. The flag-blessing ceremony was particularly impressive."

Sonnenblum made another effort to rise above the past. "I'm only a humble servant of the Führer—or was—but you'll always find me on the side of decency and reconciliation."

Never one to rouse a sleeping dog, Bachus turned hurriedly to address the betrothed couple. He spread his arms wide. "May God bless your union, my children! Ask, and it shall be given you; seek, and ye shall find. The Church's succor and support will always be yours in time of need."

Sonnenblum yawned. The scent of his mother's culinary masterpiece was making his mouth water. He yearned to eat and drink, especially drink. Total oblivion was his overriding desire, but the sixth member of the party had yet to appear.

When he did, Sonnenblum could hardly believe his eyes. As if he hadn't already plumbed the depths of affliction, the latecomer turned out to be Richard Breitbach, his archenemy, yes, but the father of his daughter's intended and his mother's invited guest.

While bowing to the inevitable, Sonnenblum manfully set his face against any display of false bonhomie. He rose and ostentatiously retreated rather than shake hands. The two men *hurrumphed* malevolently at each other until Gertrude reduced them both to silence with a summons which, in a land where mealtimes were still as good as sacred, could not but pacify the bitterest foes.

"Dinner's served!"

They ate with silent and single-minded concentration. It was only when the dessert arrived that Bachus rose to deliver his own conception of a discourse laced with humor and the common touch.

"The ways of the Lord are wonderful indeed, particularly where affairs of the heart are concerned. Thanks to the love these two young people bear one another, harmony now reigns between families who were mutually ill-disposed, at least in part. We East Prussians, with our sound and sturdy common sense, have no time for tragedies such as that of Romeo and Juliet."

"Quite," said Richard Breitbach, liberally helping himself to more Burgundy. He was looking mildly amused. "Gilgenrode isn't Verona. *We* still subscribe to certain conventions, eh, what?"

Sonnenblum deliberately ignored him. "As members of a more lucid and level-headed Nordic race, we never indulge in operatic Latin excesses. Whatever our differences, we're loving parents and responsible Germans."

"Nonsense!" growled Breitbach.

Sonnenblum looked at him for the first time. "Was that aimed at me? I'm doing my best to bury the hatchet. What more do you want?"

"From you? Nothing." Breitbach was clearly feeling frisky. "It's the other way round, if anything. I'm quite prepared to welcome your charming daughter into my family with open arms. I'm even prepared, though far less so, to

274

see my younger son take that ludicrous job off your hands. It's you who should be grateful."

"Peace be with you!" Bachus cried in tones of parsonical entreaty, probably fearing a threat to the strawberry flan and Frau Gertrude's promised bottle of genuine twenty-year-old cognac. "This is a festive occasion—a time for rejoicing and thanksgiving."

But Sonnenblum's voice was shaking with anger. "Take that back, Breitbach! Apologize at once!" He turned to Johannes and Erika. "Don't worry, you two, this is just between us; take no notice and enjoy yourselves. But you, Breitbach—" He readdressed himself to his target—"If you won't apologize, come outside and I'll knock your teeth down your throat."

"Not before coffee," Gertrude said firmly. "Till then, let's have a little self-control. You can't be quite as silly as you look, but I sometimes wonder."

With a sumptuous dinner inside them, the town's two gamecocks emerged into Market Square. Seen from a distance, they might have been taking a friendly constitutional, but their faces looked pale, tight-lipped and menacing in the light of the full moon.

Together, almost shoulder to shoulder, they stared up at the windows of the apartment where Beate Fischer lived no longer. She had left the little town, presumably for good, while the singing was in progress that morning. Although Sonnenblum and Breitbach were determined not to mention the fact, each man privately longed to do so.

The final billows of German Day broke thunderously around them. Figures lurched past, bawling a raucous song, and tottered down a side street on their way to some tavern or other.

275

"I suppose you feel you've won, Richard." Sonnenblum spoke with a trace of bitterness, but the words were aimed at himself. "All that's happening here, all this wheeling and dealing, all this back-stabbing—even Keller's murder—it's all my fault. Isn't that what you're thinking?"

"Forget it, Heinrich. This is a lunatic age, so let's hope it doesn't last too long. We ought to concentrate on other things. How about taking up chess again? We used to play a lot, remember? Failing that, we could always talk."

Sonnenblum shrugged, mulishly. "I wouldn't know what to talk about."

"Certainly not your political achievements—that I promise you—but we do have one topic of common interest: there's always Beate, the captivating little bitch. We'll never forget her, either of us."

"I advise you to treat her memory with greater respect, Richard. I was ready to marry her."

"So was I, old man, and we weren't the only ones who chased her. Beate was a woman of the world, but the pressure must have proved too much for her."

Sonnenblum was breathing heavily with his head bowed. "Be that as it may, I'll never say a word against her."

"Same here." In a sudden surge of fellow feeling, Breitbach gave his companion a hearty slap on the back.

Sonnenblum swayed and lost his balance. Feebly, he put out his hands in search of support—a tree to cling to, a wall to lean against.

Breitbach caught him and hugged him to his chest. "Too much booze?" he inquired kindly. "Too much dinner? Ah, Heinrich, a man finds it hard to digest things at our age. They tend to lie heavy on the stomach—or the heart, whichever."

"Maybe." Sonnenblum straightened up. He drew a deep breath and dabbed his moist forehead with a handkerchief.

"I don't see you laughing at me, Richard. Why the hell not?"

"Because there's hope for you yet. Tonight of all nights, you haven't said a word about your political fiasco. I've only heard you mourn one loss, and it's one we both share."

"By God, Richard, I do believe you're right." Sonnenblum made the admission with a leaden tongue. He sounded infinitely surprised at himself.

Breitbach and Sonnenblum were still standing side by side in the moonlit square, looking up at the darkened windows behind which their beloved had made her home, when German Day entered its last and most memorable phase.

More revelers staggered past, seeming to multiply in number like rabbits. Couples collided and lurched apart, semisober citizens flitted curiously about, clambering over the recumbent forms of drunks and lovers.

While all these ghostly happenings were in progress, a wild and unkempt figure started to climb the war memorial with jerky, marionettish movements. Reaching the summit, it clung to the cast-iron warrior with the tattered flag. Emil Spahn's hoarse voice rang out across the square.

"Listen to me, you race of heroes! Pipe down for a minute, however hard you find it, and suffer your little children to come unto me—if you haven't already doped them with schnapps. I want to see their shining faces! I want to see our youthful pledges of a golden German future!"

A few dozen interested spectators quickly gathered at the sound of this incoherent tirade. They crowded expectantly around the war memorial and the simian figure clinging fondly to its allegorical hero. German Day's store of public attractions seemed inexhaustible. Breitbach and Sonnenblum, now propping each other gently up, lingered in the background.

"Fellow citizens, compatriots, fellow Gilgenroders!" A fine rain of spittle glinted in the moonlight as Emil's voice cleft the air once more. "This has been a truly German day, a unique and auspicious occasion. Your bellies are well lined, your digestions hard at work, your brains pleasantly befuddled by brass bands and fine words. I, too, must give thanks, if not to God, at least to the Führer and his men.

"Why? Because all is well with our wonderful little town. We can pride ourselves on our valiant German males, who know the meaning of true patriotism and are, without a doubt, the warriors of tomorrow. I salute the future defenders of the Fatherland!

"But we must never forget that our serried ranks contain an abundance of splendid German women. They can justly feel proud of their brothers, husbands and sons—proud, too, of their daughters, who yearn, even now, to taste the joys of German motherhood. This new Germany of ours is a wondrous place. The rest of the world will soon find it hard to ignore us.

"Why? Again I ask, and again I give you the answer: because we have rediscovered our national values; because we are courageous enough to point the finger at public enemies like the eternal Jew, the slimy Pole and the degenerate German subversive who fouls his own doorstep, whether he be a carrier of religious disease or a suspected cat lover.

"One thing is certain: he who isn't for the new Germany must be against it. He's an enemy; and enemies of the Fatherland, Führer and Reich must be eradicated, eliminated, isolated, liquidated, exterminated. Sieg—"

"Heil! Heil! Heil!" Three cheers reverberated around the shadowy square. Some of Emil's audience actually applauded him with genuine and artless enthusiasm.

Sonnenblum, who had been growing steadily uneasier, said, "He's on dangerous ground. Shouldn't we stop him?"

Breitbach patted him soothingly on the back. "What's it to you, Heinrich? You're just a dentist now. This is District Director's business. Knowing Konrad as well as I do—which isn't saying much—I'd say he was quite capable of appointing Emil his director of propaganda. Mind you, he'd have to lay off the booze and forget about that cat of his."

"My God!" Sonnenblum looked genuinely aghast. "This is a plot, and I'm part of it."

Emil Spahn's ecstatic face had congealed into an idiotic grin that disguised the anguish gnawing at his heart. Susie's furry shape met his eye at every turn, but Susie was dead.

"And so, fellow citizens, compatriots, fellow Gilgenroders, the die is cast. Our fate is sealed, and woe betide those who try to dodge it—their graves are already dug. Sacrifices are inevitable—our universally beloved Führer has proclaimed this with his own lips, so be warned. As for my own pearls of wisdom, ladies and gentlemen, no need to believe a word of them. Everyone knows I'm only a poor old halfwit."

And glad to be just that, his expression seemed to say.

Epilogue

HEINRICH SONNENBLUM revived his dental practice and, being adequate at his job, reestablished himself as a citizen of repute. His nominal Party membership secured him exemption from military service during World War II.

He was killed just the same, though not on the so-called field of honor. He expired in his clinic, which he had converted into a makeshift first-aid post, during the dying days of the war in East Prussia. A shell got him as Soviet troops were blasting their way through Gilgenrode, now part of Poland. According to witnesses, his last words were, "How did it ever come to this?"

Old Gertrude Sonnenblum, his mother, was privileged to die in peace only a few years after the events described. She succumbed to a heart attack in 1937, while attending divine service. Surviving mourners state that Parson Bachus, who conducted her funeral, had real tears in his eyes.

But Gertrude did not die before she had devoted herself, heart and soul, to nurturing the marriage between her granddaughter, Erika, and Johannes Breitbach, which proved to be tolerably happy. She also lived to see the birth of two great-grandchildren, whose main resemblance to her lay in their sturdy build and robust common sense.

Johannes Breitbach produced two books during those dark years. One reviewer—writing at a safe distance from Nazi Germany—described them as "a densely woven tapestry of disturbing dreams and soul-searing visions." Shortly before her death, Gertrude persuaded Johannes to take Erika and the children on a Scandinavian tour financed by his father. From this, by prearrangement, they never returned. In Oslo they were helped by the writer Max Tau, a German Jewish *émigré*. They live there to this day, not in the height of Central European affluence but no less happily for that.

Richard Breitbach seemed to have lost his voice, at least from a political standpoint. Once a spirited warhorse, he now grazed the lush pastures of existence like a weary old nag. This, he felt, was the only way to live—or rather, survive —in relative peace. If he succeeded, it was largely because his international reputation as a master saddler made him a foreign-exchange earner of considerable importance.

It was not long, however, before he became a displaced person—one of the very first. Taking advantage of a state-approved business trip to the Argentine, he decided to stay there for good and was welcomed with open arms by his many customers in that saddle-conscious country. That was in 1943.

But the older he became the more he pined for his long-lost East Prussia. In 1968, just before he died of old age, he made a trip to Boston. The purpose of his visit was to ask a woman a question—one question only, but it gave him no rest.

The woman concerned was married to an extremely

successful American businessman who had made a fortune out of canned meat, toothpaste and plastics. His name was Green, and Mrs. Green—first name Beate, or Bea as she was generally known—had been born Beate Fischer. She was a stunningly attractive woman even now, with a dark and sensual beauty that owed its conservation to a thorough mastery of the cosmetic art.

"No regrets?" Breitbach asked her, but only after they had spent some hours reminiscing and poring over prewar snapshots yellow with age. "Are you—" he hesitated—"are you happy?"

Beate stared at him wide-eyed, looking almost childlike despite her years—she hadn't lost the knack. "What do you mean, happy? Sure, I do recall a few brief moments of happiness in the old days, at least by Gilgenrode standards, but where did they get us?"

"Where *could* they get us, at a frightful time like that?" So saying, Richard Breitbach bade her a hurried farewell and fled as though fleeing from himself. He died soon afterward.

Felix Kimminger, that budding tycoon with an eye to the main chance, recorded a swift increase in turnover. He systematically expanded his business interests, and not only by acquiring the White Hart Hotel. His well-gauged services to the great new era were many and various.

Immediately after the outbreak of World War II, Kimminger started to invest his profits in the far west of Germany, mainly in Cologne and its environs. He now presides over an unrivaled network of nightspots in which the widow of Urinoco Schulze holds a substantial stake. His empire boasts whole regiments of pimps and prostitutes, not to mention strip-tease joints, short-time hotels and porno shops.

Siegfried Sass, the Jew from Gilgenrode, was fortunate

enough to die in the town he loved and so stubbornly refused to leave at any price. He was therefore spared what
followed. Not for him the cruel and relentless fate that
overtook so many millions of his blood and faith. It was
his privilege, after enjoying a bottle of Mouton Rothschild
on a glorious spring night in 1934, to retire to bed and
never see the dawn.

Parson Bachus, who had been deserted by his wife and
daughter, met his end in Lake Gilgenrode with Emil Spahn.
He did so on December 5, 1939, after a winter's night of
single-minded devotion to the bottle. World War II had
broken out, and people were starting to die like flies. Any
hope of deliverance, however slender, seemed to be fading
on the horizon.

With their arms fondly linked, Bachus and Emil strolled
across the lake's frozen surface. The ice, which was not yet
bearing, gave way. They sank, gurgling, into the depths. It
was as if the Topich—the legendary East Prussian water
sprite—had only been awaiting his moment.

But before the merciful waters closed over both men, a
chance spectator caught—or claimed he caught—their dying
words. "We're going on ahead!" cried Bachus. "They'll all
follow, every last one!"

According to the same witness, Emil called back, "We
all have to die sometime, Parson, and death comes easy to
a man who loses the dearest thing in his life. Ah, Susie. . . ."

Thanks to his indefatigable friend the count from Königsberg, Konrad Breitbach was duly confirmed in his appointment as District Director of the Gilgenrode branch of
the NSDAP. As much to his own surprise as anyone else's,
he hung onto the job for nearly nine months.

He was then brought before a Party tribunal, a far more
formidable body than any regular court, and expelled from
the ranks of the Movement. Having been officially pro-

nounced a write-off, a broken reed—an unperson—he took up saddlery again. No one could be blamed for regarding him as just another Party hack who had served his purpose and been discarded.

The only semieffective attempt on Hitler's life, which had been preceded by many other far more abysmal failures, took place at his East Prussian headquarters on July 20, 1944. Among those for whom the Gestapo mounted an intensive search in the ensuing days was Konrad. Their interest in him was justified to the extent that direct links were suspected between him and Count von der Schulenburg, who was known to have been an intimate friend of the would-be assassin, Stauffenberg.

After distinguishing himself as a Party organizer and administrator in East Prussia, Schulenburg had gone on to become Deputy Police Commissioner of Berlin and the Party's number two in Silesia. Throughout this time, nobody ever managed to nail him for anti-Nazi activities. He was one of the Third Reich's many human enigmas and, as such, a thorn in the flesh of those who preferred to see things in black and white.

Schulenburg was, in fact, "executed" after July 20—that is to say, suspended from a meat hook with a piano string around his neck and filmed for the Führer's delectation. Though horribly tortured in the preceding days, Schulenburg refused to name a single one of his fellow "conspirators." His silence extended to Konrad Breitbach and Superintendent Tantau.

Tantau fled to Switzerland on the morrow of July 20, and there he stayed. After thorough screening, he was admitted to the ranks of the internationally famous Zurich police force. Now retired, but still an object of professional veneration and commonly referred to as "the grand old man," he lives in Zurich to this day.

285

Konrad Breitbach took refuge in the boundless forests of his native East Prussia, where he lived for months like a creature of the wild. He enjoyed this in his own way. "I sometimes felt like Robinson Crusoe," he says, "like someone who had finally fulfilled a boyhood dream."

Shortly after the end of World War II, Konrad was picked up by Soviet troops and transported to Siberia. There he remained for eight long years, but even there, it seems, he retained his wry, knowing smile. He resumed work as a saddler as soon as he was repatriated to West Germany, where his unique skill has predictably earned him great commercial success.

"But what exactly *were* you in those days?" he was asked, decades after the above events, by one of the dwindling band of German journalists who are still interested in coming to grips with their nation's past. "What did you really *believe* in?"

Konrad chuckled at these questions. Crow's-feet deepened around the bright-blue eyes and the high-domed forehead wrinkled with amusement. Konrad's snow-white hair was still thick and abundant. Even the deeply etched lines at the corners of his mouth betrayed cheerful serenity. His eyes twinkled as he replied.

"My dear sir, what would you like me to say? That I joined the local branch of the Nazi Party? That I became probably the youngest local Party boss in the Third Reich? If you really want my personal confirmation you can have it."

"Those things are a matter of record, Herr Breitbach. There are plenty of witnesses around, even today, but surely that can't be the whole story?"

"I suppose you want the truth, so-called." The little man chuckled again. He could still look surprisingly schoolboyish. "For heaven's sake, why not pick whatever suits your

286

book? You can portray me as a notorious Nazi or a fearless freedom fighter. The choice is yours."

"So you won't commit yourself?"

"I suppose that's it," Konrad replied simply, with a sunset smile. "A lot of dirt had built up in those days—we were perched on the garbage dump of our national existence. Whether or not we realized it, liked it or tried to ignore it, few of us survived its collapse with clean hands."

"Is that an attempt to explain the situation?"

"No, nor excuse it. It's a straightforward statement, but no one can fully understand its meaning who wasn't exposed to the pressures of the time. Too often, life and the urge to survive were identical. All a lot of us tried to save was our skins. Some might call that a modest ambition."

The journalist stroked his chin. "It's hard to grasp, nowadays."

"Quite. That's because people are too eager to forget what actually happened, not only in Nazi Germany but at other lurid stages in human history. They banish it from their minds as quickly as possible—until next time. . . ."